DANA LECHEMINANT

The CHAD NEXT Door

a sweet romantic comedy

Author's Note

The Love in Sun City series can be read in any order, as standalones or together. Writing this series has been such a fun experience for me because the four stories all overlap and share scenes over the course of a month. Not only did I get to discover the stories, but I also got to discover them *at the same time*. It was a cool experiment to see how this type of project would work, and hopefully it gets you excited for the other stories as you read this one. I've added dates to each book to help you keep track of shared events, if you so desire. :)

Enjoy your time with the Briggs siblings as they simultaneously (and quickly) fall madly in love!

– Dana

Chapter One

Chad

October 4

IF THERE'S ONE THING I hate, it's puzzles. I used to love puzzles. I have no idea where that love came from because I'm pretty sure I haven't done an actual puzzle since I was six, but there was something satisfying about the idea of taking broken pieces and putting them together into something whole. These days it's just a chore, despite my entire life being made up of one solved mystery after another.

The broken pieces never fit quite right anymore, and I always feel like I've left a part of myself behind each time I solve a new case. Is it even worth the effort?

I've been thinking that a lot lately, and I don't especially want to know what that means for my business. I've spent the last eighteen years building up a reputation as a private investigator; I've never met a mystery I couldn't solve. I have so many people hoping to hire me that I have three different backup detectives to recommend them to whenever my client list is full. At this point, I could refuse to take on any clients at all, and the commission I get from those recommendations would be enough to pay the bills and then some.

I think that's what scares me the most. I don't want to do this, and I don't *have* to do this. But if I stopped, what would that mean for me? Where would that put me?

"Briggs? Did you just figure something out?"

I look up from the picture frame on my desk—I've been staring at it for a while—and shake my head. "Keep talking."

Gordon Thwaite has been talking at me for the last twenty minutes, telling me all sorts of "evidence" he's found when it comes to who is stealing money from him. He hired me a week ago, but I figured out the culprit about an hour after first stepping into his office. I could have told him the answer back then, but most people like to think I've done my due diligence, and they always prefer proof. He wouldn't have believed me if I'd told him too soon, so I've been biding my time and gathering evidence until I've reached a point where he'll accept the answer I give him.

He's not going to like it.

"Oh," he says. "Well, that was basically it. Do you think it's Sharon?"

His secretary is quite possibly the sweetest woman I've ever met. She's nearing seventy years old and keeps Werther's caramels on her desk, and she will talk about nothing but her grandchildren for hours if given the chance. She also happens to be married to a self-made millionaire who struck oil on their little farm decades ago. Thwaite may be a moderately successful stock trader, but his wealth is barely enough to make him a target. If he had been making more, he likely wouldn't have noticed the funds going missing in the first place, but ten million dollars made enough of a dent to send him running to me.

"It's not Sharon," I say, resisting the urge to roll my eyes. If he would open his eyes for once, Thwaite could have figured this out on his own. The signs were all there.

He frowns at me, as if annoyed that I didn't consider his theory. Honestly, I wasn't listening to his evidence anyway. "You sure?"

"Positive."

"Then who is it? Damian? Brian from accounting? The guy who cleans the—"

"It's Todd."

Thwaite's jaw drops, his face turning ashen as he stares at me. He's going to argue—I know he is—but deep down he knows I'm right.

They always do.

"Todd?" he repeats. "My brother? You think my *brother* is stealing from me?"

I don't think. I *know*. Todd used a shell company to siphon the money, but he wasn't good at covering his tracks. One transfer from the shell to his own account each time, in the exact amounts that have gone missing from Thwaite's business account, isn't exactly a mystery. Besides, the guy was shifty the moment I set foot in the office and introduced myself. He knew exactly who I was, and I made him nervous enough that he took an early lunch that day.

During his lunch break, he went to the bank and cashed out as much as they would let him take in one go. The rest went somewhere I couldn't track it.

I take a slow breath and rub the scruff on my jaw, bracing myself for a stronger reaction than this disbelief Thwaite is giving me now. "Todd has access to the accounts."

"Because we started this company together after he left his teaching position in Alabama."

"He sent a questionable email to your accounting team, telling them he noticed some discrepancies in the books."

"That's how I found out about the missing—"

"So he requested full control over the money until things were resolved," I continue. "AKA no one else could access the money. The day you hired me, Todd cashed out half a million dollars from his personal account."

Thwaite groans, growing agitated enough that he stands and starts pacing. It's sinking in now. "He gets a good salary. That's not—"

"Where is your brother now, Gordon?"

"On vacation. He lost a good deal of money at his monthly poker tournament, so he needed a few weeks to decompress."

This time I do roll my eyes. "Where is he, Gordon?" I know the answer, but I want him to come to a conclusion on his own.

Thwaite scoffs. "In the Cayman Islands I think? I don't know, somewhere tropical. Why does it..." He suddenly sinks back into his chair. "Oh."

There it is.

I give him a second to process. No one wants to find out their one surviving family member is a dirtbag, and I can't imagine this is easy. I lucked out with my siblings; I love them all to death, and they're good people. My dad, not so much, but he hasn't been a part of my life in over a decade. Finding out someone I thought I could trust had screwed me over would be a hard storm to weather, so I'm not going to push Thwaite to process this any faster. He can take all the time he needs.

"You..." He swallows. "You're really sure about this?"

I nudge a manila envelope toward him. "All the proof the police need to take him down, if he ever comes back," I say. "He is in massive debt with that poker ring, and even the money he took from you isn't enough to cover what he owes."

He doesn't even look at the envelope. "Is he in trouble?"

It's a credit to the kind of man Thwaite is to still be worried about his brother despite the unfortunate circumstances. He could easily wash his hands of this and carry on with his life without caring what happens to Todd, but he won't. There's a reason he never suspected his brother, and I admire his commitment to his family.

But there's something he needs to understand.

Sitting forward, I lace my fingers and rest them on the desk in front of me, trying to be as gentle as possible. It's not easily done for me. "Gordon, most of that money he stole came from your clients. You haven't been taking much of a salary the last few years as you build up your business, so how are you going to pay them back? Whether you care for your brother or not, you're going to have to get that money back from him or you'll be facing criminal charges yourself."

He's smart enough to know I'm right. But I hate that I'm right at his expense. That it seems to age him twenty years as he slouches in the comfortable armchair I keep on the other side of my desk. He lets out a weary breath that seems to take all of his strength with it.

There goes a bit of my soul.

I stand, picking up the envelope and placing it in his hands when he joins me at the door. "I'm sorry," I tell him, which isn't something I say often. I try to be impartial, just a man finding the facts and presenting them in the most helpful way. But I've lost track of the number of marriages that have ended in this room. Of the family members that have betrayed one another. I've lost the reasons I should be happy in a world that is increasingly awful.

Settling in my chair as soon as Thwaite is gone, hopefully to go contact the police, I let out a deep and weary sigh and turn my focus back to the one and only picture I keep on my desk. I was sixteen when I paid to have it taken, a splurge I couldn't afford back then, but I'd been so afraid of losing my siblings that I wanted a way to keep them.

Houston and Brooklyn, twins in appearance but not personality, both look confused in the picture, probably because they'd only ever had their picture taken for school pictures. Our mom was always too in the moment to grab a camera. At eight years old, they share matching awkward smiles as they look at the camera. Houston is missing one of his front teeth, and Brooklyn's hair looks pretty wild because I hadn't figured out how to do it for her and she was too interested in schoolwork to do it herself.

Then there's Micah. I had to beg her dad to let me take my half-sister for the day, and I know he was wary about letting a teenager who barely had a license drive with a kindergartener. But even if she didn't live with us, she was one of us. She's so much like our mom, though Micah barely knew Mom before she died. She has the same smile, even in this old picture. And though she stands out because her clothes actually fit and her dark hair is done up in a bow, she was so happy to be with us for the photo session. Micah is the happiest person I've ever known, and this five-year-old grin always reminds me that there is still a lot of good in the world. Especially in my family. I need that reminder more and more lately.

I can't keep doing this. I can't keep giving people bad news and expecting my life to get any brighter without something to look forward to at the end of the day.

My phone is in my hand before I've really thought this through, dialing the number I call most.

Micah answers after two rings, like she always does. No matter where she is or what she's doing, she always answers when I call, and I love her for it. "Chad! Hi!"

I relax, already feeling a little better because she's the sort of person who always talks with exclamation points, even when she's talking quietly. It's impossible not to feel better with her around. "Hey, Half-pint. How you doing?"

She clicks her tongue. "Don't you sound cheery? What's got you being Mr. Grumpy Gills?"

I've never figured out how she does that. I've gotten into the habit of keeping emotion out of my voice, but Micah always sees through the mask. "Tough case," I mutter.

"You'll figure it out!"

I already did. Therein lies the problem.

I pinch the bridge of my nose, thinking for a moment. This is long overdue, but I worry about staying away from my siblings for too long. It's not like they can't call me, right? "Hey, so, I think I need to get away for a little bit. Take a break."

She's quiet for a second, which is unusual for her. "Sorry, I think I heard you wrong. It sounded like you said you were going to take a break!"

I chuckle, recognizing her joke. "I know it's unusual. I think I need some time to myself. A chance to breathe for a bit."

"I think that's a great idea!"

"I don't know when I'll be back."

"Good!"

"What?"

Her laugh sounds like sunshine. Like someone took the warmth of a summer day and condensed it into a single sound. I don't have a favorite sibling, but Micah is my favorite for moments like this, when I feel like I'm drowning in the sludge of ugly, unwanted truths brought to light.

"Chad," she says, putting a lot of emphasis into my name. "When was the last time you took a vacation?" She doesn't wait for an answer because she knows I don't have one to give. "You deserve to have some fun! Go travel the world or something!"

That sounds like a nightmare. In order to get anywhere I might want to see, I would have to face public transportation. There are too many people in airports. Too many problems on display.

I once flew to California to see one of Houston's games when he was playing college baseball, and I was ready to pull my hair out by the time the plane landed. My seatmate spent the flight confronting her boyfriend over text, who was clearly cheating on her despite repeatedly telling her he wasn't. The kid behind me kept kicking my seat while his parents actively ignored him and each other because the husband hadn't wanted to go to Disneyland in the first place and resented the fact that *her* parents paid for the trip because he couldn't afford it. (People really need to learn to whisper quieter when surrounded by strangers in the security line.) And the couple across the aisle from me were clearly pining over each other despite convincing each other that they were only friends.

I stepped in on that one, bumping into the girl as we deplaned and knocking her into her friend's arms so he would have to catch her. I found them making out as they waited for their luggage at the carousel, so it must have worked.

That's beside the point. I'm not a fan of crowds, or people in general, so I will not be traveling the world despite Micah's excitement over the idea.

"I was thinking Laketown," I say, already smiling because I know how she'll react to that.

"Laketown? Seriously? That town is so *tiny*!"

Exactly. Micah's dad, Lloyd, always brings his whole family up to the little mountain town in Colorado each summer for a massive family reunion. Massive because he's been married six times and had kids with almost all of his past wives. The twins and I aren't technically related to him anymore since our mom died, but he still considers us his family. Plus, I think Micah would throw a fit if we didn't come, and she has her dad wrapped around her little finger.

Laketown is small, yes, but that also means it's quiet. That's exactly what I need right now.

"I need some time away, Mic," I say. "Think you'll be okay?"

"I'm twenty-five years old, Chad. I think I can handle myself."

She can, but she also tends to keep herself vulnerable. I make a note to ask Brooklyn to keep an eye on her while I'm gone since Houston is deep into the World Series with his MLB team and won't be home for a week or two. Micah is full of endless positivity, but that also makes her susceptible to disappointment bringing her down, no matter how much she pretends otherwise. I don't like leaving her alone if I can help it, and I know her dad feels the same way. The only reason he let her stay in Sun City instead of making her move with him to Diamond Springs a couple hours away is because he knows I'm here to keep an eye on her.

"You can always call me," I remind her, glad when she doesn't complain about me being overbearing. It's the problem with being eleven years older than her; I feel like I have to take care of her, no matter how capable she might be.

"What are you going to do in Laketown?" she asks. "There won't be any mysteries to solve."

That's the point. That town is as unproblematic as they get. "I'm sure I'll find something," I say with a chuckle. Hopefully that something involves a whole lot of silence. "I'll see you when I get back."

"Have fun! Be sure not to fall in love with some bright-eyed beauty and never come home!" I can practically hear her winking.

I'm sure she would *love* that. No one loves love like Micah. But unfortunately for her, I have no intention of opening my heart to anyone. I tried that once, and it fell apart in my hands when my girlfriend of six years, a woman I was fully planning to marry, dumped me out of the blue and disappeared from my life without a trace. Not that I tried hard to find her. Mercedes made it clear that I was not what she wanted, and I'm not one to force something that isn't working.

No, love isn't in the cards for me, and that's fine by me. It wouldn't last anyway.

Nothing good ever does.

Chapter Two

Hope

October 8

MAYBE MOVING ACROSS THE country was a bad idea. I thought it would be like in those movies when the struggling family packs up their car and leaves their sad life and all its memories behind, and everything is sunny and bright and new (new to them, at least, because they're always struggling for money in those movies). The move is about new beginnings, fixing what is broken, turning lemons into lemonade. It turns out that it only works when it's *actually* sunny, when the mom has an *actual* plan, when the kids are *actually* willing to make the change.

I should have factored in the idea that it's the middle of October in a small Colorado town and these kids aren't exactly on my side because they're not mine in the first place.

"Can we go home now?" Zelda has a look of utter revulsion on her face, and I'm starting to think it's her new default expression. She's only seven, but she has the spirit of a teenager hell-bent on overthrowing a dystopian government.

I mean, I don't blame her. She hasn't exactly had it easy in her short little life; I'd want to rebel too.

She stares at the rundown house that is going to be ours for the foreseeable future, and I'm pretty sure she is thinking it's probably haunted. (*I'm thinking that too, sis.*) But hopefully it's a cheerful little ghost. A Casper protégé to help us settle in and find a place here.

"This is home," I say as cheerfully as I can. It's not very convincing, but that could be because I haven't found the willpower to turn the car off yet. It's not even in park, like I'm secretly trying to decide if this is actually going to work. Maybe we need to run back to the sun.

But we can't go back. I sold the Florida house because there was no way I was ever going to be able to pay for it, and this is probably the only thing we're going to be able to afford until I figure out some kind of job. It's also the only place close enough to my Aunt Phoebe for me to feel even a little bit comfortable with our new situation.

That's a strange sensation on its own. I don't know if I've ever even had a conversation with Phoebe since my parents died eight years ago.

A little sniffle comes from the seat behind me, and I carefully glance in the mirror because the last time I looked directly at Link, he burst into tears and cried until he fell asleep. He seems okay for now, but that will probably change. He's only thirteen months younger than his sister, but he couldn't be more different from Zelda. That makes this so much harder. I think in the last three weeks he's said maybe a dozen words to me, and I have no idea what he needs. Zelda, on the other hand, tells me to the minute what I'm doing wrong and how awful everything is, which is oddly comforting as I scramble to figure this whole thing out.

"Should we go take a look?" I ask, forcing myself to turn off the car and accept that this is our new reality. No amount of wishful thinking is going to change it. I step out into the cool mountain air and take a deep breath in this tiny moment to myself while the kids undo their buckles. I don't remember the last time outside smelled this fresh, and I can't deny that I don't love the piney edge to the breeze. It's colder than I expected, though, and I shiver, wishing I had thought to buy some coats before we got here. But Florida doesn't exactly have a lot of winter gear.

A door closes somewhere nearby, and I glance over just as a man steps out of the house next to ours, a fluffy golden retriever on his heels. While these houses aren't necessarily sharing yards—one of the perks of being on the edge of a barely populated small town—the neighbor is close enough that I really hope his dog doesn't spend all day barking at squirrels.

The dog notices me first, ears perking up as he pauses his sniffing and gives me a smile. Okay, that's pretty cute. So is his owner, if I'm being honest with myself. The man—broad shoulders and scruffy beard placing him firmly in the *man* category—bends to pick up the newspaper with his coffee mug in hand, and I feel like I've entered a movie set in the nineties. I didn't know people still read newspapers. Nor did I realize people from small towns could be this attractive. He's got a whole lumberjack look to him, though he's dirty blonde rather than dark, so he can only claim sixty-seven percent of "tall, dark, and handsome." But he is *rocking* those two-thirds. Even with the small patch of gray in his beard putting him several years my senior. If this were a movie set—because even though it's overcast and the kids are whining, this still feels like the start of a movie—he would absolutely be the small-town hero who falls in love with the outsider.

It's a good thing this isn't a movie.

"Who's that?" Zelda asks, making me jump because she says it loud enough that Dreamy Neighbor glances over.

Face heating, even if he doesn't know how long I just stared at him, I give him a little wave. "Uh, hi. We're your new neighbors."

He frowns. No, it's more than that. It's a full-on scowl as his denim-blue eyes take in the picture we make: Zelda, who matches the man's scowl completely because she's angry at the world; Link, who looks like he's spent the last three weeks crying and is one refused meal away from becoming dangerously thin; and me, a twenty-four-year-old grad school dropout who has no idea what she's doing because she suddenly got custody of her niece and nephew when their mom died of a cerebral hemorrhage.

It's not a pretty sight.

He grunts, gives a short whistle, and disappears into his house with the dog right behind him.

Okay, then.

"Can I go play with the dog?" Zelda asks. She's still scowling, but it has softened in the last two seconds.

Something tells me we're not going to see much of our neighbor, which is a pity because his is one of only three houses on this lane. We passed the third on the way in, and it's a ways down so we can't even see it from here.

"I don't think so, sweetie," I tell her. "We need to unpack before it gets dark, anyway."

She rolls her eyes so hard that I'm amazed it doesn't hurt. "Fine." She hefts her backpack higher on her shoulder and stomps up the front steps with some impressive rage in her feet.

I glance at Link. "Ready?"

He nods once and then follows his sister without a word, though his lip quivers. I'm so glad I'm not a crier or his heartbreak would be my undoing. It's still painful, but at least I can keep that pain to myself.

I put in the code in the padlock on the front door and brace myself for what we might find inside. When I bought the house, I looked at the pictures of course, but I know pictures can be deceiving. My last apartment looked like a spacious dream, but it turned out to be a prison cell with a separate bathroom. This place in size alone is an upgrade for me, but I know what these kids are coming from. They're not going to love trading their massive playroom for a house that could fit inside their last one five or six times.

I can't help that my sister was a literal rocket scientist and made the big bucks. I...do not. I make no bucks, to be exact, except for the few hours a day that I used to make *Star*bucks in between classes. Bailey had a surprising amount of debt, and I have all my student loans, so after the life insurance money and selling the house, this is what we can afford while still leaving enough for the kids to go to college if they want to. Knowing my luck, in the decade between now and then, an undergrad degree will probably cost ten times what it does now. And if these kids are half as smart as their mom, they're not going to be going to community college. I see Ivy Leagues in their futures.

My bank account is weeping just thinking about it.

"Are you ever going to open the door?" Zelda asks.

I guess there's no point in delaying the inevitable. Gripping the doorknob, I push it open with gusto and then flinch as a wave of musty, dead air hits me right in the face. *Gross.* In unison, the three of us poke our heads inside, trying to see in the darkness, but it looks like all the curtains are closed.

"Anyone see a light switch?" I ask. I could just step inside and feel around, but I worry that I'll end up touching something I don't want to. Who knows what might be lurking on the walls?

Zelda lets out a heavy sigh that makes her sound like she's fifty, and then she pushes me out of the way and takes the first step inside. She finds a switch in half a second, and the room is suddenly bathed in light.

"Oh, okay, this isn't so bad." Those words are out of my mouth before I can stop them, and Zelda and Link both give me looks of horror. I mean, they should have figured out at this point that I'm out of my element here, right? Of course I was expecting the house to be bad.

Or maybe they're looking at me like that because the front room looks like it hasn't changed since 1957. The listing said this place was furnished, but I didn't realize that would mean it would look fully lived in. Suddenly I'm wondering if some old lady lived and died here and no one ever bothered to get rid of her stuff.

Let's just hope they got rid of the lady. No way am I living here if we come across a mummified body in one of the beds. I can deal with ghosts, but I draw the line at corpses.

"Should...should we check out your rooms?" I say, eyes still riveted on the clashing colors and strange furniture designs. Why is everything orange and green? Why is that chair shaped so roundly? Why are the legs on the couch such thin pegs?

Zelda clears her throat, looking at me like this is all my fault. (It technically is, but we can fix this. Eventually.) "Do we get our own rooms? Or do we have to share?"

I made sure to get a three bedroom for that very reason, though I sort of wish I'd splurged for four bedrooms just so I could have a home office and try to find some kind of remote job. I don't think I can work otherwise, though I should figure out the school situation soon. I've thought about homeschooling so they can have some more time to settle, but I don't know the first thing about teaching. They're already smarter than me as it is.

"You each get a room," I confirm and warily lead the way down the narrow hall. I honestly have no idea which room is which, so I take a guess and point to the two doors that sit directly opposite each other. "You can pick who gets what."

Immediately, they each take a door and shove them both open. In a weird synchrony that would make them look like twins if I didn't know their birthdays, they spend two seconds looking at the rooms before crossing the hall and trading places, closing the doors behind them.

I guess they picked?

That leaves the last room for me, and a strange foreboding settles over me as I push the door open. My jaw drops. Not only is this room *not* furnished, it's also the tiniest room I've ever seen. Like, it will fit a bed and a dresser and nothing else. (That's assuming I can find a place to buy those things in the first place.) I know for a fact that this house has a master bedroom, and I have a feeling that's the room Zelda picked. Link would have gone for the room at the back, which probably looks out over the woods where he can watch the wildlife to his heart's content and never interact with another human being.

This room is also *freezing*. I'm amazed the rest of the house hasn't caught this utter chill. Tucking my arms around myself, I search for the source of the cold—like a hole in the ceiling or a missing wall—but I've only been in the room for two seconds when a chilling sound hits my ears. Something is *rustling* in the closet. Straight up moving around. And that had better be a friendly ghost or I swear I'll—

Something sleek and black darts from the closet and disappears through the massive hole in the broken window, and I scream louder than I've ever screamed in my life.

Chapter Three
Chad

NEIGHBORS. I SPECIFICALLY CAME to this house so I wouldn't have neighbors because the only person within a mile radius is Hank, who basically never leaves his house except when he is completely and thoroughly blocked. I mean, who wouldn't want to share a street with a hermited novelist? That's the dream right there.

But no. Apparently, less than twenty-four hours after I settle in, someone decides they absolutely need to buy the rundown house that has sat vacant for over a year. Not just someone. A *family*. With one kid who isn't even a little bit shy and another who has the subtle signs of being a troublemaker because he wouldn't make eye contact with anyone. Their mother looks like she's barely into adulthood herself and has all the signs of an overwhelmed teen mom. She wasn't wearing a wedding ring, which probably makes her a *single*, overwhelmed teen mom, and the last thing I need is her realizing I have no need to leave the house so I'm available for babysitting or soothing her lonely heart or anything else she might be looking for.

I have no idea why a woman like her would come to a place like this, but I don't like it. I left Sun City so I could leave complicated behind.

"You'd better keep your distance," I tell Duke.

He lifts his head from where he's lying on the back deck next to me, tail wagging slightly as he smiles at me. Sometimes I genuinely think he can understand me, and right now he seems to think that I'm joking about staying away from the neighbors.

I hit him with a hard stare. "I'm serious. The minute you go over there and say hi is the minute they think we can be friends. I'd rather pretend they don't exist."

He drops his head back down with a little sigh, disappointment all over his face. Maybe I'm being harsh.

I take a deep breath, enjoying this moment of silence since it might be my last. Those kids looked the same age as the twins were when our mom died, and Brooklyn and Houston were *never* quiet. I can only imagine those two will be the same, and this could be my only chance to enjoy a peaceful morning before it's full of arguing children.

A scream pierces the air, and I jump, coffee spilling all over me. What in the... I look toward the neighbor's house just as a large animal slips out of a back window, and panic sets in. Was that a badger? Duke is already on his feet, vibrating with anticipation, and I shout, "Go!" as I leap over the deck railing. He takes off after the animal. I head for the house.

The front door is thankfully unlocked, though I nearly bowl over the boy as he hustles into the front room looking white as a sheet. The girl is right behind him, more confused than afraid, which means the scream came from their mom. I rush past them to the very back room where it sounds like she's straight up hysterical.

I find her huddled in a ball in the corner, her face in her arms as she shakes uncontrollably.

"Hey, are you okay?"

Her head snaps up, eyes wet with tears, and she sits there staring at me, completely frozen now. The hysteria in her eyes is clear as day, mixed with fear and maybe even horror.

I crouch down so I'm not looming over her. "Did it hurt you?" Reaching out, as if I haven't made things worse by barging in here, I wait for her to say or do anything.

I don't have to wait long. It all comes out in a snort followed by the most obnoxious laugh I've ever heard. She's back to shaking, but not with sobs. Laughter. Enough of it that she's crying again.

"Sorry," she gets out in between guffaws—yes, guffaws. "It shouldn't be funny. But it's *so* funny!" She buries her face again as if that might contain her laughter. Then she gasps and looks up again. "Are the kids okay? Where are they?"

I glance behind me, finding both kids peering at us through the open door. Duke, for some reason, is right between them, his fur tangled up in their little hands. Guess he gave up on the badger chase pretty quickly. "They're fine," I mutter, feeling more foolish by the second. Why do I always do this? Why do I feel like I have to step in and save the day when I don't even have the full story?

I clear my throat, standing again and moving to the window. It looks like a rock or something may have broken it, and there are bits of fur around the sharp edges. I wonder how long the badger has been sneaking in here. Based on the smell—or lack thereof—I hope it isn't long. "You'll have to get this window fixed if you want to keep him out," I say, though that's obvious. "I don't know why a badger would be living at this kind of elevation, though."

"Link says it was a wolverine."

I look behind me at the girl, who spoke. I'm guessing Link is the boy, though he's focused more on Duke than on me. The only sign I get that he may have said something to his sister is the pink in his cheeks.

"There aren't wolverines in Colorado," I say, though I'm not entirely sure about that. I've spent my whole life in New Mexico outside of the family reunions Lloyd throws here in Laketown, so it's not like I could call myself an expert on Colorado wildlife.

Link looks up at me for half a second before dropping his head again. He looks angry.

"I would listen to him," the mom says, finally getting over her laughing fit. "Link knows animals better than anyone."

"I don't know if we should be trusting a seven-year-old to identify—"

"He's six." She rises to her feet, all traces of her laughter gone.

I clench my jaw. "That makes him even less reliable."

Fire flashes in her eyes as she steps closer to me. "Oh, and you're an expert on Colorado wildlife?"

It's a simple question, but her voice carries undercurrents of accusation. Either *she* is a wildlife expert—not likely—or she has guessed right when it comes to my own knowledge and doesn't like that I've chosen to be right regardless. On top of that, I've insulted her kid. Not a great first impression.

Not that it matters. This will hopefully be our one and only interaction.

Maybe it *was* a wolverine, but I'm pretty sure it was a badger. Then again, I don't even know the difference between a squirrel and a chipmunk. Working around downtown Sun City doesn't require a thorough knowledge of woodland creatures. Maybe the first grader does know better than me. Whatever it was, she's not going to want it crawling in and out of her house. "Sorry for letting myself in," I tell the mom. "I heard you scream."

"I appreciate you checking in," she says, though she can't seem to decide if she means it as she gazes at me intently. I keep my expression neutral out of habit, which seems to frustrate her. "We can take it from here, and you can go congratulate yourself for being the big, strong hero."

I have no idea what to say to that without sounding either condescending or conceited, so I opt to say nothing. I would leave if the kids would get out of the way, but they form a wall with Duke, the girl gazing up at me while the boy pretends I'm not here. "Duke, home."

He whines, eyes darting between the two kids. He *loves* kids, and he never gets to be around them because I'm a homebody who only takes him out on my daily runs. Houston sometimes *acts* like a kid, but it's not the same.

I feel bad about it, but I need to get both of us out of there before this turns into a thing. "Duke. Home."

He does as he's told, backing away from the door and click-clacking down the hall. His retreat sparks the kids to move too, finally giving me an escape.

I make it to the front door before a soft voice says, "I'm Hope, by the way."

I glance back, trying to gauge the woman's reason for introducing herself.

She shrugs, wiping a few stray tears from her cheek. "I figured if you ever have to rescue me again, you should know. What's your name?"

"Call me Grizz." It's the name my siblings used to call me, and it feels a lot safer than giving her my real name. Safer from what, I have no idea. Maybe I just know the effect my name has thanks to the internet. I'm gruff already, but as soon as people learn I'm named Chad, they seem to think I'm some sort of dude-bro out to seduce women and flaunt my upper class, white male success.

Pretty sure hiding alone in the mountains is the farthest I can get from my name.

Hope cocks her head, probably testing out my name and trying to decide if it's real. "How long have you lived here?"

That's not a question I should answer either, though I don't want to lie to her. So I give a different truth. "I bought the house about a year ago." Hoping it would be a nice vacation home for Mercedes and me, but who needs that detail? Not me. Except, this is the first time I've set foot in the house since the contractor finished the remodel about a week before my girlfriend dumped me.

"I've never been to Laketown before last night," she says as she leans against the wall. "Anything I should know?"

Stay away from badgers is the first thing that comes to mind, but I hold that in. It's not any worse than what I actually say, though. "Keep to yourself. Everyone else does."

If only that were the truth.

Chapter Four
Hope

October 9

ALL IN ALL, THE couch isn't too bad. I thought it would be lumpy or have springs that poked me in the back all night, but it was comfortable enough that I managed a few hours of decent sleep before my growling stomach woke me up a little after five this morning.

I know the kids are sick of peanut butter and jelly, but it's the only thing we have until I can get to the grocery store. We're lucky I thought to grab a loaf in the first place, and I almost got a smile out of Zelda when I told her last night that she would have to use her hand to scoop the peanut butter because, despite the dozen embroidered pictures of ducks, the house does not have any cutlery.

They were probably silver and the only thing of value to whoever sold the house to me.

As I creep into the kitchen and look at my pitiful options for breakfast—bread, peanut butter, jam—I tell myself that this is a normal post-move problem. I just don't know if Link and Zelda will see it that way. They had a live-in nanny who often cooked for them while my sister was at work, and from what Bailey would tell me about the nanny, she was basically a gourmet chef but with kids' food. How am I supposed to compete with that?

"We can work with this," I say as I eye the bread with my head tilted to the side. "All we need is another angle to make it different."

I grab a slice of bread and press it as flat as I can get it, and then I smother it in peanut butter with one hand and jam with the other. After licking my fingers clean and then washing them in the frigid sink water—haven't figured out how to get warm water yet—I roll my flattened slice into a cute little cake roll sort of thing. I love it, but I hope Zelda and Link love it more. Especially Link, who barely touched his sandwich last night. As it's the only food we've got, they'll have to eat it so they're not miserable when we pack up and head into town for some real groceries.

As I work on making a couple of sandwich rolls for each kid, I gaze out the window at the view. I was too busy unloading the car yesterday to really pay attention, but it is truly gorgeous up here. I feel like I'm in a rustic cabin—if that cabin were straight out of a fifties sitcom—and the wilderness beyond that window feels full of possibilities.

It also feels full of wolverines, but that's a different problem.

I haven't been brave enough to see if the wolverine has returned to my tiny closet, and I don't know if I'll ever be. I'll just turn the living room into my bedroom, and it'll be fine. I don't need privacy or anything. It's not like I've spent the last six years completely on my own because I was blessed with roommates who enjoyed partying over staying in so I never saw them.

Ha.

Basically, I'm exhausted from never having a moment to myself over the last few weeks, but it's not like I would give up this chance to take care of Link and Zelda. Bailey chose me to take them if anything happened to her, and I'm taking that trust seriously.

"Aunt Hope?" Zelda blearily wanders into the front room, rubbing her eyes.

I lick off a bit of peanut butter I missed on my pinky. "Hey, kiddo. How did you sleep?"

Something snaps in her expression, like for a moment she forgot to be disgusted. "It was cold."

Right. Because I haven't figured out how to turn on the heater either. I have a feeling it's related to the lack of warm water. I Googled how to turn on the heat, but by the time we got everything unloaded, I was exhausted. Plus, I have no idea where the furnace actually is, and I have a feeling the pilot light, whatever that is, isn't lit. That seemed to be the consensus among the forums I looked at.

I don't exactly feel like taking a match to a tank full of gas should be a thing I do.

"We'll get the heat figured out, sweetie. Come eat some PBJ rolls."

Though she eyes my offering warily, Zelda sits on one of the stools at the counter and picks up one of the rolls. "This is weird," she says but takes a bite anyway.

"Good weird or bad weird?"

She thinks about that for a second. "Both."

At least she's eating it. Link will be the true test, but I've got one of his favorite granola bars as a backup, just in case. I've had it in my purse since the day I realized he likes them, just in case there's an emergency food situation.

Someone whistles outside, and I know without looking that it's Grizz. Which is absolutely not his real name. Or if it is, it's no wonder he's a bit grumpy because that's the kind of name a person has no choice but to live up to. I don't *need* to look, but I still do it because I can't get over how attractive he was up close and how much I want to know more about him.

Here are the facts I know about Grizz:

1. He is way too old for me so I shouldn't be interested in the first place.

2. He is not as old as I thought when I only saw him from a distance—probably in his mid-thirties.

3. He is still too old for me.

4. He looks like Chris Hemsworth but, like, better? Which I didn't think was possible.

5. He absolutely doesn't like me.

6. That's not a lot of things.

Moving to the window, I pretend to wash my hands so Zelda doesn't wonder what I'm looking at, and I watch as Grizz throws a ball for his incredibly well-behaved dog. Like, that dog is basically perfect, both in manners and in appearance. He and his owner match too. In appearance, I mean, not necessarily in manners. He's got that golden blond coloring that I've always secretly loved, plus he's a decent size, not too bulky but not slender either.

I'm talking about the dog, by the way. But I guess it fits Grizz too, though I would put him more on the thick side than his dog. I mean, his shoulders are the kind that work really well for chopping wood and wrestling bears and hopefully chasing wolverines out of closets. He can probably light a pilot light in a furnace too, though the jury is out on if I'll ever be brave enough to ask him.

Problem is, if I don't ask him, it means I'll have to hire someone to do it, and something tells me that won't be cheap. I don't know the odds of someone in Laketown being able to do it—but how hard can it be?—which would mean getting someone from Coleville, the nearest town with a population greater than a thousand, which is almost an hour away. Maybe I could ask Aunt Phoebe if she has a recommendation in Furley? (Also an hour away, by the way.) My goal is not to bother her if I can help it, even if she told me I can ask for anything.

It's hard to ask someone for help when they pretended you didn't exist for most of your life.

Grizz whistles that clear and piercing whistle again—how does he do that?—and the dog comes running back, plopping himself right at his master's feet. Maybe it's just me, but seeing the way Grizz has such a handle on the animal is weirdly attractive. Don't get me wrong. I am fiercely independent when I can be and don't need a big strong man to fix all my problems for me. But when most of my life has been filled with spineless cowards, seeing a man take charge with confidence has me on the edge of swooning.

"Hope, why are you washing your hands so long?"

I jump, splashing myself with frigid water. "Because I was really messy," I stammer. "Is Link still sleeping?"

Zelda shrugs as she finishes off her second roll. "He's probably looking next door just like you are."

Well, it's time to die of mortification. Thankfully, odds are extremely low that Grizz will ever hear that I spent a good three minutes watching him this morning. At least, he won't unless I ask him to help with the furnace.

Zelda keeps talking as she reaches for a third roll. "The dog's name is Duke. That's what his collar said. He's really nice."

Oh good, I can rest easy knowing I'm a dog stalker, not a man stalker. Grizz never needs to know. Ugh, I can*not* keep calling him that. It sounds like a stupid nickname a frat boy came up with, no matter how accurate to his personality it seems.

"Finish up your breakfast," I tell Zelda, pulling myself away from the window to reduce temptation to keep watching. He's probably inside at this point anyway. "I'll go get your brother, and then we need to go to the grocery store before we run out of peanut butter."

Sure enough, Link is perched at his window. He's pulled the bed directly against the far wall so he can sit and look outside. For as long as I can remember, he's always been fascinated by animals, but Bailey never let him have a pet because she worked too many long nights and wouldn't have been able to help take care of anything. But during our long phone calls, when she was stuck at the office and I was up cramming for a test or writing a paper, she would go on and on about how many animal facts he knew. We had to sell most of his books along with the house, but I've been thinking I need to get him an encyclopedia app or something so he can still learn more if he wants to.

"Whatcha looking at, bud?"

He doesn't turn away from the window, but he gives me a shrug. It's better than nothing.

I hesitate in the doorway, but he seems to be a little brighter today than he's been since I picked him up from Child Services. So I take a chance and sit on the end of his bed with him, watching him as he watches Duke play tug-of-war with Grizz. He looks so much like Bailey. He has her upturned nose and her rich brown eyes. His brown hair is lighter than his mom's, with a bit of wave to it while hers was always stick-straight, but there is no arguing that he's her son.

Sometimes, when I study the kids like this, I wonder what their dad was like. Bailey never talked about him, even when I asked, but I know he wasn't great. He couldn't be if he left her right after he found out she was pregnant with Link. With the way Bailey skirted around my questions after she told me she was having another baby—basically when she was in labor—I've wondered if Link came as a result of something more sinister than I'd like. Bai was already thinking about leaving him, whoever he was, and I get the sense that he forced himself on her. It would explain how she got pregnant so quickly after Zelda when I know she was already overwhelmed with one kid. She wouldn't have chosen to have another baby.

Not that Bailey regretted getting Link. She always fiercely loved her children and was the best mom in the world to them.

It's a lot to measure up to.

"I heard his name is Duke," I say, shaking away the bad feelings and focusing on the kid who is now mine. That part is never going to change. "What kind of dog is he?"

He glances at me, giving me a look that says I'm clearly stupid for not knowing. You would think, with how quiet he is, he would be the sweet one, but he shares Zelda's disdain. I wonder if they did this with Bailey too or if they only dish it out to me.

"Oh right, he's a golden retriever, isn't he?" I roll my eyes as if it's silly that I forgot. "Hey, I've got some breakfast ready, and then we need to go to the store before we all starve."

"I could stay here." He says it so quietly that I barely hear him, but I'm overjoyed that he says anything at all.

I ruffle his hair. "Nice try, kiddo, but I can't leave you here by yourself." I can see he wants to argue, so I give him a nudge. "Get dressed and come get some breakfast."

By the time Link has swallowed one whole roll—technically it's more than he ate last night—Zelda is practically begging to get out of the house. She says it smells like an old lady, which isn't wrong. If we get a sunny day any time soon, we'll have to air the place out and hopefully get rid of the stale perfume smell.

The drive into town only lasts ten minutes, but for a girl from the heart of Tampa, that feels like forever because there's nothing but trees in between the first house on our lane and the edge of town. And 'town' can barely be called that when it's made up of a single main street and a few offshoots that all have cutesy names like Strawberry Street and Blueberry Lane. It's a pretty adorable town, if I'm being honest. It's just so different from what I'm used to, and it will take a while for it to sink in that this is now *my* town.

"What do you guys think of Laketown?" I ask as I pull up in front of the tiny grocery store on Main Street.

"I miss Orlando," Zelda says without hesitation.

Okay, I would miss Orlando too if I lived that close to Disney World, but we're here now, and I'm not going through all the trouble of buying a house somewhere else. The only reason I could get this one was because Bailey had amassed enough equity on the Orlando house that I had a pretty good down payment ready to go. (A month ago, I didn't even know what equity was. Look at me adulting all over the place!)

"Well," I say as I climb out of the car, "maybe you can learn to love Laketown as much as you loved Orlando. Besides, think of all the fun we can have on the lake as soon as summer comes."

"Oh, honey, there's no lake in Laketown."

I spin around to face the owner of a sweet and feminine voice, finding a woman with soft gray hair and the kindest green eyes I've ever seen. She smiles at me, filling her face with deep wrinkles, before holding out her hand.

"Hi, I'm Eleanor. You must be the woman who bought the old Keller house."

That name sounds vaguely familiar, so I must be. Plus, with a town this small, I would imagine there aren't a lot of newbies moving in. "Hi, yes, I'm Hope Duncan. This is..." I gesture to Link and Zelda, who have strangely remained glued to the side of the car instead of joining me on the sidewalk. It might not be unusual for Link to keep his distance, but I have never seen Zelda be shy. "Link and Zelda."

Eleanor's smile shifts a little as she takes in the kids. "Oh my, well, those are certainly interesting names, aren't they?"

"They come from a video game," Zelda says, finally stepping back into her fearless attitude. "But you've probably never heard of it."

"Zelda, remember you need to be polite," I growl under my breath.

Thankfully, Eleanor waves my warning away and returns to her full smile. "Oh, she's right. I don't really know anything about video games. You and your husband must love them, though!"

It would be a good idea to nip this one in the bud before the whole town starts thinking anything but the truth. I don't want to have to correct a thousand different people when I could potentially start it all right here. "Oh, I'm not married. And they aren't mine." I wince as soon as I say those words. "I mean, yes, they're mine. They're my niece and nephew."

Did they notice? Link has been completely focused on the curb by his foot, and Zelda hasn't lowered her chin—she must find people who don't like video games to be inferior. It would explain a lot of her feelings about me, that's for sure. But I don't want them to think I don't want them. I do! I absolutely do. Even if I have no idea how to be a parent and less than a month ago I was a starving grad student living in a sketchy apartment with a guy who literally never left his room except to go to the clubs until long after I had fallen asleep.

"Well," I say when Eleanor doesn't seem to know how to respond to my clarification. "We should probably get some groceries. Wait, did you say there isn't a lake here? In...Laketown?" That was one of the reasons I picked this place (along with the proximity to Aunt Phoebe, but we're not counting that). I was hoping to give the kids something fun for the summer.

She laughs like I've just told the funniest joke she's ever heard. "Oh no, dear, we're drier than the Sahara Desert."

Her analogy doesn't quite work, considering the skies have been threatening rain since yesterday, but I understand her meaning. There isn't a lake in Laketown, which has me wondering if I've brought us to a backwards place that isn't as charming as it seemed on paper.

"It was nice to meet you, Eleanor," I tell her, debating if I mean that as I reach for the kids and start shuffling them toward the door.

"Let me give you my number, honey." I'm about to refuse when she adds, "I can send you all the school information. The bus runs right past your lane every day."

Okay, that would actually be really useful. Though Link gets a mild look of terror in his eyes as Eleanor types her number into my phone, Zelda actually looks excited. She must have been so bored the last few weeks with nothing new to learn. I hope, if I do send them to school, she'll be able to help her brother settle in and make some friends.

"Thank you," I tell Eleanor sincerely. "I haven't even had a chance to look at the school stuff. It's been a little chaotic the last few weeks."

She may not know any of the details of our life, but as she looks us over again, Eleanor seems to sense that we're all new to this arrangement. "We here in Laketown look out for each other," she says, pointing to my phone. "Whatever you need, I can point you in the right direction. Just give me a call!"

As she waves and walks away, toward what looks like a little bakery, I hold back a sudden rush of emotion. She is the embodiment of what I was hoping for from a small town, and I seriously hope she's not the only kind one. It's hard to be completely hopeful when Grizz is the only other person I've met so far, but I pray he's the exception to the Laketown rules. I only have room for one gruff and grumpy guy in my life when what I really need is all the help I can get.

I take a deep breath and put on a brave face. Help or no help, I can do this. "Okay, kiddos, let's go get some food!"

Chapter Five
Chad

I SHOULD HAVE STAYED home. I really have no reason to come to town—my fridge is stocked, the house is solid, there's a whole bookshelf of books waiting for me—but here I am, slowly wandering the tiny hardware store as if there's anything in here I don't already have stocked in the garage. With how much I have in my house to occupy me, you would think I spend all my time here instead of Sun City.

But I only made it two days before I started going stir crazy, so here I am.

Looking for a way to fix my neighbor's window.

"Can I help you with anything, Mr. Briggs?" A woman in her late twenties approaches me, though she's been watching me since the moment I stepped through the door. She pretended not to, but it's not like this store is very large. I watched her just as easily as she watched me, and I get the feeling I should do my best to avoid her. She wasn't running the store a year ago when I bought the house, so the only way she would know me is through gossip, which tends to move quickly in this town.

As she smiles at me, waiting for my response, I give her a quick examination. Comfortable clothes fit for her occupation while still being flattering, low maintenance hair style, no wedding ring or sign of one existing anytime recently. She must have recently moved to Laketown and is here to stay unless she finds love with someone passing through.

Someone like me.

"I think I've got it covered, Miss..."

"Oh, I'm June!" She thrusts out her hand, revealing calloused palms that speak of a considerable amount of hard labor. She's not just a pretty face to sell tools, then. Good for her. "And you're Chad, right? Sorry, that must feel strange, having everyone know your name when you don't know anyone yet."

I take her hand, still a little wary, but at least she understands the frustration of being in a small town. She must have moved from somewhere much bigger. I wonder what brought her here. It could have happened anytime in the last year, really, and for someone as young and friendly as her, my first guess would be that it was to get away from someone. Likely a romantic partner. It would have to have been a serious relationship for her to up and move to a tiny town like his.

No. Don't start digging, Chad. You're on vacation.

"It's a little strange," I say before she thinks I'm entirely antisocial. Which I am, but I don't want to make enemies while I'm here. "I'm all set, though. You can get back to doing what you need to do. I don't want to keep you."

She smirks, straightening a row of garden spades. "You must not be from a small town. This is the busiest I ever get." She gestures to the empty store. "It's always pretty quiet, but sometimes it's nice. What brought you to Laketown?"

Hope is going to need to buy a new window in the long run, but for now I could patch the hole with a bit of plywood and some plastic wrap to try to keep out the cold. I grab a roll of plastic and some assorted nails, moving toward the end of the store where some plywood sheets lean against the wall.

Thankfully, June doesn't follow, even though I expected her to. "Sorry," she says with a grin, which makes me pause. She leans her arms on top of the shelf between us. "I was like you once, and I know how hard it is to trust that no one is out to get you. I'm not going to push, but I promise you can be open with anyone in Laketown. They'll have your back. Whatever you're running from, you're safe from it here."

She heads back to the front of the store just as the door opens to let someone new in.

Am I running away? Probably. I needed a break, but I could have taken a break back in Sun City without abandoning Micah or the twins. Instead, I drove almost two hours to a tiny town in the middle of nowhere, to a house that I bought for a woman I hope to never see again. I knew even before packing the truck that I would get bored.

But that's the point. I *need* to be bored. I need to stop looking for broken things and start enjoying my life. I came to Laketown for a literal breath of fresh air, and I shouldn't pretend otherwise.

I shouldn't come into town anymore either if I want to avoid people asking questions. June was probably a best-case scenario, and I doubt the rest of the town will be as understanding if I want to be secretive.

"Fancy running into you here."

The plastic slips out of my grip at the sound of a familiar voice, rolling down my leg and flying directly toward Hope with impressive speed. She tries to catch it with her foot, I think, but she ends up stepping on it. She trips forward and flails her arms to catch herself, but she knocks boxes of nails off the shelf instead. I take one step toward her before she slams into me, shoulder ramming into my stomach and knocking the wind out of me.

And maybe it's because I can't breathe or because I don't remember the last time I had this much physical contact with a person, but I go down, knees crumpling beneath me at the same time my feet slip on stray nails. I land hard, losing any air I might have had left when my back hits the ground.

I won't even mention where her elbow lands, but I want to curl up in a ball and crawl away from this menace of a woman before she punches me in the face too. A broken nose would hurt less.

"Oh my gosh!" She scrambles to get up, taking out my spleen in the process when the palm of her hand sinks into my gut.

I grab both her arms and silently beg her to stop moving. If I could breathe, I wouldn't be so silent. I keep my eyes shut but don't let go of her wrists until I can get in a lungful of air. Then I peek at her.

Her face is beet red as she grimaces at me, but there's another emotion in her expression beyond embarrassment. One that I saw yesterday too. She's trying so hard not to laugh, and it's clearly a losing battle. The panic in her eyes tells me laughing is her default response to tense situations, which generally means she encounters those a lot. I hate that my mind immediately starts wondering why. I'm on vacation. The whole point of coming to Laketown was to take a break from reading people.

Hope is *not* a puzzle that needs solving. She's a problem I need to avoid.

"Go ahead," I grumble as I slowly release her wrists. I wince when I see the red marks I left behind with my grip, but she's already bursting into a fit of laughter that fills the whole store even when she covers her mouth with her hand.

I slowly sit up, knowing I'm going to feel every bit of this fall tomorrow while Hope will probably be perfectly fine. She's young enough to bounce back, plus I cushioned her fall. I'm going to have to ice and heat my back if I want to be able to move tomorrow, which has me really feeling my age. I try not to think about how I'm just a few years shy of forty, but those years keep creeping up on me.

What do I have to show for it?

"Is everyone okay?" June appears behind me, her eyes wide as she takes in the scene. "What happened?"

I'm about to tell her that I'll clean it all up when Hope says, "It's my fault. I scared him, and then I lost my balance trying to help."

"I'm not sure you ever had your balance," I mumble, though I don't mean it. I'll be the first to admit that I'm kind of a baby when I'm in pain, and I'm not going to be personable until I'm no longer questioning my ability to have kids thanks to Hope's elbow.

To no one's surprise, Hope doesn't especially like my comment, and she hops to her feet with a chill look in her eyes. It doesn't stop the red from spreading up her neck. "Well," she says, tugging at the hem of her shirt with more force than necessary, "you seem like you're fine."

Fine, yes. A jerk for adding to her embarrassment, also yes.

She turns her attention to June, talking over my head like I'm no longer sitting on the floor in front of her. "Hi, I'm Hope. We just moved into the Keller house, and I've got a broken window I need to fix. Know where I can start?" All of her words come out in a single breath, like she's eager to get through this conversation as quickly as possible. Probably to get away from me and the catastrophe that surrounds my aching body.

They jump right into a discussion about her options, and I sit there between them, growing more and more irritated even as the pain dulls. I just wanted a nice, quiet break from the world, and twice now Hope has brought nothing but chaos. Is this going to be my entire Laketown experience? Am I going to have her either sending me into a panic or maiming me every chance she gets? If that's what I'm in for, I might as well go back to Sun City.

Movement pulls my eyes to the next shelf over, where a fluffy head of brown hair pokes around the corner and a set of dark eyes meet mine. It's the boy, Link, and he's clutching a handsaw like it's the only thing that can give him a shred of happiness.

"He's too young for a saw," I say to no one in particular.

The women stop talking just as Link disappears like he's been caught. Which he has.

"I don't need you telling me how to raise my kids," Hope says with a huff. "You clearly have no idea what it takes to be a parent."

She couldn't have had better aim if she tried, and the sting of that insult is so much sharper than anything that just happened here in the store. She's not the first person to tell me that, but her words have no less weight to them than they did eighteen years ago.

"You're just a kid," the judge told me. "You don't know what goes into being a parent or how much sacrifice you have to make."

But I did know. I did my homework behind the counter at the drugstore where I worked after school until I realized I wasn't making enough to pay for new clothes for the twins, who were going through growth spurts. So I dropped out of high school and worked two different jobs, getting paid under the counter. I checked out cooking books from the library and learned to make meals that were more than boxed pasta full of preservatives. I took up sewing. Forged my dad's signature to let the twins go on field trips. Went to every baseball game that I could. Helped with homework. Barely slept some nights because I worked late and wanted to be up in time to help Houston and Brooklyn get ready for school. I held Brook when she cried of loneliness and taught Houston what it meant to be a man when I didn't know how myself and gave up any dreams I might have had so I could make sure my brother and sister were relatively happy and cared for.

But in the eyes of the judge, I was just a kid who was in over his head. Why should I get custody of my siblings after my dad went to jail?

Grunting, I struggle to my feet and become acutely aware of how much bigger I am than both of these women. I'm fairly tall as it is, six foot three, but Hope's head barely reaches my chin. June is a similar height, and neither woman can claim anything beyond petite. June may have some muscle on her, but they're both making me feel like a giant as I stand between them.

"Sorry about the mess," I say, even if I can't really claim fault for it. Nor can I bring myself to stick around and help clean it up. I need some distance from my neighbor, preferably forever, so I head for the door.

"Do you know if anyone around here can light my furnace?"

I stop dead. Hope wasn't talking to me, but she doesn't have heat in her house? Last night it got below freezing, and there's that hole in her window. Were they shivering all night?

June hums a little. "I'm sure there's someone. I've never done that, but one of the older men in town might know—"

"I can light it." I wince when Hope immediately glares at me across the store.

"I think I can figure it out," she says, rolling her eyes.

June, on the other hand, doesn't look so convinced. "It might be a good idea to—"

"I've got it covered."

I fold my arms, though I should have guessed she would be as stubborn as she is destructive. I glance outside, giving myself a moment to take a breath before I say something else I regret, but that glance gives me a perfect argument. "Feel free to let those kids freeze," I say and jerk my head toward the street, where light snow has started to fall.

Hope's eyes go wide, her face losing some of its color as she watches the white flakes fall lazily to the ground. "Is that...is that *snow*? But it's October!"

Where in the world did she move from if she has to ask? I clench my hand into a fist instead of grabbing my phone, telling myself I don't need to know. Then again, I just have to look outside at her license plate.

Florida. What brings someone from the opposite end of the country to a place like Laketown, Colorado?

I *do not* need to know.

"We've had snow in July here," June says with a shrug. "October is pretty normal."

"Okay, fine," Hope says with a sigh. "You can light my furnace for me."

"Don't do me any favors," I growl. Is it really so difficult for her to accept help? Or is it just accepting help from me?

She narrows her eyes at me, and I don't like the way this is heading. Needing to rescue her is one thing. Needing to rescue her when she doesn't want it is going to be another thing entirely. I don't have the patience for this.

Right as I step outside to head back home and grab the tools I need, I hear Hope ask one more question that makes me wonder how the kids have survived this long with their clearly incompetent mother: "Is there anywhere I can buy some coats or something?"

There is no way I can in good conscience ignore those kids when they clearly need some help, which means I'm going to have to start playing nice with my neighbor. And that is not going to be easy.

Chapter Six

Hope

THE SNOW ONLY LASTS for about an hour, and it doesn't stick to the ground, for which we are all thankful. Well, everyone except Zelda, who apparently has never wanted to do anything more than she wants to build a snowman. She threw a tantrum when she realized there wasn't enough—read: any—snow with which to build. That tantrum in turn led to Link bursting into tears and locking himself in the bathroom for two hours. I had to beg Zelda to let me into her room so I could use the master bathroom, and there's nothing like a screaming seven-year-old to make you wonder how long a full bladder can be held before it starts to cause complications. I may start squatting in the woods if things don't improve.

Needless to say, when Grizz knocks on my door just before dinner time, I am not in the mood for his beautiful, grumpy scowl.

"Took you long enough," I say, even though we never decided upon a time for him to come over and light the furnace. Zelda's screaming has me on edge, and apparently I get snippy when I'm stressed. That's new. And it only seems to happen around him...

I did some more Googling and seriously thought about lighting the furnace myself, but there is still that real fear of making the house explode, so I swallowed my pride on this one and left it alone. It *is* cold, though, and that's not helping the sobbing children situation. We bought some coats before heading home, but we can't feasibly wear them 24/7.

Grizz grunts and glances past me, eyes twitching a bit as he listens to Zelda's impressive shrieks. "Rough afternoon?"

"Don't start. Can you help with the furnace or not?"

I could almost swear he smiles a little as he steps inside, brushing past me because I don't exactly move out of his way. Maybe I'm being petty, but I hate that he doesn't think I can do this whole parenting thing when he has no room to talk. From all the gruffness I've seen so far, I doubt he has ever interacted with a kid, so he has no idea how hard this can be. Honestly, I don't think *I* know how hard it can be. All things considered, Link and Zelda have been way easier than I expected, which makes me think they're just holding out on the real difficulties until I'm a little less prepared for them.

I don't even want to think about the upcoming teenage years, mostly because I still feel like I'm a teenager myself. It's only been five years since I was a teen, which isn't very long at all.

"Where's your furnace?" Grizz asks, though his eyes are locked on the hall where the screams are still coming. He stands with his hands on either side of the walls, directly in the entrance to the hallway which is exactly where I need to go to show him the furnace.

The mature thing would be to ask him to move. Instead, I slip under his arm. But I misjudge the space between his ribs and the wall, colliding painfully with the sharp corner of the wall and bouncing directly into him. It's probably instinct that has him wrapping his arm around my shoulders and pulling me safely into his side, but heat still floods my whole body at the contact, just like it did at the hardware store today.

I have spent enough of my life being on the clumsy side that I don't easily get embarrassed, but when I took him out today, I wanted to bury myself in a hole and die. Not only did I make a huge mess that June refused to let me clean up, but I am well aware of just how thoroughly I injured both his body and his pride. I've never been much of a flirt, but I'm pretty sure hitting a guy in the nuts doesn't count.

And let me be perfectly clear: I have no intention, nor will I ever have it, of flirting with Grizz the Grump. I'm barely capable of taking care of myself let alone these kids, and throwing a guy into the mix, especially an older man, would do nothing but complicate things.

Does that stop me from taking this miniscule moment to nestle myself in his arms and enjoy the solid warmth of his body? No. No, it does not. It really is cold in here, okay? No one can blame me for taking advantage of a moment of clumsiness. And no matter how old he might be, that doesn't change the fact that he's all sorts of good-looking, to the point where I'm almost angry that there are people in the world who age this well. We're talking George Clooney levels here, though the only sign of gray on Grizz so far is in his scruff. Still. The man looks—and feels—good, and I refuse to let that go to waste.

Grizz clears his throat, and I step back, pretending there was nothing weird about that moment just now.

"Balance and I aren't friends, as you well know," I say, glad to see him pink a little. At least he knows he was rude earlier. "Furnace is this way." I open the closet door and wave my hand at the big appliances that are currently the cause of many of my woes.

He glances at me. "Water heater too?" he guesses, and I appreciate the wince he gives me when I nod. "You should have told me yesterday. Were the kids okay last night?"

"They were a little cold, but not too bad. I think we'd all like a shower, though."

He grunts again, and I'm starting to understand where the nickname Grizz may have come from. I'd still like to know his real name, but with the way he seems to keep to himself, I have to wonder if anyone would even know it. June told me she'd only just met him today, even though he bought the house a year ago. Maybe Eleanor would have better info? I have to ask her about the school situation still anyway, so I could just throw that in and—

"Done."

I blink. "Wait, already?" Sure enough, a little flame glows from the furnace, warm and bright. I hear the heater kick on, and suddenly I relax. "It was that easy?"

There's that almost-smile again, and I am so curious to know what his smile would look like if he let it loose. He's got that permanently grumpy look that a lot of people have in their resting expressions, but the wrinkles around his eyes tell me he's not *totally* against smiling. When he's this handsome, he either has a perfect smile or a terrible one; there is no in between with this kind of guy. If it's terrible, I can see why he would hide it from people he doesn't know. (For the record, there's no such thing as an actually terrible smile. A smile is a smile.) But if he has the kind of smile that lights up his face and makes rainbows appear, I desperately want to see it, just to say I did. So, the big question is which is it?

"Do..." He hesitates, glancing at me as he opens the panel on the water heater. "Do you want me to show you how to do it in case it goes out again?"

If it means I can avoid asking for his reluctant help again, then absolutely. But I play it cool and shrug one shoulder as I say, "Sure. If you want."

I'm not sure how that warrants an eye roll, but he gives me one anyway. "First, you want to make sure there isn't any gas floating around in there. The valve was already off, so we should be good, but if it goes out later, you'll want to turn it off for about ten minutes."

"So we don't go boom. Got it."

That throws him off, pulling his eyebrows down low as he tries to see if I'm serious or not. I am, which makes this funnier. "Then you'll want to turn it down to the lowest temp." He shows me, twisting the dial. "Newer models have a button you can push to ignite the light, but this one is, uh, pretty old. You should probably get a new one."

Yeah, that's not happening anytime soon, but I'll add it to my list of things I need to buy if I ever find a job. It can go alongside a bed and dresser for my tiny room which, I'll be honest, is likely still inhabited by our wolverine friend.

"Noted," I tell Grizz, just so he'll keep going.

"Then you take your lighter, and..." He holds the flame toward the place where I assume the pilot light is supposed to be, and it ignites immediately. "It's pretty simple, so you should be able to handle it."

"Because I am only capable of simple things," I agree as seriously as I can manage.

This time he turns more red than pink. "That isn't what I meant," he growls.

"I'm having a hard time figuring out what else you could mean. Thanks for your help, but I think I can take it from here."

He seems to fully agree because he turns without a word and heads for the door. But he gets stopped by Zelda suddenly opening her door as he approaches it. I knew he was big, but seeing his broad silhouette next to Zelda's thin frame makes him look exceptionally huge.

"Did you turn our heat on?" Zelda asks him. There's a bit of anxiety in her face as she looks up at him, like she's also realizing how big this man is now that he's standing so close to her.

And then Grizz does something that I never would have expected. He crouches down so he's at her same height. "I did," he says, speaking with impossible gentleness in his voice. "Is it starting to feel better in here?"

Zelda smiles—smiles!—at him. "Uh huh. Was it hard to turn it on?"

"Nope. And I showed your mom how to do it."

"She's not my mom. My mom is dead."

I watch as both of them react to that statement. Grizz stiffens, shoulders going tense and his hands curling into balls where he holds them in his lap. Zelda droops, her face going slack as if for a moment she'd forgotten that her mom is gone and she's stuck with an incompetent aunt who's trying her best but absolutely failing.

Tears pool in my eyes as I stand there frozen, wishing I had a way to change reality so Zelda would never have to say those words.

Grizz, on the other hand, reaches up and brushes a tear from Zelda's cheek with a big finger. "My mom is dead too," he says, and then he stands up and walks out of the house without looking back.

Well crap. Now it's going to be so much harder to dislike him.

Chapter Seven
Chad

I ONLY MAKE IT a couple of hours before I see Hope again, which isn't nearly long enough. After a phone call with Micah that left me feeling more frustrated than I'd like, I've been sitting on my porch watching the sunset fade to dusk and trying to reconcile what I thought I knew with the new information that has come in. If Hope isn't the mother of the kids, what is she? She looks similar enough that I'm guessing she's family. Probably too old to be a sister, though it's not impossible. Aunt is the most likely explanation. But why would she be the person taking care of the kids if they've lost their mom? She's so young, and on her own, and I don't especially want to think there isn't anyone else in the family who could have taken the kids because that would make them so alone.

I know how that feels. I wouldn't want that for them.

How long has Hope had the kids? Did they move because she got them? Is she going to have them forever, or is this a temporary situation? Does she have any help at all? Single parenting is difficult no matter what, but when you aren't prepared for it?

I forced myself to leave my phone inside so I'm not tempted to see what I can dig up, but my resolve is slipping. If I know the situation, I'll know if she even needs my help. She might be perfectly fine, and that's why she's getting so irritated with me stepping in. But she also might be drowning and too stubborn to cry out for help. I told Micah that I wasn't going to pay any attention to my neighbor, but maybe if I can just get a little more information, I'll scratch the itch enough to leave things alone.

I'm halfway out of my seat when Hope appears next door, stepping out the back door and into her sorry excuse for a backyard. Being right at the edge of the open forest here doesn't exactly lend itself to having a manicured lawn, but she doesn't even have a patio or a deck. It's not very kid-friendly, something she may not have thought of when she bought the house. Houses closer to town are a little more suburban, but she didn't pick one of those. She picked this one, so she's going to have to get used to the kids driving her crazy inside or running around the woods.

I shudder. Maybe I should suggest they borrow Duke if they ever decide to do that. I don't want to know what would happen if he came across a mountain lion, but I would rather he take the fall than the kids.

Duke lifts his head with a whine, as if he can read my thoughts.

I scratch his ears. "Don't worry. I doubt she would accept your help any more readily than she accepted mine."

But now he's seen her, and his tail starts thumping as he watches her wrap a blanket around her shoulders and pick her way through the stick-strewn area to a worn and warped bench that sits at the edge of her property.

Curiosity gets the better of me, and I mutter, "Go get her."

Duke gladly hops up and scurries over to her, startling her until she realizes it's not a woodland creature creeping up on her. A smile lights up her face as she reaches out and pets his head, and she laughs when his tail wags so hard that his entire rear end is wagging with it. I'm pretty sure she doesn't know I'm out here or she wouldn't be showing my dog this much affection, but I'm not going to change that fact. Not yet. I'm going to use this moment to watch her before it gets too dark, and then I'm going to go inside and pretend I don't have internet access so I can't research everything about this woman.

I should turn my internet off entirely until the itch goes away, but I worry that won't happen anytime soon. Every time I see her, I'm going to want to know more.

Hope is undeniably pretty. She has a girl-next-door vibe—I'm ignoring that irony—the kind of beauty that is natural and easy. So far, she's worn her dark hair long and free. It has a little wave to it that gives it some life, and I wonder if it's as soft as it looks. Her heart-shaped face is young and full of life, with all the signs of her being quick to smile. I think her eyes fascinate me the most, if I'm giving myself this moment to catalog everything about her. They're a rich brown, warm and soft and bottomless. Even when she's glared at me, I've felt her gaze deep in my bones, like she's lived a thousand lives in her short lifetime.

There's a story in those eyes, one I wouldn't mind knowing.

I curse under my breath and shake that thought away before it latches on. I came to Laketown to simplify my life, and that means staying away from something as endlessly complicated as Hope and her little family.

I'm safer without her around, both physically and emotionally.

"Has anyone ever told you your dog is perfect?"

I swear again, this time a little louder, and then cringe when I realize she's standing just a few feet from my deck and looking up at me. "Sorry," I say and make a note to be better about my language, especially when the kids are around. I should be better in general—my mom hated swearing, and now Brooklyn does too. "Uh, yeah, he's a good dog."

I can't decide if I should be glad or mad that he brought Hope over here, but he looks a little too pleased with himself as he grins at her side, tongue lolling out of his mouth.

Hope rolls her eyes. "*Good dog* applies to basically every dog. Even the bad ones. Duke is, well, perfect. I mean, he doesn't even *smell* like a dog!"

Oh, he smells. Just not after I've given him a bath, like I did today after he decided to roll around in the mud that came from the snowfall. I would have been over to light the furnace sooner if I wasn't afraid of Duke sneaking under my covers like he likes to do when it gets cold. I've found mud in my sheets more than once.

"Uh." Apparently I've forgotten how words work now, though I can't decide if it's because I'm thinking about dog smell or because she looks cute bundled up in her blanket like that. And I shouldn't think about how she's cute because I've already given myself too much liberty when it comes to Hope tonight. Right, I was going to tell her she can borrow Duke. Which sounds weird. I shouldn't say it that way. "If the kids are ever playing outside, they should come grab Duke if I'm around. It would be safer."

She stiffens. "Safer? How so?"

"There might be mountain lions."

"Mountain lions?" She jumps back a step, which startles Duke and makes him bark and lick her hand to make sure she's okay. "Are you serious?"

I could tell her that they probably won't come this close to the house, but I can't say that for sure. We're in a pretty remote area, and I know Hank down the road said he's seen one or two in the few years that he's lived on this lane. It's better if I give it to her straight, especially when she has a badger climbing in and out of her window.

"It's possible, yeah. I think Duke would scare one off if it ever came close, but you should tell the kids to keep an eye out if they're ever out here on their own."

A shiver runs through her, and I don't think it's from the cold. Did she really not do any research before buying the house?

"Did you figure out your badger problem?" I ask.

"Wolverine," she replies.

"Right," I say, even though I did a little digging and learned there hasn't been a wolverine sighting in Colorado for over a century, so it's probably a badger. This is not the hill I need to die on.

"No," she says after waiting to see if I'll argue about the species any more. "I haven't even had a chance to fix the window yet."

"You'll want to get a new—"

"New window, yeah. I know. I've put it on the list."

She has a list? I wonder how many of those things on her list are things I could help her with. Save her some money. Then I wonder if she would even let me help. Probably not. Next time she goes into town, I'm going to walk around her house and make sure it's structurally sound and only the one window needs fixing.

"Is the ba—wolverine back in the house?"

Her lips twist up in a little smile, though it's almost too dark to see it now. "I have no idea. I've been too afraid to look, but it's okay. I don't have a bed in that room yet, so I've been sleeping on the couch anyway."

My thoughts turn to the three guest rooms I have in my house, all of them fully furnished in case my siblings ever want to come stay for a few days. I keep those thoughts to myself.

"I'm sure Duke would love to scare it out," I tell her, and I swear the dog knows exactly what I say because he turns to look at Hope's house, suddenly tense. I know dogs are smart, but sometimes I think he's *too* smart. But then he'll go and roll himself in roadkill, so that intelligence only goes so far. "You'll want to make sure it isn't inside before you patch up the window until you can get a—"

"I *know*, Grizz."

That name is so stupid. I should just tell her my actual name, but I don't want to. "I'm just trying to help," I say, keeping my voice from shifting into frustration.

Hope, on the other hand, lets her own frustration color her words with enough acid that it's like she's trying to hit me with it and melt me into a gooey mess. "If I need your help, I'll ask for it."

"I won't hold my breath."

"I'm going inside now."

"Do what you want."

She groans and stomps back to the house with the same temper Zelda seemed to show earlier.

"Inside, Duke."

But the dog stays put, his eyes locked on the door that Hope disappeared through as he whines. It's like he has already decided she is his new favorite person.

That's going to be a problem.

Chapter Eight
Hope

October 10

AFTER STUFFING A BLANKET against the bottom of my bedroom door, the rest of the house stays a little warmer. Despite telling Grizz that I am perfectly fine to handle everything on my own, I haven't worked up the courage to check on the wolverine, which I need to do before I cover up the hole in the window. So I'm just going to wait things out until I'm hit with a sudden burst of bravery. Maybe that will be never. The couch really isn't all that bad, and the kids have been spending most of their time in their rooms today, giving me a chance to get them signed up for school and even research a few remote jobs I could possibly do.

Not that I found much. When I had plans to study the stars and figure out what actually happens inside black holes, typing out captions on TV shows doesn't exactly sound like a thrilling new career choice. I gave up on that hunt pretty quickly and put my focus more on the school side of things.

When I called Eleanor, she told me that she'd already mentioned the kids to the principal and they're excited to add to their small numbers, though it sounds like there are some kids that get bussed in from almost an hour away. Despite being tiny, Laketown is in a pretty central location, so we have a grade school and a high school that serves all of the surrounding small towns. Eleanor also told me about the summer carnival, though I don't know why I need to know about that in October. Apparently it's a whole thing and people come from all over. There's a Christmas festival, farmer's market in the fall, and a tulip festival in the spring, and it all sounds pretty great. Maybe coming here wasn't such a bad idea after all.

Signing the kids up for school was the easy part, though. Telling them about it is going to be rough. Zelda will probably be happy, but I have no idea how Link is going to react. I figure if I take them into town to the little ice cream shop I saw on Main Street, I can soften the blow a bit.

Link, as usual, is sitting on his bed and staring out the window like he might find the answers to the universe out there. He hasn't said anything since before we went grocery shopping yesterday, but he ate the chicken and potatoes I made last night, so I'm not going to push him. One step at a time is the way to go with this kid.

"Hey, kiddo. Anything interesting out there today?"

He shakes his head, even though his eyes are riveted on the trees. I don't think he's spent much time away from this window since I told him about the possibilities of mountain lions being out there. I'm pretty sure he would love to see one, which has me a little bit terrified. Grizz did offer up his dog, but I don't know what a golden retriever could do against a big cat with claws and fangs. I don't want to be the woman who's known for letting her nephew get eaten by a mountain lion, so I'm going to be extra cautious about letting the kids play outside.

"You know what I think?" I say. "I think we should go into town for some ice cream. Celebrate our third day here. What do you think?"

"Of course we want ice cream," Zelda says from the doorway, and I have to wonder how long she's been standing there. I have a nagging feeling that she tends to keep a close eye on me whenever I'm around Link, like she thinks she needs to protect him from me. I have no idea why she would think that, and I hate that she doesn't trust me yet. I don't think either of them do, but they're smart enough to know they don't have a choice.

I paste on a smile and clap my hands. "Well, then let's go!"

There are a good number of people in the ice cream shop when we arrive, probably because it's the only dessert place in town, but I'm not complaining in the slightest when it makes both kids scoot up against my side and hold on to the edges of my coat. They haven't been touchy feely even a little bit, and it's killing me not having someone to hug. I'm a glutton for physical contact—case in point, the way I mauled Grizz with a hug yesterday—and it's been literal years since I had someone I could interact with. Hopefully these kids will learn to love me enough to start actually touching me, but I won't hold my breath. They haven't before, so why would they now? They might just not be huggers, and I will have to be okay with that.

"You guys can choose whatever flavor you want," I tell them when it's our turn up at the counter, and their eyes bug out of their heads a bit when they see the number of options. There are only six flavors, but apparently that's more than what they're used to because they practically press their faces to the glass and start drooling.

I know for a fact that Bailey was obsessed with ice cream, so this feels weird.

"What does that one taste like?" Zelda asks, pointing to the vividly blue flavor.

The teenage girl behind the counter smiles. "Do you want to try it?"

Zelda's jaw drops. "I can try it?"

"Sure." She grabs one of the sample spoons and pulls out a little bite.

My heart melts a little when Zelda hands it to her brother and then requests another sample. She's such a good sister, even though I know she's having just as hard a time as Link is. She learned that from Bailey, who was always looking out for me when we were growing up, even when things were tough.

Once both kids have tried every flavor, Zelda asks for cookies and cream and tells me that Link wants the blue cotton candy kind, even though I have no idea how he told her that because he hasn't opened his mouth except to put ice cream in it. They must have some sort of silent communication style going on. Maybe I can learn it if I study them long enough, though with my luck it's probably Morse code or something. They seem like the sort of kids who would know that kind of thing.

Once we have our loaded cones, we find a seat in the corner next to the big windows that line the front of the store. It isn't quite dark yet, and there are a lot more people outside than I would have expected. I guess it's not so cold that no one wants to be out in the elements, but I never really figured a small town like this would have a thriving downtown scene. Most of the people wandering Main Street look on the older side, like retired couples who are now empty nesters and want to enjoy a more peaceful life away from the hustle and bustle, but there are a good number of young people too. Like, *teenager* young, not *the sort of people I could become friends with* young. And while it wasn't on my radar in the slightest, I can forget dating in Laketown.

June told me there are two single men under fifty in this town—I promise I didn't ask her for this info—and both of them live on my street. One of them, an author, is basically a hermit and rarely comes into town or even leaves his house, while the other is my charming, friendly neighbor Grizz. She called him that too, by the way. Or, I think she did. She was sweeping up nails as she talked, but I'm pretty sure she called him Mr. Grizz. Maybe it's his last name?

It doesn't matter. There could be a hundred eligible men in Laketown and I still wouldn't be interested in dating any of them. Not for a few years, if even then. More than likely, I'll be on my own until the kids are grown up with families of their own. I've never had much time for dating anyway, so I don't feel like I'm making much of a sacrifice by focusing on the kids.

"So, what did you want to tell us?" Zelda says.

I nearly drop my ice cream. "What?"

She points to her own cone, giving me her signature *Are you stupid?* look. "You have bad news, right?"

Seriously, this kid is a little terrifying sometimes, and I genuinely wonder if she's actually seven or if she's seven hundred and trapped in a little kid body. "Are you psychic?" I ask her.

She scrunches up her face. "What does that mean?"

"Never mind. Why do you think I have bad news?"

"Because Mom always got us ice cream when she had bad news."

Oh. I wish I had known that before I suggested this. Apparently Bailey and I think alike, though. "I have news," I say carefully, "but I don't think it's bad news. At least, I hope it isn't. I signed you guys up for school."

I brace myself for another tantrum, hands on my keys in case we need to make a run for it.

But the kids just blink at me for a second before returning to their ice cream. "Okay," Zelda says.

Really? That's it? "You're not mad?"

"Why would we be mad?"

I'm not sure how to answer that one. I guess I was just going off of my own experiences. I was the kid who couldn't wait until summer vacation came around so I could have freedom again. It's kind of funny that I willingly paid a lot of money to keep going to school year after year up into my master's program, all things considered.

I sit back in my seat, turning my gaze back out the window so I can smile without them seeing. "I guess I thought you guys would like being out of school."

"We don't have anything to do here, and you just want to read books all the time. It's boring." Zelda is not one to mince words.

My eyes catch on a man directly across the street from us. He walks slowly, hands in his pockets, until he looks over and sees the ice cream shop, and then he stops with a surprised expression on his face. It's gone a moment later, but there is something familiar about him. I must have seen him in town yesterday without really noting him.

He seems to be watching me right back, though, like he thinks I look familiar too. Maybe we met somewhere else? He's probably somewhere in his later thirties, though his curly brown hair is streaked with gray. Unless he was a professor or something, I don't know where I would have seen him before, but there's definitely something… A moment later, he blinks and keeps walking, pausing to talk to someone as they cross paths. He's gotta be a local then, and he must have one of those faces. I'll probably see him around again, and we'll have one of those conversations where we list a bunch of places we might have met and realize we have literally never been in the same place before now.

The kids finish off their ice cream, and though Link cries a little when his cone breaks in his hand, all in all the night is a raging success. They agree to try taking the bus in a week or so after they've gotten used to being at school—I'll drop them off tomorrow and get them checked in—and they both brush their teeth and go right to bed.

I send Bailey a quiet prayer of gratitude for raising such good kids, and then I settle on my couch bed with a book, drifting off to sleep before I even get through a chapter. For the first time since the day I got the phone call about my sister, I sleep peacefully.

Chapter Nine
Chad

October 11

I HAVE A PROBLEM. And I *know* it's a problem because I've lost track of the number of times Houston has gotten mad at me for digging into people's lives—especially his. Though no one can beat Micah in optimism and cheer, my younger brother is one of the most happy-go-lucky people I know. Nothing gets to him, so when something has him bothered, I've learned to pay attention. Especially when that something is me.

I looked into Hope. I couldn't help it. When I get that itch, that need to fix a problem, I can only resist it for so long before it starts to drive me crazy, and I was at my wit's end.

Strangely, I couldn't actually find anything on Hope, but I found the kids. The school records were a little too easy to access—I'll let them know so they can get a better firewall—and there aren't exactly a lot of kids named after video game characters in a little town like Laketown. Link and Zelda Duncan, six and seven years old, transferred from a school in Orlando. Their mom died about a month ago from an unexpected cerebral hemorrhage, and from the sound of things it was Link who found her on the floor in her bedroom when she hadn't come downstairs for school. He alerted the nanny, who called 911, but at that point it was too late. Kids were sent to CPS, and from there I couldn't follow the trail. Hope Duncan wasn't listed anywhere, but she could easily have a different last name from the kids.

All in all, I didn't learn much, and it only partially satisfied the itch. But now I know way more about my neighbors than I should. That'll get me into trouble if I'm not careful, hence this being a problem.

Those poor kids. Especially Link. I sat in the hospital room when my mother's cancer eventually took her away from us, and I was fifteen at the time. Old enough to understand what was happening. And it still gutted me. The twins were even worse off because they were only seven, too young to really grasp the concept of why she had to die. They were so convinced she would get better until she didn't. I can't imagine what went through Link's head when he tried to wake his mother up, and I'm starting to understand why he's so quiet.

Still feeling like I need to finish the rest of the puzzle—I seriously hate that I'm like this—I decide to go for a run before the weather turns too cold for that kind of thing. I change into shorts and a tank quickly and set out with Duke at my heels before my computer pulls me back to dig some more. Maybe I can blow off some steam and get over this insane need to know everything.

I think it's a control thing. So much of my life was out of my control and beyond my abilities to take control, and that feeling of helplessness still haunts me now and then, like if I let things slip I might lose someone else I love. It's not even like I've lost all that many people, but two is still a lot. I lost my dad first, when he got into some bad stuff and made the decision to cheat on my mom, and his life went downhill from there until he ended up in prison. Then Mom got sick, and I had to lose her slowly, piece by piece as the cancer wore her down to nothing. I guess I can count losing my siblings for a little while, when they went to live with Micah's dad, Lloyd, after the judge denied my custody appeal. I visited them all the time, but for a few years it was like they weren't mine anymore. Plus, Houston was getting into his baseball ego phase and was too cool for me, which hurt more than I'll ever tell him.

I don't like that the thing that brought my brother and me back together was a tearful phone call—on both our sides, I'll admit—after he blew his chance for a scholarship his senior year when he showed up to a game hungover and got benched when he could have been playing for a scout. He thought his life was over, and I had to talk him down to make sure he didn't do anything stupid before I could talk to Lloyd and see if he could use his influence to get Houston another shot.

My brother lost some pride after that, which was a good thing, but that didn't stop him from becoming one of the MLB's most celebrated players over the last few years. He's got one of his last Series games tonight, and I have a feeling he's going to pull his team to a World Series victory for the second time since he got drafted by the Sun City team eight years ago. If not tonight, for sure the next time he pitches.

I don't know how long I've been running, but Duke is slowing down, which means I've gone too far. I come to a stop and force myself to take some deep breaths and stretch out my burning limbs, pretending that I'm taking this pause for the dog's sake, not for mine. I'm getting too old to push myself this hard, which is as depressing as it is true.

In fact, Duke is still grinning as he sprawls out at my feet, happy as can be. He's only seven years old, after all. I will never admit it out loud, but the only reason I got him in the first place was because Micah graduated high school and was heading out into the real world, leaving me without anyone to look out for. It was awful, I was lonely, and he and I made eye contact in the shelter. I knew immediately I needed to take him home, and he's been at my side ever since.

Except now, apparently. Without warning, he gets up and trots off behind me with a bigger grin than before. Before I can turn to see where he's going, a car honks, making me jump a mile in the air because it's right behind me. I press a hand to my chest, knowing before I even turn around that I'll find Hope behind the wheel, laughing at me.

There she is, a huge smile on her face as she hops out of the car and starts petting Duke the traitor. He could have warned me she was pulling up behind me. "Sorry!" she says when I pull out my earbuds. "I thought for sure you would have heard me stop. Did you run all the way out here?"

Wherever *out here* is, it must be farther than I thought, though I don't have my phone on me to see what time it is. Which, honestly, is pretty stupid of me, but I was determined to keep to my own business, something I would not be able to do if I had any kind of network. As I wrap my earbuds around my iPod, I glance down the street, hoping to see some sort of mile marker, but there's nothing but trees. The one thing I *do* know is I ran in the opposite direction of town, so there's really no reason for Hope to be out this way.

Was she following me?

"What are you doing out here?" I ask, folding my arms as Duke rolls over beneath her vigorous rubs and offers his belly for sacrifice.

She giggles, rubbing him even faster before she looks back up at me. Then she freezes, her eyes locking on my arms for three seconds before she meets my gaze again. "I got distracted by your muscles—I mean by Metallica. I missed the turn." Red blossoms on her cheeks as she turns her focus back to my ridiculous dog.

I'm so tempted to call out her slip, but I'm more curious about the other part. "Metallica?"

"It's my belt band."

"Your what?"

She snickers before hopping up to be more at my level. "You know, the band that you sing along to so loudly that you lose your voice? Belt band."

"I don't think anyone calls it that."

"How would you know, old man?"

"How do you even know who Metallica is?"

"I'm not *that* young!"

I scoff, flexing my arms a little just to see what she'll do. "How old are you, anyway?"

She's pretty good about ignoring my biceps directly, but that doesn't stop her face from heating more. "I'm twenty-four."

Hmm. She almost looks younger than that. "I was listening to Metallica before you were even born," I say, which might be true. My dad loved metal bands, so there were probably some moments when I was younger that I heard a few songs. But now I'm thinking about how I was twelve the year Hope was born. That was the year Mom married Lloyd and found out she was pregnant a few months later. The twins were horrified and cried for days, but I was excited.

This really isn't helping the whole *old* situation. Twelve years isn't a lot, but it's...a lot.

She folds her own arms, though I'm not sure what she's hoping to gain by matching me. She's still tiny, and now she's got Duke pressing himself up against her leg begging for more ear scratches. "And how old are you? Fifty? Sixty?"

"Forty-seven." I don't know why I say that. Maybe it's a defense mechanism of some sort, even if it makes absolutely no sense. But I can't complain about the outcome because her jaw drops, her bottomless eyes going wider than I've ever seen them.

"Seriously?" When I nod, she claps a hand over her mouth. "Dang, you look good for your age, Grizz!"

"Chad." I hold out my hand, unable to stop myself from grinning. "My name is Chad. And I'm thirty-six." I should be concerned that she didn't really question the almost-fifty thing.

Though she takes my hand, she seems weirdly fixated on my smile. What, do I have something in my teeth? No, because I haven't eaten anything today, something I'm feeling now that the adrenaline of my run is wearing off. Still, my smile drops under her examination, which breaks the spell, and she grimaces.

"Sorry," she says, almost in a whisper. "You just...you have a really good smile. I wasn't sure if you would."

"What is that supposed to mean?"

Chuckling, she shakes her head and takes a step back. I'm not sure she realizes she's still holding on to my hand, stretching our arms out between us. "Nothing. Just a theory I have. I should let you get back to your run."

I tighten my grip on her hand before she can walk away. I'm almost enjoying this civility, and she's excellent at distracting me from my wandering thoughts of things I can't control. I can't control her either, but she's the only one who has all the answers I want. Maybe, if I can be nice for long enough, she'll give me some of them.

"Where are the kids?" I ask.

She looks down at our clasped hands. "School. I figured they were probably ready to start back up again."

"I'm sorry about their mom." I almost let out a curse before I remember Zelda told me that part so it's okay that I know it. At least I didn't find anything on Hope, so there's no chance of slipping up there.

Hope blinks, looking back up at me with a lot of emotions swirling in her eyes. No tears, though. "Thanks. Me too."

"When did...?" I know this answer already, but if Hope is willing to give me some info on her own, I'll have less to hide.

She wraps her other arm around her middle and shivers a little. She's probably cold, but I think there's some emotion coming through with that movement as well. "It was about a month ago," she says. "Really sudden. And my sister decided that I should be the one to take them if anything happened to her."

Sister. So she *is* their aunt, which must mean she has a different last name. The kids likely took their dad's name, though I didn't find any info on him either. Hope would know, though now isn't the time to ask something like that. Nor is it my business.

Is that going to stop me from digging? Probably not.

"So, is there a reason you're holding my hand?" Hope nods toward our hands hanging between us, a little smile playing on her lips. "I mean, it's a good hand, I know. But if you need help crossing the street, you only have to ask."

She's really going to lay into those old man jokes, isn't she? I won't let them bother me, even if they do.

"I can cross on my own, thanks." And yet I still don't let go. Why am I not letting go?

Lifting an eyebrow, she glances around the empty road as if searching for someone to help her out of this situation. Though, I don't think she's uncomfortable. She's not giving off a wary vibe, just a confused one. I'm confused too. The last time we spoke, we both ended up frustrated.

"Are you scared to be out here all alone?" she asks.

I roll my eyes. "I'm not alone. I have Duke."

"Ah, yes, the vicious retriever."

The vicious retriever who is currently resting his head on her feet like they're the best of friends now. It's usually my feet that he's warming, and I don't like the jealous feelings creeping up in my chest. They're feet, for crying out loud, and I'm usually more annoyed with him than anything when he does it. But Duke doesn't like my siblings this much, let alone a woman he barely knows, so I have no idea what he's doing right now. I've always been his favorite.

"Were the kids excited about going to a new school?" I ask, mentally kicking myself for making this even weirder than it already is. Why would I need to know that? I wouldn't. I don't. But I still want to know. And now I'm wondering if Zelda is making friends or if her strong personality is making her a target because a bully can get a reaction out of her. Is Link going to talk to anyone, or will he be as quiet as he's been with me?

Hope swallows, her hand tightening around mine though she's looking at Duke below us. "They were pretty on edge this morning, actually. Link wouldn't let go of my hand when I dropped them off, and Zelda threw a fit when she found out they would be in different classes even though they've always been in different grades."

"Oh." I clear my throat, finally relaxing my hold. To my surprise, Hope hangs on. Maybe she needs the reassurance that she's not failing as a parent just because her kids were afraid of a new situation. "When my brother and sister went to middle school, my sister Brooklyn had a meltdown. She and Houston were always in the same class growing up, and suddenly she had all these new teachers and none of the classes were with him. She didn't know how to handle that for a while."

When she looks up, there's a bit of hope in her eyes, like she desperately needs to know that the kids are doing normal kid things. So I keep talking.

"Houston was fine, but he's always been good on his own. He's the most independent out of any of us, which is good because he's on the road most of the time." I cock my head. "Though, I guess he's got his team with him."

"Team?"

This has nothing to do with Link and Zelda's situation, but Hope seems to be brightening back up again. I didn't mean to bring her mood down, so I'll do what I can to pull it up where it belongs.

"Yeah, he's a baseball player. For the Red-tails."

Suddenly Hope's other hand is on my arm so she's holding me with both hands and staring at me with wide eyes. "Wait, is your brother Houston Briggs?"

A smile breaks out of me, and I tell myself that it's because she's so excited. Not because she is apparently someone who enjoys sports because it doesn't matter if she likes sports. It's not like this is a relationship that will ever grow beyond this weird hand-holding thing we're doing on the side of the road.

"Does it make me cool or lame if I say yes?" I ask.

She jumps up and down a couple of times, to Duke's displeasure. "Definitely cool! I mean, I'm a Burrs fan myself, but that doesn't mean I can't love Houston Briggs too."

I groan. "I can't believe you just said that. You do know that the Burrs are playing my brother's team in the World Series right now, right?"

Though she can't help but grin, she tries to turn incredibly serious as she says, "Yeah, okay, well, it's unfortunate that the Red-tails are going to lose tonight, but it's still—"

"Excuse me? Have you seen them play?"

Honestly, I don't care if they lose. Of course I hope they win, but if they don't it means Houston only has to pitch one more game before he can get some real rest because he stresses over the games regardless of whether he's pitching. He won't admit it, but he's slowing down, and I have my suspicions that he's hiding an injury. He's had a few odd throws recently that don't make sense outside of an underlying issue that he's probably ignoring because that's what he does. He ignores problems and works himself harder, and one of these days something is going to snap.

Hopefully it isn't one of his tendons doing the snapping.

Hope pulls me back to the present—literally pulls me closer—and narrows her eyes at me. "Yeah, I've seen them play, and they've lost two games already. Tonight's gonna be the third, and then we're only one game away from winning."

"You mean the Red-tails?" I counter. "Yeah, you're right. They'll win tonight, and then Houston will be the starting pitcher again in Game Six. Your little Burrs are toast."

Surprisingly, she seems to see some sound logic in my argument. Houston is pitching tonight, and he hasn't lost a single game this season when he's the starting pitcher. Barring something catastrophic, the Red-tails are going to win.

"How about we agree to disagree?" Hope says with a roll of her eyes.

"Seems to be a theme with us," I reply.

She grins, and I'm mesmerized by her smile. Despite losing her sister and taking on a couple of kids who are dealing with a lot of trauma, she has such an open and honest smile. The world hasn't broken her yet, and I wish I could protect her from the inevitable heartbreak that comes from being alive. I wish I could keep her happy like this because *someone* deserves to feel that way.

A brisk breeze blows over us, winding its way inside my tank and chilling me to my core. That's when I realize that at some point over the last couple of minutes, I've adjusted my hold on Hope's hand so that it's pressed between both of mine and held against my chest in such a way that I could easily caress her fingers. Press a kiss to her palm. Pull her those few inches closer and see if her lips are as soft as they look.

I drop her hand like I've been burned and take a couple of steps back, wishing I could take back the last few minutes because I don't want her to get the wrong idea. There may be attraction here—I'd be stupid to admit otherwise—but there are so many reasons why it has to end there. I could make a whole list.

In fact, I do make a list as I brush a hand over my hair and pretend nothing just happened.

1. She is twenty-four years old.

2. Link and Zelda need some stability in their lives.

3. She's twenty-four. Twelve years younger than me.

4. I only planned to stay in Laketown for a few weeks. Maybe less.

5. TWENTY-FOUR

6. I got my heart broken six months ago, and I don't think there's enough of it left to give it to someone new.

Okay, so, I'm not sure I realized that last one until just now. I knew Mercedes hurt me, and I knew I was okay with being on my own because I don't want to experience heartbreak again. But this is different. This is me suddenly realizing that my own pain is not my biggest motivator for staying solitary.

I don't think I can love anyone the way they'll deserve, which means I need to stay far away from Hope. She deserves more than what I can give her, no matter how much I feel a pull toward her.

"Well, I'll let you finish your run," she says, and her face shows all of the awkwardness I've caused by forgetting for a moment who and where I was.

"Hope?"

She turns.

I give her a sad smile. "Think you could give us a ride home? This body isn't what it used to be."

Thankfully, that gets a grin out of her, but she also gives me a full perusal from head to toe, which sends a shiver through me because she seems to like what she sees. Her eyes go a little glassy at the same time her cheeks turn a flattering shade of pink. Then she clears her throat and the moment is over. "Get in the car, old man."

Duke interprets that for himself and hops through her open door before I can even move, and I am more certain than ever that staying away from this woman is going to be a lot harder than I would like.

That's not going to stop me from trying.

Chapter Ten

Hope

October 17

I HAVE NEVER BEEN more thankful for Zelda's nonstop talking. It has been a whirlwind week with getting the kids back into the habit of school—for Link, this year is his first time doing school full-time—and I've barely had time to breathe, let alone think about my neighbor whenever the kids are home. Zelda keeps that theme going tonight, forcing my focus to remain on her as she goes on and on about a girl at school while I make spaghetti. I listen hard because I want to make sure they both had a good day and are making friends. And, honestly, anything is better than the last several days, during which I pretended to clean up the house when really I was just thinking about the way Chad—so much better than Grizz—held on to my hand on the road last week.

And more than that... I've never had a man look at me the way Chad looked at me. Over the course of a few minutes, he went from exasperation to irritation, sympathy to excitement, appreciation to...dare I say it? Adoration? Admiration? Attraction? Any of the A words, that was him. What does that even mean?

We haven't interacted since the road, but that doesn't mean I haven't seen him. He tends to be outside a lot, playing with his dog or cleaning up his yard. At one point he was stringing lights on his deck, and I may have had to sit on the kitchen sink to get a good view out the window, but I enjoyed the view a little too much. The way his arms—I will never get over his arms—stretched over his head as he attached the lights. The man has phenomenal arms. They're the kind of arms I wouldn't mind wrapped around me for an extended period of time.

"Did you hear me, Hope?"

I absolutely did not. I was dreaming about a man's biceps while stirring the spaghetti sauce. "Sorry, sweetie, what did you say?"

"I said that the man who lives next to us is outside if you want to watch him again."

"What?" My hand slips, catching the handle of the saucepan and knocking it off the stove, sending warm tomato sauce everywhere. All three of us scream out of reflex, probably because Link and Zelda get splashed too even though the bulk of it hits me in the chest. Thank goodness it wasn't hot yet, but that doesn't make this much better.

I stand there, arms dripping with sauce and my eyes shut tight because I got a fair bit in my face too, and heaven help me I'm going to start laughing even if this is so not the time. I really do try to hold it back, but when it breaks from me with a splutter and sends sauce flying out of my nose, I lose all control.

Then I slip.

That's how a breathless Chad finds me, flat on my back on the massacre that is my kitchen floor and laughing like a maniac. *Of course* he came running when he heard us scream, and I can only imagine his first thoughts when he sees the red liquid everywhere because this must look like the most gruesome murder scene in the world. But there I am, laughing my head off because I am such a sad excuse for an adult that the only thing I can do is laugh.

He mutters something under his breath as he slips his phone into his pocket, clearly exasperated by my incompetence. Even though I'm still overcome with my laughing fit, I hear him ask if the kids are okay.

"It's just sauce," Zelda tells him. "Is Hope okay?"

Chad looks down at me, and he seems less panicked now that he's taken in the scene. And what do you know, he's just as handsome upside down as he is right side up. Typical. "I would ask if you need help," he says, "but something tells me you'll say you've got it handled."

I deserve that, and I really could handle it. But I feel like something changed between us last week, and he made me feel like I don't have to be a perfect parent when he told me about his siblings. So, despite my inner voice telling me that asking for help is not how I operate, I shake my head. "Actually, I would love some help."

His eyebrows jump up—down, from my perspective—and he doesn't seem to know how to respond to that. But then he holds out his hand

and grasps my wrist, and with a little twisting maneuver he has me on my feet a moment later. Naturally, my foot slips again and knocks me into his chest, which I marginally feel bad about because I just covered him in sauce. The other part of me is thrilled.

"Thanks," I breathe while I'm still pressed up against him. Gotta get my fill while I can since he'll probably freak out again. He's so warm and solid. I want to fall asleep with his broad chest for a pillow and his arms as a blanket and the sound of his heartbeat as a soundtrack to my dreams. Yeah, that sounds nice.

"Go take a shower," he grunts, gently pushing me away from my little cuddle fantasy. "I'll clean up in here."

Okay, I know I asked for help, but that's just ridiculous. "But—"

"Go." He points, but it's the strength in his voice that gets me to move. It's that sense of command that had me so fixated on our first morning here, and I hate how much it works on me now. But at the same time, I don't hate it. I want to salute and say, "Yes, sir," and maybe do an experiment with his lips because I can only imagine the way he takes charge with something like a kiss.

Hope Duncan, what in the world is wrong with you?

I pause at the edge of the hallway and look back to make sure the kids are okay with me leaving them here with Chad, but there is no way I can focus on the kids right now because Chad is pulling his sauce-covered Henley over his head, and his t-shirt didn't get the memo that it was supposed to stay put. That t-shirt deserves a medal for failing so miserably at hiding the complete *man* lurking beneath it.

It's not like he's all jagged edges and perfectly cut abs—the abs are there, I promise. He's most definitely strong, but it's the solid kind of strong, where you only see the muscles as he moves and shifts and—*oh my stars he's looking at me*. My face goes up in flames because I've been caught staring—and probably drooling because for the last six years I've been surrounded by frat boys who think strength comes from zero percent body fat so you can see every ab, like one big Lego piece pressed onto an otherwise flat stomach. College guys never really did it for me, and now I can see why. There's a difference between looking strong and being strong, and Chad Briggs is undeniably *strong*.

This, ladies and gentlemen, is a purebred man.

"How's that shower treating you?" Chad asks, the corner of his mouth twisting up in a smirk. He has a right to smirk when he looks like that. And I'm not sure how he expects me to leave this room when now he's in a tight white t-shirt that hugs every ridge and curve. It's borderline cruelty.

"Hope, why are you all red?" Leave it to Zelda to snap me out of a moment I was thoroughly enjoying.

"It's the tomato sauce," I lie, and then I do give Chad a salute, because why not, and head into the shower as the sound of his laugh echoes down the hall.

And oh boy, do I really like that laugh.

I'm in trouble.

I'm definitely going to have to fix the wolverine problem sooner than later because as it turns out, having my clothes still in suitcases in the living room presents a bit of an issue when there is suddenly nothing but a towel between Chad Briggs and all of my dignity. I realized the problem as I was rinsing the conditioner out of my hair, but so far I have yet to find a solution, even though I've been standing in the steam-filled bathroom for five minutes now, trying to telepathically tell Zelda to grab me some underwear at the very least. That's still more than I would like a certain manly neighbor to see, but it's better than just a towel.

When I'm finally convinced that Zelda is not, in fact, psychic, I come to the conclusion that my only chance is to try to sneak past the opening between the couch and the kitchen and hope Chad is too busy cleaning up to notice me. I'm not sure I like my odds—luck has not been on my side when I'm around this man—but I don't have much of a choice. I'd rather take my chance than have him come looking for me.

Turning off the hall light, I make sure everything is tucked away and my towel is secure. Batten down the hatches, so to speak. With my tendency to fall around Chad, I am taking no risks. I creep slowly, listening to the sounds of the kitchen for any signs of what may be happening in there because I'm going to have a narrow window to make it to safety. I vaguely realize I will have to make it *back* to the bathroom after I grab my clothes because no way am I changing in the open living room, but I'll think about that after I have something to wear. For right now, I'm focused on the sounds coming from the kitchen because something is off.

There's soft music playing, something that's familiar but not something I could name. I feel like it's a band from the eighties, but it doesn't really matter what it is because louder than the music is the bouncing, uncontrollable laughter of a child. Zelda, to be exact, though I haven't heard her laugh since I was in Orlando for Christmas last year.

Poking my head around the corner, wondering if this is all a weird dream, I set my eyes upon the scene and feel my heart swell inside my chest like an expanding balloon.

Link is sitting on a stool at the counter, right where I left him, but he's no longer splattered with sauce. Instead, he's carefully shredding cheese onto a plate and grinning. I don't think he's smiled like that even once since Bailey died, but he can't seem to stop now. I only have to wonder what's so amusing for a second because my eyes fall next on Zelda, who sits on the counter with Chad right in front of her. He has placed cooked spaghetti noodles on his face, a ring around each eye and one hooked over his lips like a tiny walrus mustache. He shaved today, but something tells me the scruff will be back by morning. Not that that's important, but I want to note it. With his noodle accessories, he's making ridiculous faces at Zelda, who sounds like she's laughing so hard that she's in danger of falling off the counter, which of course she won't because Chad has a hand on her leg, ready to catch her.

I don't think I've ever seen anything more beautiful than this, and I genuinely don't know what to do with the emotion pounding through my chest right now because I don't know if I can put a word to it. Whatever it is, I don't want to let it go.

Chad picks up another noodle and carefully places it above Zelda's lip to match him, and she starts laughing so hard that she collapses against his chest. When he wraps an arm around her and pulls her in for a hug, I'm pretty sure my soul leaves my body.

Here lies Hope Duncan: died of cuteness overload.

Chad looks up, and at some point I must have stepped out from the hall because his eyes go wide at the same time the noodles fall from his face. "Hope!" His voice cracks, and he immediately drops his gaze. "Uh, we were just waiting until you were done. The food is ready, but, uh, you're clearly not."

Why am I still standing in plain view? I slip into the dim living room and head for my stuff, feeling way calmer than I would have expected. Honestly, this could have gone so much worse, and it's nice to know he's a decent guy who won't try to catch a peek as I dig through my suitcase and grab the first clothes I can find.

"I still need to buy a dresser," I explain as I dart back into the hallway.

Right before I close the bathroom door, Chad mutters, "Must be on the list."

When I emerge fully clothed, Chad has set both kids up with a plate full of spaghetti (with a lot of veggies in the sauce, I notice) and some garlic toast (which I did not have ingredients for). Both kids—even Link—are chowing down while Chad leans his elbows on the counter across from them and tells them some kind of story. I walk in slowly so I don't interrupt, but that doesn't mean Chad doesn't notice me. His eyes travel from my head to my toes as I approach, but it's so quick that I almost miss it.

I could never miss the zing from his gaze, though, and this has officially become the weirdest day. It started with Zelda screaming and Link sobbing (like it has all week), and now it looks like it's ending with a giggly family dinner way better than anything I would prepare on my own, and Chad's eyes giving me the visual equivalent of a classy kiss on the hand. Without missing a beat in his story, he hands me a plate loaded with the best-looking spaghetti I've ever seen and keeps talking to my enthralled kids.

"And then Houston had the bright idea to pull off one of his shoes and get rid of the spider once and for all."

"Did he kill it?" Zelda asks through a mouthful of noodles.

Chad slams his hand on the table, making us all jump. Then he grins. "He missed. And do you know what the spider did?"

Link shakes his head, eyes wide.

"It jumped right onto his hand, trying to get away from the killer shoe! Houston ran outside screaming and shook his hand so hard that the spider flew off, and he's been afraid of them ever since."

I'm a little worried Link and Zelda will now be afraid of spiders too, but Chad isn't done with his story.

He puts his hand on an upside-down cup that's sitting on the counter nearby. "That's why it's always better to take them outside instead of trying to hurt them. They just want to live their lives in peace."

"Can we take it outside right now?" Zelda asks.

That's when I figure it out, and I nearly drop my plate. Chad's hand is there to catch it, his palm cupping around the back of my hand as he steadies my food before it ends up on the floor. He barely even looked at me, so I have to wonder if he anticipated that reaction. Who in the world is this guy?

"Yes, there's a spider under there," he tells me calmly, and he meets my terrified gaze. "I'll take it outside on my way out." His stare calms me down pretty quickly, or at least calms my spider fear because my heart is still pounding. I'm blaming that on the warmth of his hand under mine. And the way he's somehow so good with these kids despite my initial assessment of him. And the soft blue of his eyes that have me mesmerized.

"You're a spider tamer too?" I whisper, sounding ridiculously breathless considering I'm just standing here. "I would have screamed if I saw it."

He smiles, though it's nothing like the grin he gave me on the road last week. Still, I like this smile. It's gentle, like the bridge between the rough and gruff man I met when we got here and the guy who will wear a noodle mustache to entertain a kid. "I know," he says, his voice rumbling. "I figured I'd save myself the trip."

"Chad, are you and Hope going to kiss?"

I would have *definitely* dropped my plate if Chad wasn't holding it with me. Of all the things Zelda could have said right now, why did it have to be that?

Somehow, Chad barely reacts. He takes my plate from me and sets it safely on the counter, and then he gives his full attention to the seven-year-old who is doing her very best to give me gray hair before I hit twenty-five. "Only people who love each other kiss," he says matter-of-factly.

Zelda glances between us. "Don't you guys love each other?"

Oh, could this get any worse? "We barely know each other," I argue.

"But you look at him like you love him!"

I drop my face into my hands. I didn't think I would be explaining the concept of love to either of these kids anytime soon, but apparently that's what I get to do tonight.

"I know it's confusing," Chad says. I look up, curious about how he's going to handle this. "But you love your brother, right?"

Zelda looks at Link and then nods. "Yeah, but I don't want to kiss him."

"And I love Duke, but I don't want to kiss him either. There are all different kinds of love. When it comes to kissing, I only kiss people I want to marry."

Is that really true? Or is that his version of a kid-friendly explanation? Because despite how so very far away from even a mention of marriage Chad and I are, I would very much like to kiss him. Maybe not so much if there's a marriage stipulation in there, but it's not a deal-breaker. If he really is the kind of guy who kisses with intention, I can absolutely get behind that.

Zelda processes Chad's explanation, still glancing between us. I think she gets it, though there's something she's still trying to figure out. "So..." She scratches her nose. "Do you want to marry Hope?"

Chad's careful calm finally cracks, and he looks at me with a curious expression before stepping back and tucking his hands into the pockets of his jeans. "I should head back over to my place and check on Duke," he says, wincing a little.

"You can bring him over here!" Zelda offers, but I already know he's going to decline. Just like the other day, things got too close, and he's pulling back.

It's probably for the best, but that doesn't stop me from trying to keep him here a little longer. "You're not going to eat with us?"

He reaches over, silently showing Link how to twist the noodles onto his fork. It's like he's done this a million times, and suddenly I want to look up how old Houston Briggs is. He has to be under thirty if he's still pitching in the major leagues at the level he is, and if Chad is thirty-six... That's a pretty big age gap. Either he did a lot when it came to raising his siblings, or he has his own kids out there somewhere.

Why do I not like that idea? Probably because it would mean someone out there has been loved by Chad Briggs, and I am apparently extremely prone to unwarranted jealousy.

"I came over to make sure you were okay," he says with a shrug, and it's like he's put on a mask, hiding the way he really feels about leaving. Maybe he's eager to get away from my drama. Maybe he thinks he's in danger of doing something he shouldn't if he stays.

There's usually a difference between what we should do and what we want to do, and I've learned that life is a lot happier when the *wants* outweigh the *shoulds*.

Still, I *should* follow Chad's lead. Not only is he older and clearly wiser than me, but I feel steadier when I know he's nearby. That's not something I want to risk by being greedy and driving him away. "I'll walk you out," I tell him. "Don't want your old man eyes getting you lost out there in the dark."

He scoffs but holds the back door open for me, which is a good sign.

I'm just about to pass him when Zelda says, "Wait! The spider!" And she picks up the cup. The enormous black spider goes scurrying across the counter, and Zelda and I both scream and scramble to get away. She hides behind the counter, and my scrambling is directly into Chad's arms. Like, *in his arms*, my own arms locked around his neck and my legs wrapped around his waist to keep myself protected, like he's some tree I just climbed like a baby bear. He's certainly big enough.

Link grabs the cup that Zelda dropped and impressively traps the monster again, turning to Chad with wide eyes. "What do I do with it?" he asks. *At full volume.*

I squeak but force myself not to say anything because I don't want Link to suddenly become self-conscious about really talking for the first time in weeks.

Despite the fact that I'm clinging to him like a baby koala, Chad grabs a paper towel and steps over to the counter where Link patiently waits for instructions. I hold on to him tighter the closer we get to the creature whose sole desire is to crawl into my mouth while I'm sleeping.

"We're going to slide this under the cup," he says calmly, and then he tucks his chin over my shoulder so he can see what he's doing. The fact that he hasn't asked me to move has me feeling all sorts of feelings, chief among them a wild attraction that will not be tamped down if I stay here for much longer. He smells *so good*, like a combination of fresh mountain air and something I can only describe as *primal*, and I breathe him in without shame, even though his heart rate picks up speed against my nose where it nestles in his neck. He knows what I'm doing, and he doesn't seem to care.

More than that, he seems to *like* it.

Whatever he and Link are doing with the cup, I refuse to look, and I just pray Chad isn't the type of guy to want to tease me badly enough that he drops the spider onto my head or down my shirt or something.

"See how we have him trapped?" Chad says. "Now, you just have to hold on tight and make sure there aren't any holes as you take it outside and put it in the bushes."

"Far, far away from the house," I recommend.

Chad snickers, and then we're on the move. The temperature drops significantly as we pass through the door, which makes me nuzzle in even closer, and he wraps both his arms around my back. Whether it's to hold me in place or keep me warm, I don't care. I just don't want him to let go.

"Where should I put it?" Link asks, his voice a little wobbly from the cold.

"Put it in that bush!" Zelda says. Oh, she's here too? I should have told them to put on coats because they don't have a big, burly man to keep them warm.

Chad holds me a little tighter, as if he can read my thoughts. "That's a great place. There you go. Alright, kids, head back inside and close the door so you don't let all the heat out," he says in that commanding tone of his. "I'm going to, uh, let your aunt walk me home."

"You can put me down," I whisper, even if I don't want him to.

"Why would I do that?" he replies, just as quietly. He doesn't move until the back door shuts, throwing us into semi-darkness with only the kitchen window giving us a bit of light. When he does start walking, it's slowly, like he is taking as long as he can to cross the distance between our houses.

I shift a little, my arms getting tired from holding on so tight, and he adjusts his arms more securely around me. I've got my legs around his solid waist, and I feel like I need to break the silence before I start getting any crazy ideas about the things I can do while in this man's arms. "What were you doing outside before I summoned you with my saucy screams?" I ask, wincing immediately upon hearing myself. "I meant saucy like tomato sauce, not..."

"I know," he says with a little chuckle. "I was talking to my sister, helping her with some relationship problems." *Aww.* "Then I was going to chop some wood before your scream summoned me."

Okay, I know I had a bit of a lumberjack fantasy when I first saw him, but that's just pushing things too far. "You can't be serious."

"Why? Because I'm too old to be doing manual labor? I'm carrying you just fine, aren't I?"

"Are you calling me heavy?"

He groans. "You know that's not what I meant."

"Do I know that? Because it sounded like you're calling me heavy."

"Do you willfully misunderstand people, or is it just part of your personality?"

He doesn't sound annoyed enough to really mean what he's saying, which makes it easier to keep the teasing banter going as he crunches his way into his yard.

"It's a gift, I guess. But seriously, if you're tired, I can—"

"I'm fine, Hope."

Oh, I like the way he says my name. It sounds like a little prayer. A warm breath. I wish I could see the way his lips form the word because if we said it at the same time and got close enough, it would be a kiss.

Naturally, I decide to make things awkward as we reach his deck. "My name is actually Karen. Hope is my middle name."

He pauses. "Your name is Karen?"

Though I would gladly stay in his arms forever, I drop my legs and let him guide my feet to the step in front of him, which puts me closer to eye level with him instead of having to look up to meet his gaze. "Karen Hope Duncan. I never liked the name Karen for myself. While I've known some lovely Karens, the name always made me feel like I should be perpetually forty and getting mad at janitors. Even when I was a kid. And yes, that was before the meme. I'm not *that* young."

He chuckles. It's not the laugh I heard before my shower, but it's still a beautiful sound because it comes with a little half-smile that keeps my attention riveted on his mouth. "You keep saying that, but you're the one who was afraid of a tiny spider."

"That thing was huge!"

"It was the size of a nickel."

"Exactly!"

He reaches his hands out, one on each railing on either side of me, and it feels like he's pinning me in so I can't run away. Who in the world would ever run away with a man like this beefcake staring them down? "Rewinding a little bit, I really *was* about to chop some wood because we're supposed to have a storm coming in this weekend. The power lines aren't great out here, so I want to be prepared in case we lose power. I'll chop some for you too."

My heart jumps into an eager rhythm that probably isn't healthy. "Wait, are you going to chop some right now? Can I watch?"

He drops his head, shaking it a bit before he looks back up at me. "Do you say every thought that comes into your head?"

His voice has gotten growly over the last couple of minutes, and I resist telling him how much I like the roughness of it. The same way I like the roughness of his cheek, though I have yet to actually touch it. But to argue his question, no. I don't say everything that comes into my head, or else I might lose the chance to examine his face right now as he waits for my answer.

The lights from his house throw his features into sharp relief, highlighting each line and wrinkle and making his blue eyes brighter than normal. His eyes are rimmed with navy on the outside and almost gray in the center, and they seem to see everything as he studies me in turn. He really isn't that old, but parts of his face tell a different story. The way his eyes pinch at the corners, laugh lines spreading out past his nose and around his mouth, a scar stretching the skin right above his left eyebrow. There are a lot of stories in his skin; I can feel it. I want to know them all.

"I only ever say things I mean," I say eventually. "And there are a lot of things I still don't say."

"Things you don't mean?"

"Things I'm afraid to let anyone hear."

He leans in, and my breath catches. "Are you afraid of me?"

I'm terrified, but not because he's gruff or strong or commanding. Not even because he's so much older. I'm afraid of how quickly I've fallen under his spell in a way I'm not sure I'll ever break out of. I don't even know this man, but I feel like I should. I know I *want* to know him, which is enough for me.

He doesn't wait for my response, taking my hands and stepping back once, pulling me with him so I'm forced off the step and once again below him. Then he presses the softest of kisses to my forehead, making me melt beneath his gentle touch.

Yeah, I'm pretty sure I'm done for, and I don't even care.

Duke barks in the house, and Chad takes another step back with a little shake of his head, as if he needs the distance to remember where he is. "Goodnight, Hope," he says, the words rumbling through him, and then he steps past me and disappears into his house.

I stay outside for a few minutes, but the brisk fall air does nothing to cool me down.

Chapter Eleven

Chad

October 18

I HAVE NO IDEA what I'm doing. If all of my trauma stems from losing control, my all-too-beautiful next-door neighbor is going to be a major trigger point when it comes to my sanity (or the soon-to-be lack thereof). She's too unpredictable. All week, I've been watching her closely, trying to figure her out, but there's never been any sort of pattern. Outside of school, the kids have no sense of structure because Hope parents so gently, which tugs at my heart in a way I'm not willing to examine. It's not how I would do it, but she really listens to those kids. It makes me wonder about things I shouldn't be wondering about, but I can't stop. That's why, after a week of doing my very best to not think about her—a failure if ever I saw one—and an evening falling in love with her kids, I spent the night running through a list of things she could use, things that I could help with if she would let me.

I have four different dressers in this house, most of them empty. She can have one of them. Same with beds; technically, my siblings don't even know these rooms are set up for them, so they won't miss one of the beds. Honestly, I could even buy a full set of furniture for Hope's house and not feel the sting of spending that much because I've saved up so much with nowhere to put it all.

Sometimes I wonder if Mercedes would have stayed if she knew how much money I've saved over the years, and every time the thought crosses my mind, it makes me want to throw up because she probably would have. If I had bought her a fancy ring and promised to buy her anything she wanted, she would have said yes, and I would have been miserable because in hindsight I know she never loved me. She loved my loyalty and adoration. She loved how quickly I stepped in every time she got herself into trouble because I was friends with the cops who regularly arrested her for disorderly conduct or driving under the influence. She loved how I never questioned her commitment even when I should have.

For a guy who is so good at following the signs of cheating, there's a lot about my relationship that I refused to see until she opened my eyes by leaving.

I've been lying in bed for hours now, even though the sun has been up for a while. I'm starving; I never got around to making myself dinner because nothing sounded quite as good as spaghetti, and my only jar of sauce went to Hope. I wanted to stay and learn more about the little family next door, but that overwhelming desire is what held me back. Just like it did all week.

I'm getting in too deep. That need to rescue, to help, to feel *needed* again has been growing exponentially since the moment they moved in, and I am very much in danger of falling into the same trap that kept me with Mercedes for so long. Do I actually feel something for Hope? Or am I thriving off of the high that comes from fixing? Being the daring hero, even if it's just by cleaning a kitchen or trapping a spider, makes me feel important in a way I haven't felt in years. I worry I'm just chasing that feeling and not being fair to the woman who has yet to be shy about expressing her feelings. I can trust her when she says she's attracted to me—not that she's said that directly, but she knows her way around indirection.

It's me I can't trust. It's the hollow space in my chest where my heart should be. It's the last six months—honestly, the last six years—of solitude catching up to me.

Duke whines in the other room, telling me in no uncertain terms that he's let me sleep in long enough and I have to get my butt out of bed unless I want to be cleaning up after him. I groan because I barely slept at all, but I might as well get up and finish prepping for the storm.

Slipping into a coat and a pair of boots, I open the door for the dog and can't help but smile when he gives my hand a grateful lick before he darts outside at breakneck speeds. I lucked out with the mutt, and I know it, especially because he saved me from giving Hope more than a chaste kiss on the forehead. As much as I wanted to see if her lips were good for more than calling me old, that would have been a bad idea.

Duke does his business, and then he scurries around the side of the house like he's on a mission. He doesn't often leave my sightline.

"Where are you going?" I mutter, reluctantly leaving the covered deck and stepping out into the thin layer of snow that started falling last night. There must be some sort of critter wandering around, and I'd rather Duke didn't do anything that might require a bath when the temperature seems to be dropping. It feels like full winter this morning, so I guess they weren't kidding about the storm. "Duke!"

He comes back around the corner of the house, nose pressed to the ground as he follows a line of footprints.

I pause, looking down at my feet. The footprints go all the way around the house, and they're a different tread than mine, even though they're similar in size. And I haven't walked on this side of the house since moving in.

These tracks are fresh as of yesterday, but not so fresh that they haven't been covered by a dusting of snow. That means whoever was wandering around, they were here last night.

A chill runs through me. What if that was why Duke barked? I thought it was because he saw me on the deck with Hope, but he sounded like he was deeper in the house. Like, at the front door. The only time he ever barks is when he notices something or someone he doesn't like, and my dog tends to have a pretty good sense of judgment.

I curse under my breath and head back inside, double checking all of the locks on my doors and windows, even though I know they're all good because I checked when I got to town last week. This wouldn't be the first time someone has come after me after I ruined their life through a case, but I have no idea how they would have found me all the way out here.

Grabbing my computer, I check to see when my security cameras are supposed to be delivered—not for a few more days—and then I head back outside to make sure the intruder kept to my house and didn't go anywhere near Hope's. If he was sneaking around while I was out there, he may have seen the two of us on the steps, and I don't like the idea of someone thinking they can get to me through Hope.

Thankfully, the tracks seem limited to my house for now, but I quickly check Hope's locks anyway. Everything seems pretty secure outside of the hole in the back window, but I know better than to fix it for her while she's in town dropping the kids off for school. I'll have to wait until she gets home, but I'll need to convince her to get it fixed sooner than later without telling her why. No point in worrying her for no reason. She's stubborn, but hopefully she'll listen to me without much issue.

As snow starts to fall in thick flakes, I tell myself that I've done everything I can for now and head to the backyard to get some logs chopped in case the weather channel is right for once about the storm being a big one. If it is, it will keep anyone away unless they're completely stupid, but it could also mean other problems to deal with, like losing power and pipes freezing. I'll need to prep for the worst, especially now that I have more than myself to worry about.

Whether it's a hero complex driving me or actual interest in Hope, she's going to need my help. And I intend to follow through.

Chapter Twelve

Hope

I STAY IN TOWN for a while after dropping off the kids, not because I'm avoiding Chad but because...well, okay, I'm avoiding him. It's weird, I know, but I'm still figuring out how I feel about that man of a man, and it's a lot easier to think straight when he isn't around. I spend a good chunk of the morning with June at the hardware store because she's the only person I've met so far who feels like an outsider, like me, and she's more than happy to let me wander the shelves and borrow her computer to watch a few tutorials on fixing the window until a new one gets in.

"You know," she says at one point, "I bet your neighbor could help you. Mr. Briggs seems to know his way around a hammer and nail."

Her unfortunate choice of words gets me laughing so hard that I cry, which probably means it's a good thing that I no longer live in an apartment building full of college boys who seem to make dirty jokes for a living. It isn't even that obvious of an innuendo, but it still cracks me up.

I *could* ask Chad to help, but I do want to try doing things myself sometimes. I want to be able to provide for the kids without relying on someone else, though I'm not opposed to asking for help if it's beyond my capabilities. Like spiders, for instance. Thankfully, June has some spider spray, and I buy a couple of bottles before heading to the diner to grab myself some lunch.

On my way back to the car, the school calls and tells me that the kids are going to be let out early because of the storm. Snow has been falling all morning, but as I drive the couple blocks to the school, it has started to fall thicker and faster. It's beautiful, but not exactly something I want to learn to drive in on the fly.

We're only home for about ten minutes before someone knocks on the door. My heart does a flip—who else would be out this far if not

Chad?—and a smile breaks out on my face when I open the door and see him standing there.

"Hey," I breathe, itching to climb right back into his arms.

He stuffs his hands into his pockets as if he knows exactly what I'm thinking and wishes to avoid that. He said he was fine, but I can't imagine it was easy holding me that long. "Hi," he says back. "Uh, I came over to make a suggestion, but I don't want you to think I'm telling you what to do."

I wouldn't mind if he told me what to do. I know I've responded poorly in the past, but I'm learning to love the way he takes charge and has so much confidence in what he's doing. Do I tell him this? Of course not. "Well, that's a terrible start to a conversation," I say, leaning on the door frame with my arms casually folded.

A breeze blows past him, sharper than I expected, and he huddles up closer to himself. "Hear me out, okay? This storm is looking like it's a pretty big deal, and I'm not sure how well your house is going to handle it."

As if in response to that comment, the wind blows again and whistles through a part of the house behind me. Probably through the hole in the back window. I cringe, all stubbornness gone as I imagine how cold it's going to get if that wind keeps blowing. "What's your suggestion?" I ask, now folding my arms for warmth instead of looking cool and casual.

Chad takes a step forward, almost like he's thinking about wrapping me up to keep me warm, but he thinks better of the idea and remains where he is. A pity. His eyes still wander over me though, like he's imagining the gesture anyway. "I'm proposing the three of you spend the weekend at my house," he says with impressive gentleness, like he knows that this is a big ask.

It should be an easy choice. This should be a no-brainer because his house is clearly bigger and nicer than mine, and I highly doubt he has a wolverine-sized hole in one of his windows to let in the chill. I guess not *all* of my stubbornness went away because instinct is telling me to say no and tell him we'll be perfectly fine, especially because he stacked a bunch of wood on the side of our house this morning.

Another breeze wanders through the house, this time moaning from the fireplace that I don't even know how to use. I've seen movies where they don't turn a lever or something and all of the smoke comes into the house instead of going outside, and I'd rather not be that person just because I'm too stubborn to let a big strong man help me.

I shiver, both from the cold and because I actually like the idea of letting this big strong man take care of me. Take care of *us*. He proved he's good for my family last night, and if he could get Link to talk to a near stranger in a single evening, I can't imagine what he might do for my kids over the course of a weekend.

"You sure you can handle us for a whole weekend?" I ask as casually as I can. I don't actually want him to say no.

He smiles, only one side of his mouth curling up. "I can handle you just fine."

Oh goodness, the way he says that sends a shiver running through me that has *nothing* to do with the cold. It's the growl in his soft words that undoes me, along with the way his eyes search my face with a sort of hunger in them. We'll probably make it through the storm, no problem, but that doesn't mean I'm going to survive this weekend if he's going to be looking at me like that. Whatever switch flipped in me, I'm going to hazard a guess that his flipped too.

"Okay," I breathe, arms dropping to my sides because I can't hold them up anymore. They were already tired after last night's jungle gym adventure, and something about this man just makes me weak. I feel like I'm swooning, which is the stupidest thing I've ever heard, yet I absolutely love everything about it. This is my life now—swooning over my ridiculously attractive man of a neighbor who less than a week ago looked at me like I was the bane of his existence and now seems to be devouring me with his eyes.

"You'll want to pack some clothes for you and the kids," he says after a long moment of silently gazing at me. "I have plenty of blankets and food and things."

"You didn't let me watch you chop firewood," I say, cringing be-cause—*what*? Am I really that creepy?

Thankfully, Chad chuckles and shakes his head. "I'm sure you'll have another chance. I'll be next door prepping some things, and you should hurry." He glances up, where the sky has gotten heavy with snow. "The storm's coming in fast."

By the time we make it over to Chad's and knock on the front door, Zelda is screaming because I won't let her build a snowman until it stops snowing and Link is crying because he's afraid it's the end of the world or something. I'm at my wit's end, but at least they have enough clothes to last them a few days. I don't even know what I packed in my own bag because I was so busy trying to calm my emotional kids, but hopefully it's something I can actually wear. If not, I can brave the elements long enough to get back over to my house and grab something else. Mostly, I wanted to make sure the kids were set and that we didn't take too long to get over to Chad's in case he took back his offer.

He wouldn't do that, but he hasn't fully experienced this side of the kids. So maybe he would if given a chance.

Chad opens his door quickly, bundled head to toe in snow gear. Should I have been preparing for the apocalypse? Or was he coming to rescue us? Seeing my questions on my face, he gives me a quick smile and gestures for us to come inside. "I want to go check on Hank down the road," he says. "He didn't answer his phone, and I worry he's too busy writing to notice how bad the storm's getting."

He knows our other neighbor? I don't even know the guy beyond what June has told me, and I'm way friendlier than Chad. I would say it's because he's been here for a year, but June told me earlier this week that Chad moved in just a couple of days before we did, which brought up so many questions that I'll probably end up asking this weekend while we're trapped together by the snow.

"The TV is all yours," Chad tells me, pulling gloves over his hands and looking insanely sexy as he prepares to head out into the elements on his rescue mission. "Feel free to use the Nintendo or anything. I shouldn't be gone long, but if for some reason we lose power while I'm out, the fireplace is prepped and ready to go. You just have to light the kindling."

I haven't said a word since he opened the door, but he doesn't seem to mind as he watches the suddenly calm kids settle on the couch, already turning on the game console as Duke snuggles up beside them. A delicious little smile plays on his mouth as he takes them in, which has me feeling all sorts of feelings again. Apparently, he is not just okay with us invading his house during the storm; he *wanted* us to come over.

Is this man actually real? Because I'm starting to think he's just a manifestation of the dream guy I didn't know I had. Maybe I wouldn't have picked someone so much older than me, but then again I've always felt older than I really am.

"I'll be back soon," he says to me, and then he gives me a quick kiss on the cheek before he slips outside and climbs into his truck.

Placing a hand over the warm spot he left on my cheek, I watch him drive away with a nervous ball forming in my gut, and I have to wonder if this is how it feels to watch a loved one drive away. That would be crazy to feel that strongly for him, and yet...

Two hours later, I'm pacing. Hank's house is less than a mile down the road, and even if the truck got stuck or something, there's no way it would take that long to walk. Granted, I've never walked in snow before, so maybe it does take that long, but right now I'm picturing Chad lying dead and frozen on the side of the road, buried under a snowbank so deep that no one will find him until everything thaws in the spring. If I had his number, I would try calling his phone, but despite how comfortable I was clinging to him for a solid five minutes last night, we haven't reached phone number sharing levels in our relationship. Neighborship. Whatever this would be called.

Something tells me Chad isn't much of a texter, and I picture him with a flip phone that's almost as old as me.

The kids, thankfully, haven't noticed how long Chad has been gone. We still have power, and they've been so deep into Mario Kart that I doubt they are even aware of the storm anymore. I've thought about asking if I can join, but not only would they completely demolish me, but they would also pick up on my nerves if I ended up being that close to them. Right now, I'm pacing in the kitchen, away from where they can see, and I'm immensely glad Duke has decided to pace with me so I don't feel entirely alone.

When I think I hear a sound outside, I pause, and Duke whines a little next to me. But it's just the wind and its relentless attack on the side of the house. The snow is so thick that I can't see out of the windows anymore, which is kind of insane.

I grab another mini donut and stuff it into my mouth, and the dog gives me a bit of side eye that I don't appreciate. Okay, so maybe I've eaten most of the bag, but I need the pacing fuel. Besides, Chad doesn't seem like the kind of guy who would miss powdered donuts. He is way too fit for this to be a regular snack, and they were front and center with a bunch of other junk food that makes me think he raided the grocery store before he even invited us over.

"He can't be this good, can he?" I ask Duke as I scratch his ears, though all of my words are muffled because I'm still chewing the donut.

He does that little huffing sound, like a mostly noiseless bark that feels like he's trying so hard to talk to me. I swear, there's something way too perfect about this dog, just like his owner is way too perfect to be real.

Just like this *house* is perfect, a mix of modern and rustic, with all the bells and whistles but still with a very homey, lived-in feel. Everything is bright and open and warm, with several bedrooms fully furnished and waiting for occupants. I know they're probably for his siblings, though I can't really picture someone like baseball star Houston Briggs spending a lot of time in a little house like this. But at the same time, everything about this house feels...ready. Like Chad is just waiting for a family to fill it.

I shiver at the thought right as the front door flies open with a flurry of snow and two silhouettes hurrying inside.

I may not be able to see their faces because they're so wrapped up, but I know the big one is Chad. Without thinking, I rush toward him and jump into his arms. He grunts on impact but wraps his arms around me anyway, holding me tight as he heaves for air.

"I was worried," I murmur.

Somehow, he manages to hold me even tighter. "Sorry for scaring you," he says, though it sounds like he can barely get the words out. He's shaking as he holds me; he must be freezing!

"The truck slid into a snowbank," the other man says brightly, like it's the greatest thing in the world to get trapped out in a blizzard. "We tried to dig it out, but we gave up and walked the rest of the way. Good thing Briggs here had snowshoes in the back of his truck."

"Always prepared," I say with admiration. Seriously, who could ever think poorly of this man who goes around rescuing hopeless women and solitary men? "Are you cold?"

A shudder runs through Chad, but he says, "Not anymore."

"I'll make you some tea." I reluctantly slide back to the floor, even though my brain has started getting wild ideas about opening his coat and climbing inside with him still in it. Oh mama, that sounds so nice. "And you should take a shower while we still have power."

He pulls off his hat and the scarf that was obstructing his face, giving me a strange look as I slowly back into the kitchen. "Are you telling me what to do, Hope?" It's like he's never had anyone do that before, and he can't decide what to make of it.

I grin. "Maybe I am. But if you don't want to get warm, you don't have—"

He growls a little and disappears down the hall, shedding his winter gear as he goes.

The other guy chuckles as he politely hangs his coat on the hooks near the door. He doesn't look nearly as frozen as Chad did, which doesn't make a whole lot of sense because he's a lot smaller. In fact, he's wearing several layers, each of which takes away from his bulk as he unloads and leaves himself in just pajama pants and a sweatshirt.

"Hi, I'm Hank," he says when he catches me staring at him. "You must be the frustrating neighbor, Hope."

I frown. "He thinks I'm frustrating?" That shouldn't surprise me, but I don't like that someone else knows it too. Am I so frustrating that that's all I'll ever be?

Grinning, Hank joins me in the kitchen and helps me fill the kettle with water, since I haven't gotten that far yet. "Yeah, but I think for him that's a good thing. He's incredibly...stubborn. He wouldn't let me help dig the truck out. He literally locked me in the truck with the heater on while he tried to get it free."

Snorting a laugh, I search all the cupboards for the tea because I've forgotten where I saw it when I did my initial snooping as soon as Chad left. Finding it in the cupboard by the fridge, I pull it out and settle on a stool to wait for the water to boil. "Yeah, that sounds like him."

"Have you known him long?"

"A couple of weeks." Even though I spent most of last week avoiding him. (AKA growing more and more attracted to him from a distance.)

My answer seems to amuse Hank as he glances toward the hall where Chad disappeared. I know he's somewhere in his thirties thanks to June, but beyond that, I don't really know anything about Hank. He lives alone, obviously, but he seems too friendly and kind to be living a hermit lifestyle. Chad, with all his gruff surliness, makes sense, but Hank does not.

"What about you?" I ask, though really I want to order him to tell me everything about himself. I don't think my orders would have the same effect as Chad's, but I did manage to get Chad to go shower.

We're not going to talk about how he would have showered even if I hadn't told him to.

Hank grins, adjusting his glasses as he sits beside me. "I met him last year, when he bought the house."

"But he just moved in?" I'm trying to make sense of the mystery that is Chad Briggs, but this is only making things more muddled.

"There was some remodeling happening," Hank says with a shrug. "I watched the trucks and contractors drive past the house for a while. I'm guessing he bought it to be a sort of summer home, though. He's got a house in Sun City as well."

The man has two houses? "Is he super rich or something? What does he even do for work?"

"No idea."

"Hmm."

"This weekend feels like a perfect time to do some investigating," Hank suggests, and he seems just as excited about the idea as I am. As if he can sense my confusion, he chuckles and shakes his head. "Occupational hazard. I'm a mystery author, and men like Chad Briggs are fascinating to me. He'd make a good main character, don't you think?"

He's already become a main character in my life, and that's without knowing anything about him. "Yeah, he would," I agree.

"The quiet and mysterious mountain man full of secrets," Hank says, "reluctant to let anyone into his heart."

I know he's just speculating, but it feels so spot on that I can't help but ask, "Why do you think that is?" One second Chad is flirting with me, and the next he's closing himself off and running away, and he smiles so rarely that there has to be some underlying pain in there somewhere. Maybe he just needs reasons to smile, but maybe something in his life has taught him that there's no point in being happy.

Hank shrugs. "I'm totally guessing here, but if I were writing a character like him, he would be closed off because he's been burned before. Maybe recently. Not many people are good at opening their heart again after a loss. He could still be licking his wounds."

Anyone who gives up a guy like Chad is an idiot, but if Hank is right and someone hurt him, I want to find her and punch her in the nose. And then thank her because now I have a chance to fall for him because it brought him here to Laketown.

The kettle whistles, and Hank gets up to finish the tea for me. (Probably a good idea; I've never been known for making good tea.)

"If you were writing his book," I say before I can stop myself, "what kind of love interest would he have?"

Grinning, Hank gives me a look that says he knows exactly what I'm fishing for. "Someone who challenges him and isn't afraid to tell him what to do."

Chapter Thirteen

Hope

THE POWER GOES OUT around eight o'clock, which is a lot later than I expected. At Chad's insistence, I spent the afternoon curled up in the armchair with a book, while he and Hank kept the kids entertained. I'm not sure how Hank got roped into it too, but both men seemed more than happy to play Candyland and lose at Mario Kart over and over. The kids got to help make dinner, and they even helped clean up after we were done, something they've never done at our house even though I've tried to teach them how to do dishes and wipe down the counters. Chad makes cleanup with kids look easy.

When the lights flicker out, Chad doesn't give Link a chance to get worried. He immediately turns on a lantern and asks the six-year-old to help him light the fire while Zelda climbs onto Hank's back and decides they are adventurers exploring a deep and dark cave. It's like I'm living in a dream, and I wish I had more than words to express to Chad how grateful I am that he had the foresight to bring us over here. I can't imagine what it might have been like over at my house, where a hole in a window would have us freezing our butts off, even if I'd managed to make a fire. I don't have a fancy gas-powered lantern I can light to keep things comfortable and bright, and I would have gotten tired of entertaining the kids long before now.

Chad's tired. I can see it in his eyes and in the set of his shoulders, but he hasn't stopped once. I know I need to rescue him and give him a break, but I can't stop watching the way he's so good with Link even though Link hasn't said anything since the spider incident last night. Chad explains the proper way to build up a fire so it will keep burning long into the night and keep everyone warm, and he lets Link hold the lit match, keeping a careful eye on him so he doesn't burn himself. He grins when Link's eyes light up at the same time the logs catch fire, and my heart swells as I watch them.

Not long after he gets the fire going, Chad gets a call that immediately wipes the smile off his face. "Micah?" he says as he answers, and he moves over to the far side of the room. "Are you okay?"

Nerves settle in my stomach when his expression tightens, growing more tense the longer he listens. Is something wrong? Who's Micah?

"Hey," he says gently. "Hey, breathe, okay? You're okay. Take a deep breath with me. There's my girl."

A sharp pain forms somewhere under my rib cage. I'm making assumptions, and I really shouldn't, but suddenly I don't want to know who Micah is or what she means to Chad. Old girlfriend? *Current* girlfriend? A daughter he has hidden somewhere else? Does his second home hold a second family? Maybe that's why he's so set up for a family. Maybe he has one waiting for him in Sun City and all of this has just been him being nice.

"Tell me what you're working with," Chad says, his voice low.

I shift my focus to Zelda and hope she can distract me enough that I'll stop jumping to conclusions. "How about a dance party?" I ask her; she looks like she's growing tired of the explorer bit.

Her face brightens as she drops from Hank's shoulders. I know she used to have dance parties with her mom all the time, but we've been so busy trying to get things packed up and moved and unpacked that I haven't had any time to do anything like this. "Yeah! Can I choose the music?"

I unlock my phone, and together we find a dance mix that has all her favorite songs. We hit play right as Chad ends his call, and I'm grateful to Hank for asking the question I'm too scared to:

"Everything okay?"

Chad nods, though his face says otherwise. "My sister's stuck in the storm too, apparently." I immediately feel stupid for assuming the worst about who Micah might be, especially because he seems so worried. "She's at a closed lodge about an hour away, and I guess there's a whole tour bus of people that have taken shelter there."

"The lodge is closed?" Hank says, frowning.

Chad shrugs, rolling his shoulders a bit as if he's trying to rid himself of some of the tension that has shown up since his phone rang. It doesn't seem to be helping. "I guess her company is doing a grand reopening for the lodge next week, so they were there for a planning meeting. She's...she doesn't do super well on her own. She's trying to take care of everyone, but it pushed her into a panic attack. She needs... I need to..."

He has his phone to his ear again, and I hear him say hi to someone named Blondie before he disappears down the hall and shuts a door behind him. I glance at Hank, who shrugs before joining Zelda's dance party and giving me a look that says I should go check on Chad.

I give him a few minutes—mostly because I'm nervous about interrupting when he's clearly stressed—and then I pad down the hall and knock on his door. He grunts, which I take as a sign that I can enter, and I find him sitting on the edge of his king-size bed with his face in his hands.

"Everything okay?" I ask, even though I know it isn't. I settle myself next to him and put an arm around his broad shoulders.

He looks over at me, his eyes full of worry in the dim light coming from the hall. "I hate that I'm stuck here," he says, and then he winces. "I don't mean... I'm glad you're here. I meant..."

"I know what you meant," I tell him with a smile. "Wanna talk about it?"

He sighs. "Micah was only four when our mom died, and her dad isn't..." He shakes his head. "He loves her to death, but he doesn't really know how to show affection. And when Mom died, he was pretty beat up about it. I think Mic often felt lonely because the twins were back with our dad and her closest sibling was Sam, who..." He grimaces. "I really don't like Sam. He's kind of the worst."

I snort a laugh, even though it's not really appropriate for this moment. Story of my life. But I also rub my hand across Chad's broad shoulders, and that seems to make him relax a little as he leans closer to me. "Who's Blondie?"

"Brooklyn. My sister."

"One of the twins?"

"Yeah, with Houston. I asked her to check on Micah as soon as the storm passes and she can get through since I can't... Micah gets these panic attacks if she's alone for a long time, and I'm worried she..." He groans and falls backward onto the bed, throwing an arm over his face. "I shouldn't have left Sun City. Micah needs me, and I can't..."

Though I love seeing how much he cares about his family, I hate that he's suffering so much. I can't do anything to help his siblings, but maybe I can help him. Hopping up, I grab his arm and tug it away from his handsome face. "You know what you need?"

He scrunches up his expression, rightfully wary of the crazed look I probably have. "I'm afraid to ask."

"You need a dance party."

His eyes go wide, and he shakes his head. "You really don't want to see me dance."

"Oh, now I really do. Come on, old man. Show me your moves." I try to tug him up, but he weighs so much that he doesn't even budge. "Okay, sasquatch, you're going to have to help me here."

"If I do that, then you'll make me dance," he argues.

"Sure will. Up you go!"

But instead of sitting up, he tugs me forward, pulling me off balance until I land on top of him with an *oof*.

"That one was your fau—" My words get cut off as soon as he tucks some hair behind my ear in the softest of touches, his fingers lingering in my hair. Then his thumb brushes my cheek, leaving me shivering with anticipation.

He gives me a little smile that I can barely see in the darkness. "Thanks for listening," he murmurs. "I worry about them, you know?"

"I know. And it's nice that you care about them. But I can't be mad that you came here." Partly because I'm really enjoying the feel of his hard chest beneath my hands, but that's just a superficial reason. I'm glad he's here because I would have been completely lost without him and I'm terrified to think what we might have been dealing with if he hadn't been here to rescue me over and over. I already knew I was in over my head with the kids, but he has made that even more painfully obvious over the last couple of weeks.

Chad leans closer, his eyes dropping to my mouth for half a second. But instead of kissing me, he brushes his nose against mine, tempting me to do the deed myself. "If I come out there, will you slow dance with me?"

I smile so wide that it hurts. "That depends."

"On what?"

"On how much you're willing to bust a move first. Zelda won't let you do otherwise."

Though I'd rather stay where I am, I slip off the bed and hold out my hand to help him up. He takes it, thankfully sitting up on his own, and together we head out into the living room where Hank is trying to teach the kids "the lawnmower" dance move. Chad and I join in—he's laughably bad at dancing and clearly knows it—and for the next hour, I don't think about the storm. I don't think about Bailey. I just think about how much fun this is and how much I would love to do this all the time, just like this.

But then the music switches to a slow song, and everything changes.

Without hesitation, Chad reaches out his hand to Zelda and directs her to step on his feet after giving her a spin. He mutters something to her that makes her grin wide, and then he scoops her up into his arms and does a twirl before setting her back down. She's beaming, stars in her eyes as she looks up at the man who came out of nowhere and caught us all by surprise.

Something tickles my cheek, and I brush it away only to realize it's a tear. I almost never cry, but these happy tears aren't going away because how am I supposed to handle seeing the tender way Chad is dancing with my kid?

Chad sees me crying, and he immediately tenses up. Thankfully, Zelda doesn't seem to notice. Chad keeps his eyes locked on me as the two of them sway, concern wrinkling his brow, but then a tiny little voice pulls my attention away.

"Wanna dance with me, Hope?"

So much for holding in my tears. Link is right in front of me, his little hand held out in the same way Chad held his hand out for Zelda, and I have most certainly died right here in the living room. Swallowing, I nod and take his hand, letting him lead me closer to where Chad and Zelda are. Though he can't quite figure out the stance, Link does his best to mimic everything that Chad does, every once in a while glancing over to make sure he's doing it right. I'm pretty much sobbing now because at this point I'd almost given up hope that Link would ever be very affectionate with me. Now, he's holding both my hands and smiling up at me, and I'm doing everything I can to smile back.

The song ends, transitioning to another slow song, and I glance over at my phone because I don't remember there being anything but beat-heavy dance songs on this playlist. But my phone isn't on the end table where I left it. Instead, it's in Hank's hands as he sits in the armchair, and he winks at me as he slowly turns the volume down and holds his arm out for Zelda to climb into his lap. Wait...

"Mind if I cut in?" Chad says, tapping on both Link's and my shoulders. Link relinquishes his claim on my attention and scurries over to join Zelda with Hank. Chad pulls me in with deliberation, sliding his hand into mine as he wraps an arm around my back and nudges me deeper into his hold.

"Did you plan this?" I ask, gladly sinking into his arms.

He chuckles. "No, but we happen to have a meddling neighbor who puts as much romance into his books as he does mystery."

"Sounds like my kind of book."

"You like mysteries?"

"I like you, don't I?"

He hums, pulling me closer. "Why are you crying?" He shifts our clasped hands so he can brush my tears from my cheeks with his thumb, even though they're going to keep coming now that they're free.

"Because I never really thought about how Zelda's never had a father figure in her life until I saw her with you." I know that's a big thing to say to him, and it might scare him off. But I want him to know the truth, to know exactly what he's getting himself into before he does anything he isn't ready for.

Chad stiffens a little, but when he pulls me closer, I think his reaction is more of surprise than fear. "What about her father?" He's dropped his voice to match mine, but Zelda seems riveted on whatever story Hank is telling the kids.

Tucking my head against his chest, I shrug. "I don't even know who he is. Bailey never told me, and he's not listed on their birth certificates. I don't think he was a great guy, and she knew even then that they were better off without him."

A growl rumbles through him, making me laugh.

"Easy, tiger. We don't need you fighting our battles for us."

"But I could," he says, almost too quietly for me to hear him. "You don't have to be alone."

"Something tells me you'd be a pretty good knight in dented armor."

"Why is my armor not shining?"

I laugh again at the indignation in his voice. "Because you're the one taking all the hits for me. Obviously."

"Obviously," he repeats as if it isn't obvious at all. He rests his cheek against my head, and we dance like that for a while, even when the music ends and only Hank's soft voice fills the silence.

I feel so safe in his arms, like the world could never touch me if Chad is nearby. I've never felt this way, at least not that I can remember. With everything that's happened—losing my parents, losing Bailey, getting the kids, the apocalyptic storm outside—safe feels like a miracle.

Eventually, Hank clears his throat, and we look over to find both kids asleep in his arms. It's adorable, though he looks ready to fall asleep as well as he silently asks for help. Chad picks up Link, I grab Zelda, and we each take a kid to one of the guest rooms. Zelda murmurs goodnight as I tuck her in, but she's pretty out of it after her wild dance party. I kiss her on the forehead, brushing her hair away from her face, and wonder for the first time if she needs a dad in her life. I thought for sure it would be better with just the three of us since she's used to only having her mom, but I can't get over the way she looked at Chad when he danced with her.

Maybe Chad's right. Maybe I don't have to be alone. Outside of Bailey, I've been alone for so long, and I've always been comfortable with the way I live. Yeah, it gets lonely, and yeah, I've dated to fill the void. But no one has ever been permanent in my life. Not even my parents. They stuck around for sixteen years, and then a car accident took them away, and my sister was starting her college career. She could have looked after me, but she and I agreed we would be walking through life on our own. She was pregnant with Zelda at that point and knew she couldn't be there for me as anything more than a sister, and I was fine with that.

I've always been fine. But it might be nice to be more than fine.

I lean against the door frame of Link's room—that's how I'm going to think of it now even if this isn't our house—and watch as Chad gently runs his fingers through the boy's hair as he watches him sleep. Though it's pretty dark so I can't see much, he looks so concerned about Link, the way a father would be about his kid. It's so similar to the look he had when he was telling me about his sister that the tears are coming right back.

"How is he?" I ask quietly, wondering if Chad can see how restless Link tends to be when he sleeps.

Chad's response comes in the form of a soft whistle, which makes zero sense until Duke appears between my legs and the door and hops onto the bed. He settles himself next to Link like he's done it a million times, and to my surprise, Link turns over and wraps his little arms around Duke's neck. They both sigh in unison, like it's a pairing that was always meant to be.

Instead of waiting for me to move out of the way, Chad wraps his arms around me and picks me up, carrying me back to the living room just as Hank passes us on his way to the bedrooms.

"Goodnight, you two," Hank says with a wink.

I snort a laugh as Chad groans and places me back on my feet. "I like Hank," I say while Chad crosses the room to turn off the lantern, leaving us in nothing but firelight. It's romantic and cozy and exactly what I want right now.

"He has his moments," Chad admits, and then he stalks back toward me, a man on a mission. He grabs me, basically tackling me into the couch, but twists as we fall so he lands first and has me pinned against his body in a move so smooth that it has me swooning again. "I'll take the couch tonight," he says as I snuggle in, my head against his chest. "You can take my room."

"Or I could stay here," I suggest, which sounds a whole lot better than whatever he just said.

"Nope." The way he growls that word leaves little room for argument. "I'm giving you half an hour before it's your bedtime."

"So bossy." Maybe, if I can fall asleep within his time limit, he'll let me stay. Or at the very least he'll carry me to bed like he did with Link, and I'd be perfectly okay with letting him tuck me in. But how am I supposed to fall asleep when I've got this man holding me? Now that we're alone, I feel like every place he touches lights on fire in the most delicious way, leaving me in a state of excitement and anticipation that has driven away any hope of sleeping tonight. His heart beats loudly in my ear anyway, moving too fast for me to think he's remotely calm right now.

Running his hands through my hair, Chad laughs a little. "I'm starting to think you like me being bossy. Not what I expected from you."

"It's the weirdest thing."

"What scares you, Hope?"

The question is so out of the blue that I lift my head so I can see him. "What?"

He tucks my hair behind my ear. "Micah is afraid of being alone. I think Zelda is afraid of being forgotten. What are you afraid of? It's clearly not being told what to do."

Everything that comes to mind is something stupid, like spiders and jellyfish, and that's probably not what he's looking for. I still don't know what sparked his question, but I take a moment to really think about it. If he wants to know what scares me so he can protect me from it, so much the better. And maybe he'll trust me with his own fears if I let him in to mine.

Resting my head back on his chest, I take a deep breath and try to decide if I'm ready to admit this out loud. "I was in the middle of my last semester of my master's program when Bailey died. I was going to be an astronomer. Study the stars and find new planets. But then I got the call in the middle of class, and at first I thought someone was pranking me when they said I was the person listed as the appointed guardian for Link and Zelda. It's not like I have my life together or anything, and my entire adult life has been focused on school. But Bailey trusted me, out of everyone, to take care of her kids, and I don't want to let her down."

"But?" Chad brushes his palm against my cheek.

"Does this mean everything I was working toward is going to be for nothing? Maybe I can finish my classes online while the kids are in school, but I don't want to be an absent parent and so focused on that instead of on them, especially right now. And then what? Then I have to get a Ph.D. And after that? It's not like I can get a fellowship as a single mom and move them across the country every time I have to chase an opportunity. I love those kids too much to do that to them. So is this it? Am I going to spend the rest of my life a few feet from the finish line, watching my dreams slip away until it's too late?"

I'm crying again, and I hate that I sound so pitiful and selfish. "I'm a parent now. That means I have to put the kids first. I know that. But that's what I'm scared of. I'm scared I'm going to lose myself in them and never find me again."

Chad shifts beneath me, propping himself up against a pillow and then lifting my chin so I have to look at him again. There's nothing but sympathy in his eyes as he brushes his thumbs against my cheeks to dry my tears. "I always wanted to be a teacher," he says, eyebrows furrowing. "But when my mom got sick and died, the courts sent us to stay with my dad even though he was too far gone to take care of us. I had to get a job to make sure the twins had dinner, and I ended up dropping out of high school so I could work more. I still don't have my diploma. But even if I had the chance to go back and do things differently, I wouldn't do it. I made a choice to make sure Houston and Brooklyn had good lives, and they were happy. Most of the time. I would never trade their happiness just for a chance to have my own."

I sniff. "That's really depressing, Chad."

Laughing, he brushes my tears away again. The way he's looking at me sends a shiver through me, and I'm so glad for the warmth of his body beneath mine. "I know. Being a parent is the hardest thing in the world, but it's the most rewarding too. You have to find the balance between the bad and the good and choose which direction you're going to look. Are you going to focus on the hard days that leave you feeling like a failure, or are you going to look back at all the amazing little moments that make it all worth it?"

Where did this man come from? It's like he appeared out of nowhere, a manifestation of the perfect person to protect me from all my insecurities before my new life swallows me whole. He's watching me just as closely as I watch him, his blue eyes pulling me in, and I'm not sure he's even breathing. We're suspended in time unless one of us breaks the stillness.

I'm more than happy to be that someone.

"I'm a big fan of little moments," I say, and then I press my lips to his.

At first, I wonder if I overstepped because he doesn't move. But then his fingertips find my forehead, my temple, slide into my hair and pull me closer. The pressure of his mouth changes, growing harder as his kisses become hungrier. He sits up, hands moving to my waist and tugging me as close as he can get me without once interrupting the way his lips find mine again and again like he needs to test every little point of contact to see if it feels different than the last. For me it does. Each kiss is a new step down a path I am desperate to explore, each new taste another answer to a question I didn't know I had.

I knew his sense of control would make for a good kiss, but this is beyond anything I could have imagined. The man *really* knows what he's doing.

Chad tucks his fingers around the base of my skull, tilting my head and deepening the kiss, and my whole body responds to him, eager to get as much as I can. I run my fingers through his hair and down to his broad shoulders, overloaded with all sorts of feelings as his kiss takes over my senses. I've got nothing but time to explore, and I intend to be thorough.

Suddenly he stops, his body tense beneath my hands and his eyes shut tight. "Hope," he whispers against my mouth, and it's almost a groan.

I grin, even if he can't see it. How is he this good of a guy and still single? Has no one ever thought to lock him down? Still, I kind of hate that he's being the adult right now. "I know," I grumble. "It's my bedtime."

He finally looks at me, his eyebrows low and his eyes pained. "You have no idea how much I want you to stay," he says as he tucks some hair behind my ear. He means it. "But this isn't just about us."

"I have Link and Zelda to think about."

He nods. "And my siblings need me. I know it's not the same as—"

I cover his mouth with my hand, which seems to shut him up more out of surprise than an actual inability to speak through my palm. "Your brother and sisters are just as important to you as my niece and nephew are to me. Just because they're adults, it doesn't make them any less deserving of love and concern. And I love how much you care about them. They're so lucky to have someone like you looking out for them."

A tear slips from his eye and lands on my fingers, catching me by surprise. I've expected a lot of things from Chad, but this? He reaches for my hand and carefully kisses the tear away. He kisses my palm. My wrist. Then he finds my mouth again, this time giving me the gentlest kiss I've ever received. It's a whole different kind of intimacy from the last kiss, everything about it full of meaning and intention. A shiver runs through me at the way he touches me so carefully, and I know I will never be the same after this.

This man just let me into his heart, and I'm pretty sure not many people have been given that honor.

He picks me up, and it's like I weigh nothing as he carries me to his bedroom without shifting his gaze away from mine. His eyes say so much in the darkness, and even if I don't know exactly what he's saying, I feel every bit of it in my chest, like he's buoying up my soul with each second of eye contact. As he places me on top of the bed, he presses his lips to my forehead, yet again completely melting me with that gesture. I had no idea such an innocent touch could be so affecting before I met Chad.

I don't want him to go—my hand grabs his before he can step away—but I know he needs to. Letting him leave feels symbolic of something and has nerves building in my belly. Maybe it's the storm. Or the kids. Whatever it is, I wish he could stay with me and hold me until I fall asleep. I don't want to have to say goodbye to this man.

"I'll be right down the hall," he murmurs, bending to kiss my forehead again.

Then he finds my lips one more time, and the way he dives into this kiss feels as if he's reminding himself that I'm different from the child he tucked in earlier. I'm overwhelmed by how much I love the way he kisses without hesitation, to the point where I no longer have the strength to hold myself up anymore and I slip onto my back. Chad comes with me because I've gripped his shirt, his elbows sinking into the mattress on either side of me as his weight presses me down, but he groans against my mouth before tucking his head into my shoulder.

"You are the worst sort of distraction," he growls, and I feel the words rumble through him, both because he's still on top of me and because I've conveniently slid my hands up along his sides so I can know just how strong he really is. Very. Very strong. This is a solid man, just as I suspected, and he is exactly the sort of man I would want to spend my life with if things were different. Maybe even if they weren't. Chad seems like the kind of guy who might make a great husband and father.

Who am I kidding? I just spent all day watching him with my kids. I *know* he would make a great father.

"You're the one who kissed me," I remind him, stroking his short hair until he presses a kiss into my neck, and then I'm suddenly immobile, like he found a secret button that makes me completely powerless to resist.

"You did it first," he complains, now trailing kisses up to my ear.

"Yes I did, and I'll do it again."

"Please don't."

"You know you like it."

"That's the problem."

I laugh, though it comes out almost silent because his lips are so dang distracting. "I could have come to the room on my own," I say breathlessly. I don't want to argue, but it's the only thing that will keep me from begging him to stay. "You didn't have to carry me."

"Would you have come if I didn't?"

"No."

He chuckles and kisses my cheek. "Just as I thought." He kisses my nose. "I'm going to go back to the living room." Kisses my chin. "And you're going to stay here." Kisses my lips. "All night." Another kiss. "With the door closed." Then he claims my mouth with a longer, languid kiss, one that makes it difficult to want to do what he's saying even though he's using that commanding tone of his. His kisses speak louder than any orders to stay away.

"I'm getting mixed signals here," I whisper when my mouth is free again.

He groans. "You are not allowed to leave this room until the sun is up, Hope Duncan."

"What if I have to use the bathroom?"

"It's right there." He probably points, but I've just discovered how much I like rubbing my fingers against his scruff, and all of my focus is now on his face. "*Hope.*" The exasperated way he says my name doesn't stop me, so he grabs both my hands with one of his and presses them into the mattress above my head, stealing my breath when his eyes lock on to mine. For a moment, everything stops. Neither of us breathe, our eyes locked together as if we're both waiting for the other to choose what happens next. Chad's grip tightens around my wrists as he takes a breath, the fingers of his other hand brushing against the skin below the hem of my shirt. And then next thing I know, he's on his feet, putting some space between us and leaving me feeling cold and empty.

"Do you have to go?" I say, even though I already know the answer.

Another growl rumbles through him, but he keeps his distance. "We have some things to talk about tomorrow."

Good things, I hope. Things like how we're going to make this work and when the wedding will be and how does adoption work when it comes to this kind of custody? I don't know if that is where his thoughts are going, but I hope it is. I hope he's running through all of the scenarios of what this could be and seeing the brightest option as the one he wants to take.

I've never felt like this about anyone, and I don't know if I can ever let him go. Maybe it's crazy, but I've already lost my parents and my sister. I don't think I could lose him too. I've never felt as safe as I do with him, and the thought of being without that leaves me hollow. I don't just mean physically safe. I haven't been brave enough to admit even to myself how scared I am of the future, but I trusted him with my vulnerability. And he validated everything I told him in a way that made it all feel like it could be okay someday.

Chad saw me in a way no one ever has before.

"Goodnight, Hope," he says and heads for the living room.

"Chad?"

He pauses in the doorway, though I can barely see his silhouette in the glow from the fire down the hall.

My heart is pounding like crazy, but I don't let my fear keep me from saying the words. "Remember what you said to Zelda yesterday? It's the same for me. I only kiss someone when I..." Nope. Can't say it. It's too crazy. But I feel like I have to say *something*, so I start rambling.

"I feel like I always do things out of order. The wrong way, you know? I didn't choose a major until I took a class that I really liked my sophomore year. I legally became an adult before I went to junior prom. I became a mom of two elementary kids without ever having a real boyfriend. And I fell for a really great guy before I even knew him. Even when he's so much older than me." I swallow. "Most of those things have worked out for me so far, even if it's not the way regular people do things."

Though he doesn't say anything, he stands there long enough that I can practically feel him soaking up my words. I may have said it indirectly, but I mean it. I think I love him. Or I'm well on my way to that. I know nothing about him, but there's something deep in my chest telling me that he and I are destined. Written in the stars.

I've learned to listen to the stars.

He also said he only kisses people he wants to marry, and I think I might agree with that too. But I don't want to say anything else crazy tonight. Even if it's true.

"Goodnight," he murmurs again, and then he's gone.

Chapter Fourteen

Chad

October 19

I'm an idiot. A complete and utter fool. Stupid, selfish, impulsive, thoughtless... I could go on and on. And yet knowing this doesn't change the fact that I kissed Hope last night, which is quite possibly going to be the biggest mistake of my life. And I didn't just kiss her. I *kissed* her. I carried her to my bed and almost ignored the warning bells clanging in my head, telling me that certain things cannot be undone and I need to be careful.

By some miracle, that warning won out in the end, and I don't want to think about what might have happened if it hadn't. I've been down that road before, and I've seen the danger that comes from moving into things too quickly. I won't let that happen again. I can't. If I'm going to be with someone, I can't risk her taking my heart when she leaves, and she deserves more than halfhearted commitment on my end.

"She's twenty-four," I growl as I scramble some eggs because apparently I need the reminder.

"That didn't stop you last night."

My head snaps up, but it's just Hank, who looks a little too amused for my liking as he sits at the kitchen table.

I grip the whisk a little tighter. "I didn't—"

"I know," he says, holding up a hand. "My door was open to let in the heat from the fire, so I heard...well, everything." He turns a bit pink, though I can't imagine what he heard could have been worse than some of the things he's written in his novels. Still... "There's no question that the two of you have chemistry."

"She's twenty-four," I repeat.

He chuckles. "So you've said. That's not that big of a gap, you know."

"Twelve years."

"I've seen worse."

I growl, which is as ridiculous as it is unhelpful. "She has the kids."

"I barely know you, Chad, but even I know you want kids."

"I'm only in town for—"

"Why are you looking so hard for reasons that it won't work?" Hank asks, raising an eyebrow.

I wish I had an answer that sounds better than, "I don't know if I can love her." Apparently I just said that out loud because Hank's other eyebrow shoots up to match the first. I lean against the counter, taking a deep breath and double checking to make sure Hope and the kids haven't left their rooms yet.

"I've been in love before," I mutter, folding my arms like that might protect me. "It's only been a few months since she broke my heart, and I don't think I..." This feels strange, baring my soul to a guy I barely know, but I can't keep holding on to this and expecting the wounds to heal. "I'm not sure I have a heart left to give away. And Hope deserves so much."

She basically said she loves me last night, which sounds impossible but weirdly feels...plausible. And it's not because I'm so great and lovable; I'm pretty much the opposite. Somehow, she's worked her way into my life just like I've apparently infiltrated hers, and that makes this all so much scarier. I'm not afraid of much, but I am terrified of loving and losing.

Hank smiles like I've just told him I'm scared of roller coasters (which I am, by the way—I don't trust them). He thinks I'm being overdramatic, but he understands that this is a real fear. For a guy who keeps to himself, he seems to understand people pretty well. "I'm no expert in love," he says gently, "but I watched you with that family last night. You have plenty of heart in you, and it would be stupid to throw something like this away just because you're scared. Yeah, you might get your heart broken again, but I think that's the point of love. It's taking a risk even when you know it could end badly. But when that love endures and grows into something eternal? That's got to make all of that risk worth it."

I've never seen love reach that point. I've helped end too many marriages in my job. I watched my own father break my mother. Even Lloyd, who fiercely loved my mom, ended up heartbroken when she died. Every relationship has problems, and in my experience, even the ones who make it end up slightly bitter at the end of the day because nothing is ever perfect.

"I'm not going to tell you what to do," Hank says, adjusting his glasses, "but from an outside perspective, you and Hope could be really good for each other. In other words, you seem like you could use a little Hope in your life. Get it?"

"Har har," I grumble, but he's right. I don't remember the last time I ever felt hopeful, but she makes it so easy to dream about a better future for myself. One where I'm not alone. It's so easy to imagine having the kids every night. Getting to dance with them in the firelight. Making breakfast for more than just myself. I have wanted that so desperately my entire life, and for the first time in a long time, it feels like it could be within reach.

That sounds insane, and I know it. I don't know enough about this woman to think I have a clue who she is. Apparently she wants to be an astronomer, but beyond that? I don't know her dreams or her worries. I don't know her favorite color or what she likes to eat. I don't know what she would do if something put her in danger, or what makes her laugh, or when her birthday is. And yet my chest still aches to keep her in my life, like she was made for me and something is pushing us together.

Duke lifts his head, tail wagging as he looks toward the bedrooms, which means this heart-to-heart is now over because someone else is awake. With the way my heart rate kicks up at the thought of seeing Hope again, I know Hank is probably right about all of this. That doesn't make this any less terrifying, and if last night was any indication, I clearly don't know how to take things slow and be cautious. I can't jump into something without both of us being on the same page.

I shouldn't jump into something to begin with. Not without certain commitments. Call me old-fashioned, but I want to do things right this time around.

"I can't tell if the sun is up," Hope says, poking her head around the corner. "Am I allowed out of the dungeon?"

My whole body relaxes at the sight of her messy hair and tired eyes. I don't realize how tense I've been this morning until she makes it all go away with her little smile. I know she's remembering last night as much as I am because her cheeks slowly burn brighter red as we watch each other, and I wonder if she dreamed about it too or if that was just me. Then there's the fact that she is wearing one of my sweatshirts even though it drowns her, and my heart throbs at the thought of her rummaging through my things and picking out her favorite.

Now it's my favorite.

Hank clears his throat, and when I look at him, he rubs his jaw. Probably means I'm smiling like the idiot that I am.

"Hungry?" I ask Hope.

"Starving," Zelda says, appearing behind her. Link is with her, suddenly making the kitchen feel crowded. "Is the power back on? Duke!"

Duke hurries forward to greet the kids, while Hank says something about grabbing a sweatshirt and disappears down the hall. I figure I have maybe ten seconds before the window of distraction closes, so I jerk my head and smile when Hope scurries forward and into my arms.

Her kiss is already familiar, like a language I've been speaking my whole life but she's the only one who understands. As I run my fingers through her hair and explore her lips, her hands spread over my chest, pressing against my heart like she knows how fragile it is. Part of my armor breaks, falling away with her touch and leaving me exposed.

"I told you you love each other!" Zelda shouts.

Hope breaks away so quickly that it hurts, and I stumble forward a step, desperate to have her back in my arms. These kids are going to test my patience, but it's best to keep them around as much as possible. They'll make an excellent buffer.

I rub my mouth, grimacing when that makes Hope laugh.

"You were right," she says to Zelda, ruffling the girl's hair. "So, what are we doing for breakfast?"

For the next half an hour, Link and Zelda help me make eggs and chocolate chip pancakes while Hank and Hope go through my bookshelf, discussing who knows what as they share favorites or laugh at my choices. I'd be jealous if Hope didn't constantly send little smiles my way while Hank smirks at me multiple times and keeps a decent distance between himself and Hope as a courtesy. Apparently, he is now our biggest fan, but I can't wait for the snow to clear enough for him to go back to his own house. We have plenty of witnesses as it is, and I can't send the other two back to their own house.

In fact, I don't *want* to send them back to their own house. While it's functional, it's not exactly a kid-friendly place, and the hole in the window is making me cold just thinking about it. There may or may not be a badger living in the closet, and there's a whole lot of space between Hope's house and mine that I'm not all that fond of anymore. It's more than the possibility of someone lurking around and me wanting to keep them safe; I just want them nearby. Within arm's reach at all times.

Hank is right, and I should stop looking for reasons why this won't work. I want to start looking for reasons why it might. The fact that I'm even thinking about asking Hope and her kids to stay when the whole reason I came to this house was to get away from other people is a pretty big argument for this turning out to be good.

Breakfast is full of laughter and smiles as Hank tells us about a time he was traveling in France and tried to order pancakes but said something completely wrong and got four whole loaves of bread. Even Link laughs a couple of times, which has Hope tearing up with a broad smile, and I can't help picturing this being my life every morning.

Preferably without Hank.

I grab Hope's hand under the table, and she gives me the warmest smile meant just for me. It attacks my armor with a jackhammer, breaking away chunk after chunk with no sign of giving up until it's all gone.

Maybe I'm okay with that. I don't need armor if Hope is going to keep my heart anyway.

The storm officially stops late that morning, and Hank offers to help me dig my truck out on his way back home. He seems just as eager to be home as I am for him to leave, so I agree.

I get the kids set up with a video game and then pull Hope aside, trying to find the best way to ask her not to go back to her own house. She waits expectantly, her dark eyes big and wide, and suddenly I'm nervous.

"You..." I clear my throat, still debating if this is a good idea. She might laugh in my face. "You could stay here. My house is warmer, and..." Oh, for the love of—it's not like I don't know what she's going to say. Setting my shoulders, I give her my best taunting look. "It would be a lot easier to rescue you if you were already in the same place as me."

She narrows her eyes playfully, leaning up on her toes until she's only a breath away. "That's true, but you'll also be in a lot more danger if I'm around all the time."

"I'll take that risk." I press my lips to hers, drinking her in while I can.

It's Hank who interrupts us this time, clearing his throat by the front door, where he's bundled up and ready to go. "If you want help getting your truck out," he reminds me.

I quickly kiss Hope's nose. "Stay," I mutter before grabbing my coat and following Hank out into the cold.

When I get back a couple of hours later, she's asleep on my couch with the kids curled up next to her, and I've never seen a better sight in my life.

Chapter Fifteen

Hope

AFTER A DAY OF making the biggest snowman I've ever seen—not hard considering I've never seen one in my life—and a snow cave that fits all four of us *and* Duke with room to spare, I experience what might be the easiest bedtime of my life. There isn't a single complaint from Zelda, who tends to try to stay up as late as she can, or any sign of a tear from Link, who is happy to lead Duke to his bed again and cuddle up with him. They both fall asleep with smiles on their faces, which is quite possibly the best sight I've ever seen in my life.

Well, maybe a close second to the sight of Chad watching Red-tails baseball highlights from Monday's game. He's settled on the couch with two mugs of hot chocolate in front of him, complete with mini marshmallows. He wears sweats and a t-shirt, freshly showered and looking completely at ease as he laughs at something on his phone. Then he looks over at me, and his smile grows even wider.

"I'm guessing they fell asleep quickly?" he says, holding his arm out in a clear invitation.

I snuggle right in. I've borrowed some of his clothes again—turns out I packed myself some terrible options—and I have never been comfier despite his shirt being way too big on me. "I'm surprised they stayed awake long enough to brush their teeth. And don't worry; I brushed my teeth too."

"I wasn't worried." He proves it by kissing me softly, adding to this already great day. We focused more on the kids today, making sure they were warm and happy as we played in the snow, so I haven't kissed him since this morning. Way too long. "I'm sorry about the Burrs losing, by the way."

I shoot him a mock glare. "You're not sorry at all. Your brother pitched a good game, though."

"Yeah." He frowns at the TV, watching a replay of one of Houston's pitches. It's a good pitch, but Chad doesn't seem to like it. "I think he might be injured. He didn't throw as well as he usually does."

Well, that doesn't sound good. "Why didn't they sub in a different pitcher?"

He rolls his eyes, like I've asked a dumb question even though teams have multiple pitchers for a reason. "Because my brother likes to play the hero. Or, in this case, the martyr. He's good at hiding when something's wrong."

The camera does a close up of Houston, who looks tired but as determined as ever. I'm pretty sure he usually pitches whole games instead of subbing out halfway through the game. The Red-tails probably would have won by more points if they had let a relief pitcher come in and close out the game.

Chad runs his fingers along my arm as he watches Houston strike out the Burrs player up at bat. "He didn't lose a game this season," he mutters. "The fact that his team was losing probably made him play harder in the last inning as a matter of pride."

"Isn't that dangerous if he's injured?"

"Yep."

"Do I need to distract you, or do you actually want to watch the highlight reel?"

He chuckles. "What did you have in mind?"

Oh, I have a lot of things in mind, but the deeper we get into this thing, the more I want to know about this man who has stolen my heart. "What was so funny on your phone?" And can I replicate it so I can enjoy his laugh more often?

He grabs it, typing in the surprisingly complicated password to unlock it and holding it out to show me. That wasn't what I was intending, but I love that he has nothing to hide. A group text thread sits on the screen, full of messages from everyone but him. I even scroll up to see when he last sent a message, but I don't find one. Scrolling back down, I read through a few of them from last week, my smile growing with each one.

Half-pint:

Good luck with your game, Houston! Break a leg!

Texas:

That only works in theater, Mic. I don't particularly want to break my leg tonight.

Half-pint:

You know what I meant!

Blondie:

Be nice, Hou. You're lucky she remembered you have a game tonight in the first place.

Texas:

She's the only one.

Blondie:

Chad will probably watch it.

Half-pint:

Unless he's too busy falling in love!

Blondie:

Twice that he'll of

Blondie:

Oops.

Blondie:

I meant to say falling in love with who?

Texas:

How do you even mess up that bad?

Texas:

And you guys need to stop distracting me. My game starts in like an hour.

Half-pint:

> I warned him that if he went to a small town like Laketown he was going to run into a woman who's magically perfect for him and they were going to fall in love.

Texas:

> You do know life isn't a Hallmark movie, right? I need to know that you know this.

Texas:

> I'm turning off my phone now.

Blondie:

> Good luck, Hou?

Blondie:

> That wasn't supposed to be a question. *face palm emoji*

The next batch of texts came in about half an hour ago, picking up right where they left off last week.

Half-pint:

> By the way, I was totally right about Chad!

Blondie:

> Nice job winning the Series, Hou.

Texas:

> You only know I won because Jordan told you. What's going on with you and Jordan, anyway?

Blondie:

> Nothi

Blondie:

> I don't know what you're talking about.

I snort a laugh. "His woman, huh?"

Shrugging, he pulls me in tighter against him like he's worried I might run away after reading that. "I take no responsibility for what they may do or say. For the record, Micah is inferring everything. I haven't said anything about you other than we were caught in the storm together. She was worried I would be alone, and I assured her I am not." With that, he nuzzles his nose into my hair and kisses my temple while I read the next few texts. I love the way his siblings interact with each other; they're clearly close.

"I'm not sure if I should be offended or glad about your silence," I mutter, handing his phone back.

"I'm not good at sharing." Whether he means that in the sense of being open about telling his siblings things in general or in the sense of he doesn't want to share *me*, I'm not sure. Part of me hopes it's the latter if only because it gives me a firmer idea of how he feels about me.

"Who is Jordan?" I ask, maybe a little too interested in the drama of Chad's siblings. "Outside of the fact that he may or may not be dating Brooklyn, I mean."

"Houston's best friend."

"Sounds like a recipe for disaster. And this Fischer guy that Brooklyn says Micah is crushing on?"

"He was at the lodge with her yesterday."

"Sounds like everything went okay on that front. Is Houston dating anybody?"

He laughs, the sound deep and full. "Why are you so convinced I know everything about my siblings' lives?" When I don't say anything, he rolls his eyes. "No, he's single, which is weird for him. And no, you're not his type."

I gasp. "Meaning what?"

"Meaning there's no point in being interested. I told you; I don't like sharing."

Oh, he is good, and I reward him with a kiss that he returns with enthusiasm. He's better at restraining himself tonight, which I both appreciate and hate, and I'm guessing a lot of that is because he's tired. He's had a big day, and he's not as young as he used to be.

I snicker at the thought.

"What are you laughing about?" he asks.

"Nothing."

"Mm hmm."

"Why don't you ever text your siblings back?"

He sighs and pulls away, though his smile tells me he's not all that mad about me breaking our kiss. "If I have something to say, I'd rather say it to that person directly."

I don't know if I've ever met anyone who is so good at answering questions without hesitation. While I have a feeling there's a lot he keeps to himself, it always feels like he does everything he can to be open and honest with me, and there is so much that I love about that.

So I keep asking questions. "Is it hard, being so much older than your siblings? Bailey was only a couple of years older than me, so we were pretty close, and Link and Zelda are so close in age that they basically feel like twins."

He considers that, pursing his lips as he resumes stroking my arm like he was doing earlier. "Sometimes. Sometimes I feel more like a parent than a brother, and other times it's like we're all the same age. It was harder when we were younger, after I turned eighteen. They were just kids, and they went to live with Micah's dad because they needed someone who could actually take care of them when my dad got arrested."

I can hear the strain in his voice. Lacing the fingers of my right hand with his right hand, since his arm is around my shoulders, I try to show him that he's not alone. "Why wasn't that someone you? You were already taking care of them."

"Did you have to fight to keep custody of Link and Zelda, or did they hand them right over to you?"

I never really thought of it as fighting, but I had to prove that I was capable before CPS released them. "I guess a little bit."

"Imagine you were barely eighteen, a high school dropout, no health insurance and barely enough money to pay rent and utilities."

"Oh."

"Yep. It didn't matter if I knew them better than anyone. On paper, I was a bad fit. I'm glad Lloyd was willing to take them, or who knows where they would have ended up. But the judge was right, and they needed a real parent."

"You're a great parent, Chad." I've been watching him with my kids for the last two days, and he's a total natural.

He takes a while to respond. "I'm not a parent."

"Do you want to be?" *What in the world was that, Hope? You can't ask something like that!*

But then Chad says, "I almost was once," and stiffens. Apparently we're both saying things we shouldn't tonight. He lets out a heavy sigh, pulling his hand free as if giving me an opportunity to leave if I want to. "Sorry. That's not something I wanted to spring on you like that."

But it's something he wanted to tell me eventually? "What happened? When?"

He sighs again. "About five years ago. My girlfriend got pregnant, and we were thrilled. Then she miscarried, and she was too devastated to try again. At least, that's what she told me. Maybe she really was upset, but I think she was more relieved than anything. She said we could try again after we got married, but she kept putting off wedding talk until about six months ago when I finally figured out she'd been..." He coughs, clearly uncomfortable.

"She was cheating on you?" I hate her even more than I did yesterday when Hank suggested Chad might have an ex. "Can I punch her?"

A soft laugh comes out of him, and he kisses my cheek. "You could totally take her. You've taken *me* out several times already, so..."

"Chad?" I grab his hand again.

"Hmm?"

"Thanks for telling me. About everything. Thanks for trusting me."

"You're easy to trust. In my line of work, people like that are few and far between."

I can't believe I still don't know this yet, and I ask with more than a little curiosity burning in the question. "What do you do for work?"

"I'm a private investigator."

I sit up straight, accidentally elbowing him in the ribs on the way up. "Oops. Sorry! Really? That's so cool!"

As he watches me, he frowns as if he isn't quite sure if he can believe me. "Most people hate it."

"Do most people have something to hide from you?"

That question catches him off guard, apparently, and he has to think about it for a second. "I guess they usually do, yeah. But you don't?"

I love that he makes that a question, even though I'm pretty sure he has done some digging at some point. He seems like the kind of guy who would want to know everything about his neighbors, which would explain how he knew so much about Hank without ever really talking to him. I wonder how far he dug, but I really have nothing to hide.

"Did you find my parking ticket?" I ask, narrowing my eyes at him.

He laughs. "I didn't find you at all."

"You seriously didn't dig?"

"I didn't know your name was Karen until the other night." He tugs on my hand, trying to pull me back into his arms, but I resist, which seems to frustrate him more than the fact that he couldn't search for any of my nonexistent skeletons. "What are you doing?"

Biting my lip, I grab one of the mugs of hot cocoa and take a sip, even though at this point it's more like lukewarm cocoa. The Red-tails highlights may still be playing behind me, but this sounds like a lot more fun. "I'm going to learn everything there is to know about Chad Briggs," I tell him, settling myself on the ottoman by his feet instead of the couch.

With the way he scowls at me, I have a feeling he doesn't give many people that pleasure. "What are your sources going to be?" he asks warily.

"I only need one."

"Which is?"

"You."

Though he fights his smile, it wins out in the end as he sits up and curls one leg underneath the other. "You know," he says, taking the other mug of cocoa when I hand it to him, "I'm usually the one asking questions."

"So it's long past someone else's turn, don't you think?"

"You might not like some of the answers." Now there's vulnerability in his voice, and I can tell he wants this. He's been on his own for a while now, even if he said he was dating his stupid ex up until six-ish months ago. If she was cheating on him—how in the world could anyone cheat on *him*?—she was probably neglecting him. And this man needs to know he's worth loving. I may not know the first thing about love, but I know what I feel for him. If I can find a way to show him, maybe that smile will make an appearance more often.

That's a win-win situation right there. He gets to be happy, and I get to see one of the most beautiful smiles I've ever known. And hopefully it means more kissing because that will never get old.

"Chad," I tell him as seriously as I can, even though I'm stupidly grinning because I'm so excited. "I don't think there's anything you can tell me that I wouldn't like."

He wrinkles his nose. "That's a tall order."

"Try me."

"What do you want to know first?"

My grin grows wider. "In a fight between a grilled cheese and a taco, who do you think would win?"

Chapter Sixteen
Chad

October 20

I DON'T REMEMBER THE last time I willingly stayed up past two A.M. outside of being on a stakeout, for good reason. Sleep, difficult as it is to come by lately, is a precious commodity, and there are few things that can make up for anything less than a solid eight hours of z's. Talking to Hope is definitely one of those things.

Though at times I find myself cursing her young body and endless energy, wishing I could be twenty-four again and full of life, she always finds a reason to keep me awake, whether it's with another question—ridiculous or sincere; she has both—or by kissing me until we can't breathe. I don't know if I've ever talked this much in my life, and I certainly haven't ever kissed this much in my life, which is saying something considering I lived with Mercedes for over four years. Hope kisses the same way she does everything else: without hesitation or reservation, and that's something Mercedes never did. Not even when things were good between us.

Hope makes me feel like a new man—both the woman and the sentiment. Because she does have me hoping that this can be something. She may be young, and she may come with a lot of baggage, but who doesn't? I've got plenty of my own. Together, we might as well rent a storage locker or use it to build a blanket fort or something.

Yeah, she has me thinking about blanket forts, which I haven't made in years.

The world feels bright again, and it's all thanks to her.

She falls asleep around five in the morning after forcing me to choose a favorite book. (I picked *The Three Musketeers*, but choosing a favorite book is like choosing a favorite sibling; I can't actually pick one. I only said something because Hope told me she wouldn't kiss me again unless I did, and I wasn't willing to risk it.) She has been in every position imaginable tonight—whether cross-legged on the ottoman, lying in my lap, sitting against my legs while I rub her shoulders or braid her hair—but right now she's in my arms where she should be as we lie on the couch together. And I never want to let her go.

At this point, she literally knows me better than anyone else in the world. She knows that I broke my toe when I was ten and never told anyone, and it still aches when it's cold outside. She knows I don't like ketchup on burgers but love it on eggs. She knows I still made wishes on shooting stars until I was in my mid-twenties. (She especially loved this fact.) She knows I'm the one who caught my dad in bed with another woman when I was ten. I was too young to know anything about what, exactly, they were doing, but I knew it was bad. I told my mom about it that afternoon, and she didn't bother confronting him before she packed us up and moved out because she trusted me.

Hope knows that I cried like a baby when Mercedes miscarried and that I'm terrified of going through that sort of loss again.

I've never been known like this. Not even by my siblings. They see the man who helped raise them, who set the rules and made dinner and talked them through their tougher moments. I've always been there for them and always will be, but I've never been open and vulnerable with them. They don't even know why Mercedes and I broke up, even if I wish I had talked to them about it so I didn't have to carry that hurt all on my own.

I have always protected my heart, but Hope made it so easy to let her in that I'm not sure I'll have any armor left if this goes wrong. What will happen to me then?

I tighten my hold on her, breathing in the smell of her hair. I wonder what she usually smells like since she used my shampoo this afternoon, but this smell is so familiar that I almost prefer it. It means she's here in my life, sharing my space and my soap and my soul.

I'm in trouble.

Trying not to wake her, I crawl off the couch and lift her into my arms to take her to my bed so she can get some sleep without the kids interrupting. She snuggles into me as I walk, still half asleep, and she moans when I set her down on the mattress and step away.

"Stay," she murmurs, reaching out a hand.

I want to. I want this to be the rest of my life, but I know myself well enough to know that I've fallen so hard that I can't mess this up. I don't want another Mercedes situation where she stays with me out of obligation or some sense of duty, and I don't want Hope to think I'm only in this for the physical aspects. She is so much more than that.

After tonight (this morning?) I know her parents died in a car accident when she was sixteen and she ended up applying for emancipation instead of moving in with a relative. She wants to study the universe because she thinks it is proof of a higher power, one she wants to know better even though the hand she's been dealt in life isn't great from my perspective. She told me about how she thinks there is more to life than the space between birth and death, to the point where she almost has me convinced to believe it with her. She almost never gets embarrassed (which I already suspected) and has always been an extrovert unless she has a good book to read. Even then, she considers the characters to be real people and says it's just like being surrounded by friends. She's never afraid to try new things and always pushes back when she knows she's right about something.

I don't know if I ever pictured my perfect partner, but I'm starting to think that if I had, she would have looked a lot like Hope.

Tucking her fingers away with the rest of her, I brush a kiss against her temple and close my eyes, breathing in this moment and letting myself imagine a life with this woman. Hank was right, and I do have a heart beating in my chest because it hasn't stopped pounding since the first time I held her in my arms.

Yes, I'm talking about the hardware store. When she came into my life like a tornado and literally knocked me off my feet. I haven't been the same since, and I've been fooling myself into thinking I ever had any sense of control over my feelings for this woman. Hope Duncan is a woman who cannot be controlled, in the best way, and my life is better for having her in it.

"I love you, Chad," she murmurs, though I'm pretty sure she's asleep again.

My heart beats those words right back. *I love you. I love you. I love you.* But I can't get them to leave my tongue.

Saying it out loud feels like giving the universe the power to intervene, and I am terrified that if I do that, I'm going to lose her.

I get less than an hour of sleep before the kids are up and literally jumping on me, begging me to play outside with them again. Though I groan and grumble, they are undeterred, and somehow they convince even Duke to join in on the coercion. He gives my face a thorough licking until I roll off the couch and make an entire pot of coffee, though I'm not sure that will be enough. Link and Zelda each down a bowl of cereal while I attempt to keep my eyes open—my attempts are mostly unsuccessful—and then we're outside in the cold.

The kids play on their own, building up a fort wall with what snow is left by making bricks with a bread pan, which means I can sit on the deck and nurse a thermos mug of coffee. Duke's keeping a pretty good eye on them, but I am not going to be the guy who lets something horrible happen to a kid just because I was tired after making out with their mom all night.

"Chad, we found tracks!"

I jolt awake, unsure how long I was out but fully aware of the stream of coffee dribbling out of my mug and onto my boots. *Nice.* "Tracks?" I grunt, blinking in the sunlight glinting off the quickly melting snow.

Zelda points toward their house. "The wolverine!"

So the badger *has* been back? Now I'm happier than ever that I asked Hope to stay at my house so there's no danger of the kids running into a wild animal. Link looks way too excited about the idea of a creature climbing in and out of his window, and I should do something to make sure they don't get any crazy ideas.

"He probably got scared by the storm," I mutter, rubbing my jaw. "He must have gone back to his home after it ended."

"I thought Barry's home was in the closet," Link says with a frown.

Oh good, we've named the badger. I take a deep breath. I am not awake enough for this. "No, his home is out in the forest somewhere. Are you kids ready to go back inside?"

"We haven't done our snowball fight yet!" Zelda complains.

"Yeah, okay, fine. Do your fight. Duke, keep watch."

I fall asleep to their giggles and screams.

A pair of arms snaking around my shoulders wakes me up, and I could get used to the way Hope snuggles up from behind my chair and presses her cheek against mine. "You let me sleep in," she says, as if that's the most romantic thing I've ever done.

I need to up my game if that's the case.

"Mmm," I say. It's about all I can manage right now.

Taking the coffee out of my hands, she takes a sip as she looks out over the yard. "Zelda's getting pretty good at making that wall."

I peek one eye open. Apparently the fight is over, which must mean I was asleep longer than I'd like. Zelda's on her own, happily stacking bricks to turn her wall into a lopsided igloo. "Is Link inside?"

"I didn't see him."

I sit up straighter. Duke's gone too, which makes me feel a little bit better, but there's an unsettled feeling churning in my gut that I don't like. I'd almost forgotten that someone was sneaking around the house the other night, but that knowledge comes flooding back as I stand up and whistle as loudly as I can. Hopefully Link wasn't carried off by someone to use as blackmail against me, but I don't like the alternative any better.

A bark echoes in the distance, barely audible through the thick trees.

I curse, lifting my foot up to tie my boot because I was too lazy to do it earlier.

"What's going on?" Hope asks.

"I think Link went into the woods."

"What?" The thermos mug slips from her fingers. "Why?"

"He's looking for the badger."

"The wolverine?"

"It's a—" It doesn't matter. As soon as both my boots are tied, I stumble down the stairs and shout, "Stay with Zelda!" before whistling again, ears peeled for the sound of Duke's faint reply.

I get a few hundred yards into the trees before I finally find little footprints following a deeper trail made by an animal. Dog prints overlap Link's steps, and all in all it's easy to follow until I get deep enough into the trees that there's hardly any snow anymore. I swear again, heart pounding as I whistle once more. This time, Duke barks several times, a lot more urgency in his bark than before. He's no longer barking at me.

He's barking at something else.

Fear washes over me, making me stumble as I scramble through the thick underbrush that hasn't gotten the memo that winter is practically here. "Duke!" I shout, voice hoarse. "Link!" I keep following the sound of Duke's warning until I catch sight of Link's bright red coat. My relief is minimal because the dog is focused on something in the trees above him as he slowly forces Link backwards by backing into him.

I don't want to know what's up there.

"Link!" I shout again, but he doesn't turn. He's focused on the tree as well, his eyes wide and face pale. Instead of making a plan, I rush forward and scoop the kid up at a run, not stopping to look behind me even though a snarl cuts through the air over the sound of Duke's barking. "Duke, go!" I shout, but I don't bother checking to see if he obeys. I just run.

We're almost within sight of the houses when excruciating pain shoots up my leg. I fall, Link tumbling from my arms. I'm sure I've just been mauled by a mountain lion until I turn to defend myself and instead find a metal bear trap locked around my leg. I collapse onto my back as the pain overwhelms me, gripping fistfuls of dirt. It's not a big cat ready to eat me, but it's close.

"Chad!" Link grabs my shoulder.

"Go back to the house," I growl. "Go!"

"But what about Duke?"

"Go back. To. The house." Dizziness washes over me, and I know I'm on the verge of passing out. I can't breathe. Probably going into shock. Not sure if I'm bleeding. Does it matter? I'll freeze to death first.

Little hands lift my head, knees sliding under like a pillow. "I wanted to make sure the wolverine was okay."

Not the time, kid. "It's a badger," I growl through gritted teeth.

"No, it's a wolverine."

"It's a stupid badger, and you could have gotten yourself killed. What were you thinking?"

"I thought—"

"No, you didn't think! And now Duke might be dead because of you."

Oh, that wasn't what I meant to say. But all I can think about is the pain, and my dog, and how I'm probably going to lose my foot because the stupid kid had to go running off into the woods after a *badger*.

"Chad."

I blink and look up into Hope's blurry face, and somewhere through the pain fog I come to the realization that I've been speaking all of my thoughts out loud. *I didn't mean it*, I want to say. I don't know if that's true. No, I *didn't* mean it. I didn't want to make Link bury his face into Hope's side as he cries. I didn't want her to look at me like I've betrayed her. I didn't want to become the worst sort of man I could ever be just because I got hurt. My vision fades, my eyes focusing on the hurt in her face until everything goes dark.

Next thing I know, I'm alone on the couch, my foot expertly bandaged and the house quiet around me. It's the silence that kills me because it tells me one very important thing: I've messed up.

Chapter Seventeen

Hope

As I QUICKLY LEARN, Chad is a complete baby when he's in pain.

I shouldn't find it funny, especially given the things he said during the whole bear trap debacle, but I can't help but find his utter grumpiness absolutely hilarious, which only makes him angrier.

"I can't believe you're laughing right now," he grumbles as I try to shift the pillow beneath his foot. "Ow! You don't have to move it around so mu—I swear you're doing this on purpose."

Maybe a little bit. I'm feeling a lot of feelings and I don't know what to do with them.

I dropped the kids off at Hank's as soon as the EMTs arrived and extricated Chad from the trap, which turned out to be a lot easier than I thought it would be. Thankfully, the trap didn't do much more than bruise him because it mostly caught his boot—I think he passed out from the shock of the injury, rather than the severity—but the paramedic who talked to me before they left told me he'll probably have a hard time walking for a few days. The trap left some pretty gnarly bruising. The paramedics gave me a pair of crutches and told me they'd call in a prescription for pain meds, and then they were on their way. Their attentiveness really made me appreciate small town medicine compared to the kind of stuff I saw in Tampa because they were so thorough.

I came back to the house not long after getting the kids settled with Hank, and it's been a battle with Chad ever since.

"How's that?" I ask, giving the pillow a little wiggle that makes him growl.

He glares at me. "Seriously?"

I glare right on back, which is hard to do when I'm still feeling giggly about the way he's acting. "That's for what you said to Link," I say with a huff. "Hank said he hasn't said a word since he got there."

Chad pinches the bridge of his nose. "I said I was sorry."

"Not to him, you didn't."

"Because you won't let me get off the couch!" He tries to get up again, and I pounce on him, using my body weight to hold him down. He could easily lift me if he tried, but this seems to do the trick at keeping him in place.

"The paramedic said you should take it easy for the next two days," I remind him. Not that he heard that part himself, but I've been good about relaying the important information. Honestly, he's lucky I'm willing to be such a dutiful nurse. I genuinely thought about leaving him here alone tonight, but then I felt bad. He did kinda rescue my kid from a mountain lion and all. He and...

His expression shifts, like he's reading my mind. "Has Duke come back yet?" he asks quietly.

I wish I had a different answer. I shake my head. So much for feeling giggly. "I'm so sorry."

"I need to go look for him. He might be..."

I place my palm over his heart, holding him in place. "If he's okay, he'll make it back. You need to rest." Even if there's no actual way for me to know this, I think Duke is alive. I don't know why he wouldn't have come back to the house yet if he is, but my gut tells me that perfect dog is out there somewhere. He's fine.

Maybe I just need him to be fine for Chad's sake.

"Is Link okay?" Chad asks after a moment, and I know he's afraid to ask.

I know he didn't mean the things he said about Link. I could see the regret in his eyes, even when he was halfway gone to shock, but it's a lot harder for a six-year-old to understand that. I did my best, but Link is convinced it's his fault that Chad got hurt and Duke is missing, and he was pretty much inconsolable. Hank texted about an hour ago and told me Link hasn't moved from the couch where he's watching TV, and my heart aches for the kid. He's too young to carry that kind of guilt.

Chad knows this as well as I do. "Hope," he croaks. "I have to talk to him. Please."

"When he's ready," I tell him, which might not be for a while. "He's still struggling with his mom dying, and I think this was just too much for him to handle."

He tucks some hair behind my ear. "Do you hate me?"

It's almost like he's bracing for me to say yes. I probably should hate him, but one moment of fear and pain shouldn't be enough to discredit all of the good that makes up Chad Briggs. Everyone has moments of weakness, but it doesn't mean they're like that all the time.

I smile, even if it's not an easy gesture right now. "Do you think I would be lying here on your chest, thinking about kissing you because you can't run away, if I hated you?"

Though his eyes sparkle, he frowns. "That wasn't an answer," he says.

I give him a soft kiss. "I don't hate you, old man. I'm frustrated with you. But I don't hate you." And then, as I shift to get more comfortable, I accidentally bump his foot with mine and pull another groan out of him.

"I'm getting mixed messages," he grumbles.

Grinning, I press my lips to his again and hope it makes up for my accidental touch. "Sorry. I didn't mean to do that. How does such a big strong man have such a low pain tolerance? I am terrified of seeing you with a cold."

"Yeah, you'll want to be far away if that ever happens."

"At least you admit it."

"I know who I am."

I run my hand through his short hair, studying his face as he studies mine in turn. This weekend has felt like an eternity. Within that eternity, I've come to know who he is too, and I am terrified of how much I love him. That can't be normal, being afraid of love, but I am. It's like we're teetering on the edge of a precipice with no way of knowing what's at the bottom if we fall. We can stay where we are and play it safe, keeping everything at the surface when it comes to our relationship, or we can take that leap and see where we land.

We may end up battered and broken, but I've already had the rug pulled out from under me. My life has pivoted a hundred and eighty degrees, and maybe it looks nothing like how I thought it would, but I know it's good. I know how scary it is to fall, but I also know it's worth it.

Does he?

Is he willing to take the leap and risk it all?

I trace my fingers along his face and touch each blemish and flaw, cataloging everything that makes him unique while he lays there in quiet stillness. I'm not sure he's ready to make that jump yet, and that's okay. But I hope he finds the courage soon. I may be younger than him, but I've seen how easily a life can be cut short. I don't want to waste any time.

"I'm going to say something that you're not going to like," I whisper.

His gaze hardens with fear, but he nods. "Okay."

Getting as close to him as I can without actually kissing him, I speak against his mouth. "I am going to kick your butt in Mario Kart."

The kids go straight to bed after I pick them up from Hank's, though Zelda graciously takes a moment to ask Chad if his foot is feeling better. She asks that question while helpfully adjusting his foot pillow for him, and I'm impressed with the way he clenches his jaw and says nothing. I think he's learned his lesson when it comes to speaking while he's in pain, and he's trying.

When I'm tucking him in, Link quietly asks if Duke has come back yet, and I don't know what to tell him. "He might come back tomorrow," is what I end up saying, but I know it hits Link hard. I don't think he's going to sleep well tonight, and I don't blame him.

I go straight to Chad's room instead of heading to the living room, though I'm not sure why I suddenly want to avoid the man. I definitely didn't avoid him this afternoon. We played about two rounds of Mario Kart before Chad realized I was epically bad at the game and decided to make out with me instead, which was a lot more fun. I guess maybe everything is feeling really big right now, and I'm not sure how to deal with it, so I slide into the covers of Chad's bed and immediately start wishing I was out there with him instead.

I don't have to wish for long. I've been lying here for five minutes max before I hear the crutches clomping across the floor, complete with grunts of pain as he makes his way across the house. He surprises me by knocking, but when I pretend to be asleep, he opens the door and flicks on the light.

"Why are you avoiding me?" he asks.

I squint, temporarily blinded by the sudden light. "I'm not avoiding you." I'm totally avoiding him.

"I thought you only say what you mean, Hope. What did I do?" He cringes. "I mean, aside from all the things this morning."

He looks so pitiful and repentant that I cave immediately and reach out for him.

Sighing with relief, he hobbles inside, sets his crutches against the dresser, and then collapses next to me with his arm over top of me and his head resting on my shoulder. Cuddling like this is the last thing I would have expected from someone like him, and I love the way he isn't shy about how much he just wants to be next to me. "Thank you. I won't stay for long."

"I'm just trying to process things," I tell him, surprising myself with that admission. He always makes it so easy to be honest because that's how he is himself. "It's a lot harder to process when all I can think about is kissing you."

"Yeah, I know the feeling." He plays with the end of my hair, breathing deeply as we lie there. "Anything I can do to help?"

I think this will just take time, something we haven't had a lot of so far. It was less than two months ago that Bailey died, and I'm still adjusting to my new life with the kids. Adjusting to Chad is a whole different story, one that I really do want to see through to the end. We're in the messy middle right now, which always gets more complicated before it gets better. That's how the good stories go, anyway.

I'm not trying to compare my life to books or anything, but this will be easier if I feel like I know where things are headed.

"Do you always think this hard?" Chad asks, lifting his head and brushing his thumb between my eyebrows. "I can feel it." Then he puts his hand on my collarbone, sort of over my heart but closer to my neck. "In here. I wish I could see your heart. It's probably beautiful, just like you."

My lips twist in an amused smile. "You took the pain meds the paramedics left you, didn't you?"

"Maaaybe." He draws the word out before giving me a sloppy kiss. "I don't know if they're kicking in, though."

"I'm pretty sure they are." They must have given him something strong with the way his words have a musical lilt to them, and I wonder if they ordered more of it for him and if he'll be like this all week. I planned to pick up his prescription tomorrow, and now I definitely have to make sure I get it soon. This could be fun. "You're going to get us in trouble, mister."

He doesn't seem to care as he nuzzles in beside me, lips finding my neck. "You're the most beautiful person I've ever known, Hope. I like you lots."

Hmm, I'm not sure how to feel about his drug-addled brain sticking with "like you lots" instead of something a little more potent. I mean, it's not like I've said the words "I love you" directly to him, but I've gotten close. Is it childish of me to want him to say it first? I feel like I'm allowed to be the childish one in this relationship, all things considered.

"I like you lots too, Chad."

He giggles, which is not a sound I *ever* thought would come out of a man like him. "You do?"

"Oh, you are going to be so glad you can't remember any of this in the morning."

"How could I forget anything that has to do with you?" He nuzzles his nose into my neck again, words slurring. "You're the best part of my life, Hope. Everything is dark without you there. Life has...no meaning..."

And suddenly he's snoring.

Oh boy.

I know I should leave. Swap places with him and take his place on the couch so I can be the responsible adult that I am. But I don't want to. It's not like sleeping next to him while we're both fully clothed is doing anything scandalous, even though sharing a bed with Chad Briggs *feels* scandalous. He's probably going to be out all night after the traumatic day he's had and not sleeping at all last night, so it's not like we're going to do anything we shouldn't.

I just want to know what it feels like to spend the night breathing with him. To wake up with him by my side. To know that no matter what dreams may come during the night, he'll be there to keep me safe. Because that's what Chad is.

He's safe.

That's all I've ever wanted.

Chapter Eighteen

Hope

October 21

As it turns out, waking up next to a guy you're in love with is pretty great. Even if he snores. The sound was almost comforting, and let me tell you, that is not something I've ever thought I'd say. There's also a chance that I have never slept as soundly as I did last night, and I wake up feeling completely refreshed and ready to welcome a new day.

When I open my eyes, I realize the same is not true for Chad. He's staring at me, barely breathing, and looking horrified, like he knows he's done something really bad and doesn't know if he's going to get in trouble yet or not.

It's adorable.

"Hi," I say, doing my best not to smile.

He blinks, his eyes trailing along his arm which is still draped over my waist. I don't think either of us moved during the night, which is impressive. "Um."

"It's not your fault, Chad. I should have left."

"That doesn't explain what I'm doing on the bed in the first place."

Does he really not remember? I can only imagine how it feels to be on the couch one moment and waking up in a completely different room the next. It happens to kids all the time, but to a grown adult? "Just how strong were those pain pills?" I ask, my voice wobbling.

He narrows his eyes. "You're about to laugh right now, aren't you?"

I lose it, sinking into a fit of laughter that has me curling into his chest as if that might stop the tidal wave of amusement spilling over me. "Sorry," I choke. "I don't know why it's so funny."

"Why do I get the feeling you're going to tell me I said all sorts of ridiculous things last night?" he grumbles, sitting up with some difficulty as he tries to avoid knocking his injured foot around. He ultimately fails, hissing and groaning until he finally gets his legs over the side of the bed. "I had no idea a bear trap could be so painful, but now I remember why I don't like taking pain meds if I don't have to."

Sitting up with him, I wrap my arms around his shoulders from behind, my hands on his broad chest. I'm a fan. "I'm sorry it hurts. But you have to remember that you got pretty lucky. It could have done some permanent damage."

"Better than letting something permanent happen to Link. Can I talk to him today?"

"Not unless you're medicated."

He frowns at me. "Seriously? I promise I'll be nice."

"I would believe that more if you weren't growling more than talking right now. He just needs some time, okay? Or a drug barrier. You're so much nicer when you're high."

"There's something wrong with you."

"I love Pain Pill Chad!"

He groans, pressing the heel of his hand into his temple. "Don't...please don't make that a thing."

"Sounds like you need some more pain pills," I tease.

He must really be in pain because he nods. "Mostly because I don't want to say anything stupid again."

"I think you're prone to say stupid things regardless of being drugged or not," I remind him.

"Yeah, but you're right. When I'm drugged, the stupid things are nicer."

"That's true. I'll pick up your prescription after I drop the kids off at school, okay?" I get up off the bed, but he grabs my hand before I get very far.

"Hope?"

"Yes, Chad?"

"I really do like you lots." And then he gives me a ridiculous grin that heats my entire body because does that mean he *does* remember last night? That would mean everything he said was real, and some of the things he said...

He told me his life doesn't have meaning without me, and that may not be "I love you," but it's pretty darn close.

I smile. "I like you lots too."

Once I wake the kids up for school, I make them some Pop-tarts for breakfast—Chad gives me some impressive glares for that from his spot on the couch—and hurry them out to the car, promising Chad that I'll be back with drugs and ready for another round of Mario Kart. With the way his eyes smolder at the window, I'm pretty sure he knows I don't actually mean Mario Kart.

Zelda talks the entire drive to the school, as usual, excited to tell her new friends all about what we did during the storm. Somehow, she's missed out on yesterday's trauma and is as chatty as ever. I didn't realize it until I watched her in the rear view while waiting for a logging truck to pass on the main road, but she looks like a kid now. She's less seven going on seventeen and more the bright-eyed child she really is. Did that come from having a little bit of time to heal, or did Chad have something to do with that?

He probably did. He's changed all of our lives by making himself a part of them.

Maybe not for the better with all of us, I think, glancing back at Link. He stares out the window with so much sadness in his eyes, and I can't help but wonder if he's always going to be that way now. He was doing so well, and then...

Link shuffles inside the school when we arrive, his head hanging low.

"I don't know how to help him, Bai," I mutter, wishing my sister could tell me what to do. She was always so good with these kids, and Link could really use his mom right about now.

I'm the closest he's going to get, and I don't think I'm going to cut it.

Once the kids are inside, I head to Main Street and park outside the grocery store. I figure I should buy Chad some more donuts, since I ate them all—and yes, I plan on eating the new ones too—and maybe to find some sort of romantic lunch I can make us while the kids are in school. I don't know what constitutes romantic when it comes to lunch food, but I'm pretty sure deli meat isn't my best option.

After wandering the little store for nearly twenty minutes, I settle on a carton of strawberries and some chocolate chips. I'll make my *own* romance. The woman who rings me up—her name tag says her name is

Wendy—seems to know exactly what my plan is, and she gives me a little wink before handing my bag to me.

"I hope he likes it," she says gleefully.

I smile and hurry outside. I just hope she doesn't know who "he" is, though I shouldn't hold my breath in a town this small. I bet the paramedics have told everyone about Chad's adventure and how I was there to keep him company.

Not for the first time since arriving in Laketown, I pause next to my car and look around. It's only been a couple of weeks, and I feel like I've already seen everything there is to see. I've eaten most everything at the diner, enjoyed the ice cream, and even played all the games at the little arcade. Did this town always feel so small and I am just now starting to realize it? Or has something changed in the last few days?

I set my groceries on the front seat, but as I'm shutting the door, a strange sensation creeps up my spine, like I'm being watched. I look around, frowning because Main Street is pretty dead this time of day, and then I see him.

It's the guy from our first week here. The one who looked familiar while the kids and I were eating ice cream before they started school. He's currently peering through the window of the random antique store that is the one place I haven't been inside yet, but I have a feeling he was only recently looking at me.

That's fine, I tell myself as I head to the pharmacy. I'm obviously looking at him, so it goes both ways. Again, he probably thinks I look familiar and is working up the nerve to come talk to me and figure out why.

Not sure why that would mean he needs to look so shifty while following me, though.

I slip inside the pharmacy and veer to the left, ducking down beneath the single shelf that sits in the middle of the store, holding my breath. The door doesn't open, and I let out a shaky little laugh. "Getting paranoid, are we?" I murmur and then head to the front desk.

One glance out the window tells me the guy is still there, which brings my heart rate right back up. Trying to ignore him, I tell the clerk, who looks about seventy years old, why I'm here.

"You want what?" he asks, turning his head to point his ear toward me.

Guess he's hard of hearing. "A prescription for Chad Briggs," I say loudly.

"For bad ribs? I think you just need to ice them, dear. Take some ibuprofen."

I chuckle, and after several more failed attempts at getting him to understand, ending with me pointing to the bag sitting on the counter behind him, I have pain pills in tow and feel a lot less spooked than I was a moment ago.

Still, it might be a good idea to get an expert's opinion.

Chad answers after the first ring. "You are taking forever."

"Someone wants his drugs," I say with a laugh.

"Something like that. Please tell me you're not calling to tell me you've decided to hang out in town all day and leave me here all alone."

Face heating, I scoot toward the back of the pharmacy. This might be a bad idea, but if I don't get some reassurance that everything is fine, I'll never leave the pharmacy until the man goes away. "So, hypothetically, if I felt like someone was watching me, what would be the best thing to do in this scenario?" He's quiet for long enough that I check to see if the call dropped. "Chad?"

"Is this a hypothetical or a real question?" He sounds so official and formal in a way that I haven't heard him before, which sends a shiver through me.

"Um, the second one?"

"Where are you? I'm coming to get you."

"You're definitely not getting off that couch right now, Chadwick Briggs."

"That is definitely not my name, Karen Duncan. Where are you?"

"Disneyland."

"Hope!"

"Will you calm down?"

He growls, and it almost sounds like he's hobbling around on one crutch. "You just told me someone is watching you. I am not going to *calm down.*"

He's extra sexy when he's protective, though I keep that thought to myself. "What if I told you it's a cute little old lady watching me?" I say as I peek out the window. The man's still standing at the crosswalk like he's waiting to cross, even though there aren't any cars on the road. Only a few feet of sidewalk separate him from the door, which means he's definitely waiting for me.

"Is it a cute little old lady?" Chad asks. I think he already knows the answer to that one because he says, "What does he look like?"

"How do you know it's a he?"

"Because you're scared."

He has a good point. "I don't know if I need to be scared, though," I admit. "He just kinda seems...interested. Maybe he just wants to ask me out."

"I'm still not okay with that," Chad says roughly. "What does he look like, Hope?"

I sort of form my answer in a way that I know will frustrate him, but I also am just really bad at describing people. I once asked my freshman roommate if she'd seen the guy on campus "with the hair." "Uh, he's kind of medium build with an average face."

"You have to give me more than that," he groans.

"Why? It's not like you'll know him."

"I might."

"You never come into town, Chad."

"He's here for me, Hope. I need to know who he is."

Okay, I wasn't expecting that. I grip my phone a little tighter as I try to get a better look at the guy through the glass. "What do you mean, he's here for you?"

Chad lets out a huge sigh. "Please don't freak out."

"How about you tell me what's going on, and then I'll decide if I should freak out or not?"

"Someone was sneaking around my house the other night."

The blood drains from my face. "When? During the storm?"

"Spaghetti night."

"*Chad*. Why am I just now hearing about this? What kind of sneaking?" And seriously, why didn't he tell me? What if the kids are in danger? Should I pick them up instead of letting them take the bus home today? I have too many questions to ask them all on the phone, plus I'm mad that this is the first time I'm hearing about this.

He groans, likely sensing my anger. "I'm sorry. I wanted to get more information before I turned it into a big deal, and then the storm hit. And I might have gotten a little distracted."

"Don't go blaming this on me, old man."

"I'm not. This is on me." He lets out his breath slowly, and I can imagine him standing with one crutch under his arm as he tries to think this through. "Can you take a picture or anything? I need to know if it's someone I've worked a case against."

"You think someone would follow you all the way to Laketown?" I switch the phone to speaker so I can try to get a picture without missing anything he's saying. It won't be great through the glass and at this angle, but hopefully it's clear enough for Chad to get an idea. I hit send and wait for it to deliver.

"It's only a couple of hours to Sun City, so... Maybe. I hope not." Then he swears.

"I take it you know him," I mutter. I was hoping otherwise.

"Todd Thwaite."

"Should I know that name?" It almost sounds familiar, but in the same way that he looks familiar. Like I've met him before, or I've seen him with someone I know. It's driving me crazy that I can't put my finger on it.

"No," Chad says. "He's the brother of one of my recent clients. Technically I shouldn't tell you anything, but he's—"

"A bad guy. You can leave it at that. What should I do?"

"Can you get to your car without him seeing you?"

"No. He's waiting for me to leave the pharmacy."

He swears again. "That's it. I'm coming, and you're not stopping me."

"What are you going to do? Whack him with your crutches? Just walk me through it, Chad. Maybe I can help you figure out what he's doing here."

"I think we have a pretty good idea why he's watching you."

It's my turn to groan. "You might," I say, "but I'm new to this whole investigating thing. Why would he be watching me if he's here for you? Oh." Okay, yeah, now I see why Chad is a little on edge. "You think he's going to use me to get to you. A blackmail situation. That makes sense."

For some reason, that makes Chad laugh, which honestly helps me relax a bit. "How are you so calm right now?" he asks.

I don't really know, though I have a good guess. "Because you seem like you'd reach Liam Neeson levels if something went wrong, so I like my odds."

"Did you really just make a *Taken* reference while in the middle of being tailed? Were you even born when that movie came out?"

I snort. "You keep forgetting that I was born in the same century as you."

"Barely."

"Can we focus?"

"You make that impossible."

"Wow, someone is grumpy today. If you want me to get back there with some pain meds, you're going to have to tell me how to get out of here without being seen."

Chad hums as he thinks that through. "You're at the pharmacy?"

"Yeah, and the store clerk is starting to think I might be a little crazy, so sooner than later, if you please." Not really. I don't think the old man behind the counter even realizes I'm still here because I'm pretty sure he's just as blind as he is deaf. That has me slightly questioning if Chad is going to be taking something he shouldn't, but I'll just have to trust that the clerk isn't also the pharmacist. Then again, he did tell me to take ibuprofen for my bad ribs...

I make a mental note to check the pills against pictures on the internet before I give any of them to Chad.

"I'm pretty sure there's a back door you could take, if you manage to sneak past whoever's running the store," Chad says, and it sounds like he's trying to picture it.

I glance behind me. Sure enough, I can see an exit sign just beyond a storage closet, in a dim corner of the store. "How in the world did you know that?"

"Force of habit."

"Looking for escape routes?"

Chad grunts. "My job is about being discreet. I don't exactly want to be seen."

"But this guy Todd knows you?"

"I interviewed everyone who worked in his office, though he ducked out before I could get to him. Guilty son of a—"

I clear my throat, cutting him off in the hopes that he'll get out of the habit of swearing if I try hard enough. He's been good for the most part, but if he's going to be around the kids...

"Sorry," he mutters. "My mom would have hated some of the things I say sometimes. And Brook has the right to punch me every time I swear around her. It's a whole thing."

"I would love to meet your family." I tense, yet again cursing my mouth's ability to say the best things at the worst times. I hold my breath and wait to see how he'll deflect this one.

He responds a lot faster than I thought he would. "I think they would really like you."

Oh. That...that has to be a good sign, right?

"Can you get to the back door?"

I look at the door again, but my attention is still stuck on what Chad just said. He thinks his siblings will like me? But does that mean he wants me to meet them? Do I actually *want* to meet them? I mean, obviously I do, but what will they think of me? Houston is a professional athlete who dates supermodels and movie stars, and Brooklyn is completely gorgeous and crazy smart according to Chad, who told me she's a chemistry teacher, and Micah sounds like a literal Disney princess and probably sings to birds who do her hair and makeup every morning.

Okay, this is getting away from me a little bit.

But then there's the fact that they are *all* older than me. Chad really hasn't made a big deal about how much younger than him I am, but what if *they* do? What if they see me and immediately think I'm no good for their brother? What if they see me as nothing but someone else for him to take care of?

What if *Chad* sees me that way? I don't want him to think I'm helpless or that I can't be helpful right back at him. How would such a lopsided relationship even work? I need to show him that I'm more than a disaster and that he can let someone else step in sometimes. He doesn't have to fix everything himself, even if he's been doing that his whole life.

"Hope, are you with me?"

"I hope so," I breathe.

"How's that door situation looking?"

"Why do you think he's here? Todd?"

He groans as if he knows the real reason behind my question. "You are trouble, you know that?"

"That's my middle name."

"It's really not."

"If I go out the front door, do you think Todd will follow me?"

Another groan has me imagining him sitting on the couch now, knuckles white as he grips his phone and contemplates the best way to murder me when I get back. At the very least, he's going to try to keep me from leaving the house again. Surprisingly, he answers my question. "Probably."

"Do you think there's a way I could double around and start following him once he thinks he's lost me?"

"This is a bad idea, Trouble."

Hmm, so he's come up with a new name for me, has he? Thinks he's so clever? Honestly, I kind of love the nickname, and a thrill runs through me at the thought of playing private investigator for a day.

Still, I'm not going to be stupid about this. "Would there be any benefit to following him?" I ask.

Chad hums. Is he really considering letting me do this? "Maybe. If we can figure out where he's staying, maybe I can figure out a way to figure out what his plan is."

"How do you figure?"

He groans yet again. "How in the world are you this annoying yet so completely intoxicating?"

"Aww, you sure know the way to a woman's heart."

"If you're going to do this, you have to do everything I say. Do you understand? Hope, I need verbal confirmation that you will do everything in your power to be safe and careful and be back in my arms in less than an hour. Okay? Say it."

"It."

He swears under his breath, though I'll allow this one. He might be a little too fun to mess with, especially when he's stuck in a place where he can't distract me with his delicious kisses.

"Karen Hope Duncan, you are going to be the death of me. Forget it. Sneak out the back door and come back so I can make sure you're never out of my sight again."

What is it about a man using my full name that has me hearing wedding bells? What has my life come to? "You know," I say as I start searching the shelves for a set of Bluetooth headphones I can use—remarkably, I find some in a random corner of travel trinkets. "Two months ago, the weirdest thing to happen during my day was running into my roommate

Freddie trying to perfect his smokey cat eye while listening to a podcast that described the origin of dank memes."

I don't blame Chad for failing to come up with a response to that. "I literally have no idea what you just said," he says eventually. "None of those things are real things, right?"

"Get with the times, old man. It's not important anyway." I place the headphones on the counter, chuckling when the old clerk doesn't seem at all surprised to see that I haven't left yet as he rings me up.

"Are you trying to stall so Todd will get frustrated and leave?"

"Do you think he would?" I peek out the window as I crack open the package on the headphones. He's still standing outside, though he has his eyes on his phone now like he's just trying to kill time. Hmm, he's more patient than Chad would like. "This guy isn't dangerous, is he? I don't think you would let me anywhere close to him if he was."

"I don't think so, but I'm still not comfortable with you deliberately putting yourself anywhere that he is."

"Hang on a second." Thankfully the headphones are partially charged, and they connect to my phone easily enough. I put them on, wondering if Todd will notice them or if he wasn't paying that much attention. "Can you hear me?"

"Bluetooth?" He must have heard the sound quality change, which reminds me that he's the kind of guy who notices details and makes exit strategies. "Smart. Are you going to tell me why you brought up your weird roommate that I am definitely going to do a background check on?"

I snicker. "He's not my roommate anymore, genius."

"Don't care."

"I was just trying to say that I never thought my life would go this direction, you know? Before Bailey gave me the kids, my biggest worry was getting a paper turned in on time and doing my equations right. Now look at me."

"I would if I could. Are you going to come back home so I can?" He's used that word a couple of times now—home—and it's starting to sound familiar in the best way.

I may be grinning like an idiot—who wouldn't be with a hunk like Chad begging them to come home?—but I don't want him to know that. "Has anyone told you that you can be such a baby sometimes?"

"Houston tells me all the time."

Man, I really want to meet Houston now, and not just because he's a famous pitcher. "So, what's my plan here, Grizz? How do I follow a guy who's already following me?"

"If you can bump into him and make it seem like an accident, he'll think you didn't see him, so he won't be on his guard. Think you can do that?"

I laugh. "Have you met me? I don't need to remind you about the hardware store, do I?"

"Please don't maim him. He needs to be able to walk back to where he's staying, or this whole conversation will have been pointless and I could have been kissing you for the last ten minutes."

"Is that what you think we would have been doing?"

"Am I wrong?"

Heat floods my face, and I'm glad the only person to witness any of this conversation is my new buddy Oscar behind the counter. "Are you always such a shameless flirt, or is it just me?" I ask, unable to help myself.

Chad chuckles. "I have never been this way with anyone but you, Hope. And that's why I need you to be careful."

"I promise. I'll do everything you say. I trust you."

He's quiet for a second. "Thank you. Are you ready for this?"

"So I'm going to bump into him, and then what? Is there, like, a manual on how to lose a tail?"

Chuckling, Chad seems to have relaxed in the last few minutes, which honestly has me feeling better too. If he was still nervous, that would probably mean this was a bigger deal than it is. "Remind me to give you the crash course later. For now, you're just going to apologize and head to the hardware store. Tell June you need to go out the back way and you'll tell her why later."

Though I should wait until I have all the instructions, I shift closer to the door anyway to get ready to go. "What if she asks questions?"

"Don't let her."

"Easy for you to say! June and I are friends now."

"So tell her you're being followed. Once you're in the alley, I'll tell you where to go."

"You make this sound so easy," I mutter, sticking my phone in my jeans and tucking the pain meds into my coat pocket. "How often do you have to sneak around like this?"

He laughs. "Not as often as you seem to think. I just like being prepared in case I need to make a getaway, especially if I'm in a new place."

"Well, here I go. It was nice knowing you, Chad."

He groans.

I push through the door before I can think too hard about this, ducking my head against the cold and colliding with the man's shoulder. "Oh!" I say as I legitimately stumble forward. "I'm so sorry! I didn't see you there."

As I give him a sheepish smile, he gapes at me for a second before he recovers and flashes a phony grin. "No worries. Hopefully I didn't hurt you."

Hmm, he sounds genuine about that, though it's not like I can claim I'm an expert on people or behavior. Still, I can see why Chad doesn't think this guy is dangerous when he looks more nervous about me looking at him than he should.

I smile wider despite Chad's voice in my ears telling me to keep moving. "No worries. I'm all good. Sorry again for running into you." I head down the street, dutifully stopping at my car to drop off the meds and take a glance behind me. "Looks like he's following," I mutter, knowing Chad is probably trying his hardest not to demand a play-by-play. "So, head to the hardware store?"

"You can spend a few minutes inside before you head out the back. Make sure he sees you looking at the shelves or something."

"I feel like a spy right now."

"Yes, that is definitely what you're doing."

I can't help but laugh as I lock my car again and cross the street to get to June's store. "I don't appreciate the sarcasm, by the way. Maybe this is child's play for you, but this is way more exciting than anything I've ever done before. Just let me enjoy this, okay?"

He grunts. "You might be the only person in the world who would consider this fun instead of frightening. Are you at the hardware store yet?"

"Heading in now."

June greets me with a smile as soon as I walk through the door. "Morning, Hope! Glad to see you survived the storm. How's the whole situation with your grumpy neighbor going?"

Oh, she has no idea how much has happened since I last talked to her, and I'm tempted to stop and chat for a second. Unfortunately, doing that would mean letting Chad in on our conversation, and there is no way I won't die of embarrassment if that happens.

"I don't have time to talk today," I say, feeling breathless as my excitement ramps up. I do as Chad said and pretend to search one of the shelves like I'm looking for a specific part. "Can I use your back door in a minute?"

Blinking, June glances at the door in question as she approaches. "I guess so. Why?"

"Oh, you know, just someone following me." I glance out the window. I can't see the guy from here, but my gut tells me he's out there.

"See if she's willing to help," Chad says on the phone. "She might be able to spook him. Does she really think I'm grumpy?"

"Not the time, Bigfoot," I mutter.

June pulls her eyebrows together. "Bigfoot? Who's following you? What's going on?"

"Give her the headphones," Chad says.

"Why?"

"Because I want to know why you're acting shifty," June says.

"Let me talk to her," Chad says, more forcefully this time.

I flinch. "No, sorry, June, I was talking to..." I groan and slip the headphones off my head. "Chad wants to talk to you, apparently."

She eyes the headphones warily. "Chad, your neighbor?"

"I probably don't have much time before he comes in here looking for me," I say and basically shove the headphones into her hands. "The guy outside, not Chad. Just trust me, okay?"

Though still skeptical, June slips the headphones over her ears and listens for a minute, her face quickly shifting from confusion to surprise. She looks at me, smirks a little, and then nods. "Yeah, I can do that. Is she in trouble?" She snorts a laugh. "I can see that. I mean, she did make a mess the day we met." Another pause, during which I glare at her and she smiles sweetly. "I hate him already. You don't want me to tell her that? Why? Okay, now I really don't like him. I like you, though, Briggs.

Don't go letting my girl get into trouble, you hear?" Then she hands the headphones back to me with a grin.

"Wow," I say as I slip them back onto my head. "I hated so much about that."

"Would you relax?" Chad says, and I know he's rolling his eyes at me. "June used to work for the district attorney's office in Denver, so I thought maybe she could help us."

"And you know that how?" *I* didn't even know that about her. I knew she was new in town, but I figured she has always been a hardware gal. "Actually, you don't have to answer that. I can guess."

"He seems like a keeper," June says quietly, and then she peeks out the window at a different angle, narrowing her eyes as soon as she sees my admirer. "This guy, on the other hand..."

"What are you going to do?" I ask warily. Whatever Chad told her, she seems a little too excited about it.

June laughs. "Nothing crazy. I'll just make him question his sanity for a second. Throw him off his game and see what he does. Hopefully he'll follow me, at least for a little bit, so you can get around the corner and watch where he goes."

"How's everything looking?" Chad asked.

"I'm wishing I didn't let you talk to her," I reply. "Why am I suddenly the one in the dark?"

"Hide for a sec," June instructs, and the only reason I do what she says is because Chad growls a little, as if reminding me that I promised to do as I was told.

I duck down behind the far shelf so I have easy access to the door in case I need it, and then the bell over the door jingles as June steps outside.

"Oh, sorry," she says, sounding surprised. "I didn't see you out here. Did you need something from the store? I was just about to meet my friend Hope for lunch at the diner, but I can keep it open for a few minutes if you need—"

"No need," the man says, and he sounds both confused and frustrated. "Your friend Hope? I don't think I know her."

"Oh, she's pretty new in town. I'm running late, though, so I should get to the diner. She's probably waiting for me. You sure you don't need anything? I'll need to lock up before I go."

"No, I was just checking something on my phone. Enjoy your lunch."

Chad clears his throat, making me jump as June heads off. "Remember how I can't see anything that's happening? Are you okay?"

"Yeah, I'm fine. June just left, and it looks like he's following her now."

"Which way did Todd go?"

I hold out my hand in front of me. "Left. Wait, no. Yeah, left."

As if he can see me, he sighs heavily. "How do you not know left from right? Are you seven?"

"No, I am not. And I'll have you know Zelda is excellent with directions."

"So what's *your* problem?"

I roll my eyes, feeling the sting of his words even though I know he doesn't mean them. At least, I hope he doesn't. "Your foot is really hurting you, isn't it?"

"No." Then he lets out another sigh. The man is the king of sighing. "Yes. But I'm more worried about you at the moment. I'd feel better if you just came home. I'm sorry. I'm not trying to be short with you. I hate being stuck here and not being able to keep you safe. It's a lot harder to be rational when you're so far away."

"It's, like, ten minutes into town, Chad."

"I said what I said. I feel better when you're close."

I feel better when I'm close to him too. "So what should I do now? June locked me in."

"Back door will take you to an alley. Take a right, and you can get all the way to the diner and figure out if he's trying to find you there. He won't take long to figure out he's been tricked, so he'll circle back to the hardware store soon."

It's not that I don't believe him, but he sounds so confident for a guy currently stuck on the couch because he got in a fight with a bear trap. "How can you be sure that's what he'll do?" I ask, slipping out into the alley and double checking with my thumbs that I actually go right. I don't know how, but Chad would know if I went the wrong direction.

He seems to debate answering my question until I've almost reached the diner. "Because, in my experience, people are predictable. Especially when they're scared."

"Do you think I'm predictable?" I poke my head around the corner, grinning when I see Todd peering into the diner with increasing frustration on his face, like he's starting to figure out that he's been duped.

Again, Chad takes a while to answer. "No." I don't miss the clear and unsaid "but" at the end of that.

Because so far in this relationship, I haven't been scared. And who knows what might happen if I ever hit that point? He seems to think it won't work in his favor, so I'd better make sure I'm never scared.

"Hey, Chad?"

"Yeah?"

"How bad is it if I need to make a pit stop and use the bathroom?"

He groans. "Really?"

"Maybe." *Definitely.* Apparently I'm not all that good at this whole tailing thing. Or maybe my bladder just didn't get the memo that we were on a time-sensitive stealth mission.

Chad lets out a sigh. "Despite your name, you are truly hopeless."

I can't help but laugh.

Chapter Nineteen

Chad

October 25

THE NEXT WEEK PASSES by in a blur. Part of that is because of the pain meds that really do mess with my head enough that it's almost not worth taking them. Almost. Knowing I'm less likely to be a whiny jerk if I take them is enough of a reason to pop them in my mouth whenever Hope hands them to me. She doesn't trust me with the bottle in case I get addicted, which I appreciate, but I'm pretty sure she has a little too much fun witnessing the tongue-loosening effects of the drugs, especially about fifteen minutes after I take them, when that effect is the most potent. She only hands me the pills when she can stick around and watch me completely lose all inhibitions.

I have vague memories of calling Micah at one point and confessing how much I love her and the twins, though I genuinely don't remember exactly what I say to her. And she doesn't bring it up when she tells me she and the twins are doing trivia night without me when that's always been a thing for the four of us.

Rude. Not that I can blame them when I'm two hours away, but still. Either Micah is trying to convince me to come home, or she's telling me that they don't need me and I should stay in Laketown with Hope. Not knowing which it is makes me antsy.

A few times a day, I hobble out to the deck and whistle for Duke, though the forest remains as silent as ever. We don't talk about it, especially when the kids are around, but I know he's gone. Hope thinks otherwise, and I love that she fits her name so well, but I can't imagine my dog would be off wandering the woods so close by without finding his way back. Link didn't get all that far when he went off into the trees.

Animal control went looking for the mountain lion to try to relocate it farther from town, but they had nothing to report about Duke's whereabouts.

Hope decided that was a good sign. I'm not so sure.

There's been no sign of Todd since Hope claimed she couldn't hold it anymore and stopped to use a bathroom, losing sight of him in the process, but I'm okay with that. I'm banking on him being the coward I think he is, though I do walk Hope through the process of installing my security cameras after they come in on Tuesday. Then Hope hands me my meds and I'm useless to the world, outside of giving Hope a thorough and detailed description of the time I knocked over a display stand at the pharmacy where I worked as a teen.

For the record, Zelda seems to appreciate my drugged state as much as Hope does, saying I listen to her after school stories a lot better when I'm "silly," and I genuinely love when the afternoon hits and she comes and sits with me for an hour or so before she gets bored. Even when I'm not newly drugged, I try to stay silly just to see her smile. Her smile looks a lot like Hope's.

Link and I have pretty much been ignoring each other all week, not out of blame (on my end) but I think out of shared pain. I haven't missed the way Link spends a lot of his afternoons gazing out the back window, nor how often he cries himself back to sleep after Hope has gone to bed. I wish I could tell him that it's not his fault that Duke is gone, but every time I try, the words stick in my throat. I really don't blame him—I blame the badger—but that doesn't make my chest ache any less. Every time he looks at me, he gets teary-eyed.

After the kids go to bed, Hope and I talk. For hours. Yeah, okay, there's a lot of kissing happening in there too, but talking to Hope quickly becomes my new favorite thing. She always gets sleepy too fast, and every time I walk her to my bedroom door and kiss her goodnight, the feeling that it's not enough gets stronger. I never want to stop talking to her and sharing everything about my life, and I don't want to say goodnight to her and walk away.

If this week teaches me anything, it's how easily Hope carved her name into my heart and is going to become a permanent fixture there, whether this thing lasts or not.

By the time Friday hits, I can mostly walk without wincing and I feel confident that I don't need the pain pills to keep me civil. Hope has been letting the kids take the bus to school all week, dropping them off at the end of the lane and picking them up after spending the days with me reading or searching for a remote job she can do, but Friday she has to take them to school herself because Zelda can't decide what to wear and makes them miss the bus.

"June has been driving me crazy anyway," Hope says when I complain about her going into town. We haven't seen Todd on our street, but that doesn't mean he's gone. "She wants updates after what happened on Monday." While the kids scramble to put their shoes on, she loops her arms around me from behind where I sit on the couch—my new permanent spot, it feels like—and kisses my cheek. "I promise I'll be careful. I'm an expert tailer now."

I tilt my head up until I can reach her mouth with my own. "What if I come with you? Just in case." Hank borrowed my truck last night to pick up a new bookcase this afternoon, and I don't like the idea of being trapped here while she's all the way in town. "Please."

She glances at Link, which is exactly what I expected. "I don't know, Chad."

She's right. Ten minutes is a long time to spend trapped in a car together with nowhere to hide, and I'm not sure either of us is ready for that, even if I desperately want to fix things with the six-year-old.

"Give it time," Hope whispers, rubbing my shoulders a bit. "Everything will work out. Maybe this weekend we can try to reset things and start fresh."

She kisses me one more time before heading out, and I last maybe half an hour through a football recap before I fall asleep. (Idleness doesn't suit me, okay?)

I wake to my phone buzzing somewhere beneath the cushions. I scramble to dig it out, grinning when I see that it's Hope. "Miss me already?"

"Well, I wouldn't say that," a male voice replies.

I nearly drop my phone. "Todd?" Then it hits me, sending a jolt of adrenaline through me that shoots me up to my feet. "Where's Hope?"

"She's cute, you know. A little quirky, super pushy, but I see why you like her."

"Answer the question."

He chuckles. "Would you relax? We're just enjoying brunch, and she stepped away to use the restroom. I borrowed her phone since I don't have your number."

Does that mean they're at the diner? Or is he just playing with me? There must be more to this man than I thought if he's managed to get Hope to cooperate, and I can only imagine the threats he might have made. She knows exactly who he is and would have been smart enough to run if she had the chance.

"What do you want?" I growl, silently cursing Hank for choosing today of all days to do something with his literal stacks of books. I can barely walk, let alone run the five miles into town to get to Hope. Even making the trek to Hank's house to see if he's left yet feels like a daunting task. "If you touch her, I swear to God I'll—"

"What?" Todd asks calmly. "You couldn't even get me arrested when you had all the evidence in your hands."

"Not while you were out of the country," I growl. "Now that you're back, it'll only take one phone call to—"

"I wouldn't do that if I were you. Not if you care about your little pretend family."

His words seize hold of my heart, squeezing so tightly that I can't breathe. I sink back to the couch, gripping my phone so hard that it hurts. "Talk."

"Suddenly I find myself needing a lot of money," Todd says. "You're going to get it for me."

"I don't have..." I can't even get the words out because they're not true. Well, they *are* true. Todd owes his brother almost ten million, and I can't imagine what else he might owe to people who are far more dangerous. I don't have ten million. But I have *some* of that, and I have a ridiculously rich brother who earns that in less than six months by throwing a ball. Houston would probably give it to me without questioning it if I asked.

But what really stalls me is the fact that I am even considering that in the first place. A month ago, I would have laughed in Todd's face and hung up. But now he's threatened Hope and the kids, and I can't even think straight anymore.

Todd chuckles. "I knew you'd be smart," he says, his voice low. "Besides, all you have to do is talk to that pretty little Hope of yours. She can get you everything I need."

She can't. Hope can't even afford to fix a window in her rundown house. But Todd seems pretty convinced.

"Don't even think about touching her," I snarl, even if that's not going to do me any good. Speaking the warning out loud at least makes me feel like I'm not entirely useless. I need to make a plan. Figure out my options. But I also need more information. "How is this going to work, Thwaite?"

"I'll give you two days to get the money," he says. "I'll be at the Bird and Bend B&B, and if I don't have my money by Sunday at noon, we're going to be having a very different conversation."

He hangs up, and I sit there with my phone pressed to my ear, trying desperately to breathe as I process all of this. Two days? Houston might be my only option, and then I'll have to find a way to pay him back because no matter how ridiculous his wealth might be, he still earned it. It's not like I'm entitled to anything from him just because he's my brother.

You should go to the police, a little voice in the back of my head says, and I snap to attention, like whatever was broken inside of me just slipped back into place and I can think properly again. What am I thinking? I'm not giving that man a *cent*!

I pull up the number of a cop buddy in Sun City and flip the phone to speakerphone so I can grab the recording of the conversation I just had with Todd. Thank goodness I got in the habit of recording all of my conversations a few years ago just in case I run into moments like this.

The line connects. "Briggs! It's been a while. Got something good for me?"

"Tell me you can help me," I say and send him the file, hoping this isn't going to turn into a disaster.

I've never been happier to see Hope's car when she finally pulls into my driveway. I've spent the last two hours on the phone trying to get enough on Todd to ensure he doesn't do anything to hurt Hope or the kids, but the best I've gotten from the police is two days before they can get a warrant with the limited evidence I've got. Todd didn't technically make any threats, and the fraud case with his brother is still being built.

I'm ready to take matters into my own hands, no matter what that means for me if I go outside the law on this. I'd rather know they're safe than protect my own freedom.

Seeing that Hope is alive and well has me relaxing for the first time since my phone rang, and I don't wait until she's in the house. I run out to meet her, pulling her into my arms and crushing her against me.

"Uh, hi?" she says into my chest.

"Are you okay?"

"I'm fine. You'll never guess who I ran into at—"

"I know about Todd."

She wiggles free, looking at me like I've just told her that I dyed all her clothes black. "What? How? Were you checking up on me?"

What is that supposed to mean? "He called me," I say, as if she doesn't already know. "On *your* phone."

"Oh, he was calling *you*? I wondered about that when he borrowed my phone."

She is being way too calm given the situation. "Hope, what did he say to you?"

She *smiles*. "That's what I was going to tell you. June and I were having breakfast when he came into the diner, and I told him that he looked really familiar to me and I wanted to figure out how we knew each other."

I curse, shaking my head. "Are you insane? *You* approached *him*? Why?"

"Why are you making such a big deal out of this? It turns out he—"

"Why am I making it a big deal?" I groan, pacing a few times as I run my hand over my hair. "Hope, that was the stupidest thing you could have done."

Her jaw drops. "Excuse me?"

"Do you have any idea how dangerous that was?"

"I'm pretty sure it was fine, Chad."

I growl. "I never took you as naive, but—"

"Hold up." She literally holds her hand up, glaring at me now. "Will you just let me tell you what I found out?"

"It doesn't matter."

"Doesn't matter," she repeats. Whatever she thinks she learned, she doesn't seem to realize how much danger she might have put herself in today, and that is the hardest part. How am I supposed to protect her if she's going to walk right into the line of fire?

"Let me handle this," I beg, trying to convey in my voice how much I need her to keep her head down and let me do my job. Let me take care of her. I can't stand the thought of something going wrong and losing her.

Hope folds her arms, narrowing her eyes at me like she's trying to find something. "What if there was nothing to handle?"

If only she knew. "Hope, this is more than you can—"

"I'm going to stop you right there." She's never looked this angry, even when I've been grumpy or after I yelled at Link. It's like she's seeing me for the first time and has decided she doesn't like what she sees, and I've never felt so gutted by a look before. "You're not going to budge on this, are you?"

"How can I? I need to keep you safe."

"Even when there's nothing threatening me?"

"If only you knew what—"

"You could tell me."

"Hope. You don't know what's going on. This is just like the badger, and you can't see—"

She moves in closer, rising up on her toes to try to meet my height even though she's nowhere close. "The badger? You mean the *wolverine*? I may be younger than you, Chad, but that doesn't make you wiser. Not by a longshot. A relationship should be a partnership. Give and take. Equal sides. Yeah, things may shift from one side to the other sometimes, but they have to balance again unless you want everything to fall apart. I *know* you know that. And I know you're not stupid enough to think you're right all the time."

I don't know what she wants me to say. I'm trying to keep her safe and be everything she needs me to be. Can't she see that? "I need to—"

"You *don't* need. But clearly you aren't willing to see that."

"I don't understand," I admit. My foot is aching, my head is throbbing, and it's like there's something I'm missing that's right out of reach. "I'll tell you everything I know if you just listen to me, but—"

"But you're not going to give me the same courtesy. I know you're not." She scoffs, shaking her head as she takes a step back that feels like it puts a mile between us. "I'm going to take the kids and go stay with my aunt in Furley for a bit."

I have no idea where that is, but I already know it's too far away. "Until when?"

Tears sprout in her eyes, and that's the moment I know I've really messed up. Hope doesn't cry unless the feelings are too big for her to deal with them. "I don't know, Chad," she says just as a dark SUV pulls up to the curb in front of her house.

I tense, but the man who opens the door and looks over at us as he stands on the step is unfamiliar and smiling warmly. "Hi, I think I might have found your dog."

My heart seems to leap into my throat, choking me as I gasp, "Duke?"

The answering bark from inside the car hits me so hard that I stumble backward a step, and then a pile of golden fur scurries out through the driver's door and dashes across the lawn, leaping into my arms. Duke mauls me with kisses, his voice equal parts barks and whines, and I have never held on to anything so tight. He's too light, ribs more pronounced, and a few bandages wrap around his legs, but he's alive and happy and *here*.

"Where did you find him?" Hope asks.

I sink to the ground because I'm too overwhelmed to keep on my feet, and Duke practically hugs me as he soaks my face in slobber.

"I've been doing wildlife research a few miles from here," the man says lightly. "After the storm blew through, I was following some unfamiliar tracks when I came across him hanging out with a wolverine, of all things."

My head snaps up. "What?"

The man shrugs. "I've never seen anything like it. He was a bit mangled and pretty hungry, but it was almost like they were looking out for each other. I figured I'd better see if I could catch him and figure out where he belonged. Lost track of the wolvie, though. Shame, that."

I glance at Hope, who either looks relieved that Duke is back or angry that I couldn't bring myself to accept that a child might know more than me. It's probably both.

"You might want to check my closet," Hope mutters, folding her arms. "We've had a wolverine in and out for a couple of weeks now."

Duke decides right then that he's done greeting me and wants nothing more than to try to tackle Hope as he jumps up to give her kisses as well. She bursts into sobs—not a good sign—and then runs to her car, leaving my bewildered dog behind as she drives off.

The man clears his throat and looks at me as Duke returns to my arms. "Everything okay? What was she saying about a closet?"

Though stepping into Hope's house is the last thing I want to do right now, I can at least show him the window and the tracks leading to and from the house. Which I do, though I'm in a daze as I replay the sight of Hope driving off. The guy is thrilled and promises to come back tomorrow with a trap so we don't have to worry about a wild animal in the house, but at this point, I'm not sure it matters. I may have messed up too bad for Hope to ever want to come back.

I don't know yet *how* I messed up, but I know I did. I wouldn't feel this awful if I didn't.

I spend the rest of the day on the deck so I don't have to watch Hope pack up nearly everything I love after she comes back with the kids. I listen to them, Zelda and Link screaming with joy when they see Duke and Hope doing her best to sound excited about spending the weekend with her aunt. When Zelda asks if I'm coming with them, my heart screams for me to open the door and tell her yes. I'll go anywhere they are, no matter how far. But there's no hesitation in Hope's voice when she says I have too many important things to take care of.

The kids don't like her answer, which only makes it all feel worse because I know she's not going to change her mind.

I don't leave my chair until long after the house has gone silent, and going inside hurts even more than I thought it would. Stepping into that place where the Duncans have imprinted so many memories feels like intruding on someone else's life. Someone who doesn't do and say the wrong thing and drive away the woman who holds his heart. How am I supposed to stay here without her? Without all of them?

They'll be back. I tell myself that over and over, even if it's hard to believe. Hope is smart enough to know it's a bad idea to uproot the kids after they were just starting to feel settled. But they'll go back to their own house, which suddenly feels entirely too far away.

When Micah sends me a text, it feels like the universe telling me that it's time to wake up. The dream is over.

I sigh, fingers stiff and slow as I type back a reply. It's like my body doesn't want to admit what my mind already knows.

I smile a little, though the gesture feels forced. She's just as enthusiastic in text as she is in real life, and I love that about her. I love less that everyone is going to be paired up at our annual Briggs sibs Halloween party. That's going to feel great.

She proceeds to tell me all about trivia night and how our confident brother has met his match in the sports journalist who is known for taking down athletes and doing it with a smile. I hope he is being careful around her, and I'm glad Micah is making it sound like he might be dating someone else so there's no risk of him getting mixed up with someone he shouldn't. He's likely dating another model, though Houston has been acting strange lately, so I could be wrong. I'll have to look into it since I just promised my baby sister I would be home for Halloween next week. It will be good to be around my siblings again, though I can't like anything that takes me farther from Hope.

Just before I go to bed, I try calling her. I don't expect her to answer, but I want to try to apologize if she'll let me. I should have let her talk. I should have gotten her side of the story, no matter how scared I was.

The call goes straight to voicemail, which is a pretty clear sign that I'm not getting any second chances anytime soon. Maybe eventually, but I won't hold my breath.

I worry, if I do, I may never breathe again.

Chapter Twenty

Hope

October 26

WHEN TODD WALKED INTO the diner looking far more stressed than he'd been the other day, my gut told me that I had to take my chance. And when I invited him to join me when June headed back to her store, he looked like I had just handed him everything he could ever want. And while I knew it wasn't necessarily the smartest plan, I could see in his eyes that he was getting desperate.

I had a pretty good feeling that he wasn't after Chad at all, and it turned out I was right.

"He told me that he's Link and Zelda's dad," I tell the lawyer who came to visit me at Aunt Phoebe's. Todd is already in custody, picked up just a few minutes after I called the police while I was "in the bathroom" at the diner, AKA using the phone in the office in the back. The minute he mentioned the kids, I knew he was bad news.

Mostly because I finally recognized him from an old photo I'd seen in Bailey's stuff. Back when they were secretly dating while she was in school, apparently. Bailey had mentioned something about spending time with her professor once, but I'd never thought anything of it. It makes sense now why she was so eager to move away from Alabama after she got pregnant with Link.

"It was pretty easy to believe him," I continue as the lawyer writes down everything I tell her. "He looks just like Link, and he knows a lot about Zelda. Like her birthmark on her hip. So I didn't question him."

The lawyer nods, scribbling a few things. "That's when he asked for the money?"

"Yes. Which, I'm still a little confused about. No one has been able to tell me where it came from."

Smiling, she shuffles through her massive stack of papers and hands me an envelope. Though I try reading through the first page, it's a lot of legalese that I'm too tired to decipher. "It's a trust fund, essentially, set up by your father's family for both children when Link was born. It has been growing over the last six and a half years. I'm surprised no one told you about it when you were dealing with the custody issues, as this is an important factor in your ability to care for the children."

Uh, she can say that again. According to Todd, though I'm not sure how he knows, there's over five million in each of their accounts, which is more money than I will ever see in my life. In a weird way, it's almost going to complicate things as the kids grow up because it will be harder to raise them to have good work ethics and be generous. I'm not going to keep the money from them, but I'll have to figure out how to teach them to use it responsibly.

Unlike Todd, apparently.

"So, can you tell me why he needed the money so badly? I can imagine it was pretty bad for him to come out of the woodwork after keeping his distance for seven years. How did he even find us?"

The lawyer shrugs. "I can only tell you so much, but it sounds like he was in Laketown for some other reason. Finding you and the kids was happenstance. There is a case being put together against him in New Mexico, something that has to do with theft and fraud."

Does that mean Chad was still right? He was absolutely wrong with how he handled everything yesterday—was it really just yesterday?—but from what I gathered, Todd was pretty threatening when they talked. I understand why Chad was so spooked, but that doesn't give him the right to talk over me and refuse to let me tell him that the police had already grabbed him.

As it has since the moment I drove away, my heart throbs with the thought of leaving him behind. Getting some space for the weekend was absolutely the right decision. I was never going to be rational with the way he was acting, plus the police suggested I take the kids away from Laketown in case Todd had anyone else with him. But I miss Chad. More than I thought I could miss anyone. It feels like I left half my heart in Laketown, and I can't wait to get back.

Do I wish Chad had come with me? Absolutely.

Did I ask him to come with me? No, because I'm a coward. I was too worried that he would say no. Now that things have settled, I'm realizing how stupid that fear was. Chad would do anything for my family.

"Is there anything else you need to tell me, Miss Duncan?"

I shake my head. "The police got most of the details, and I'm too tired to think straight anymore." It's been a long day and a half, especially with all of my thoughts and feelings about Chad never leaving the forefront.

The lawyer smiles as she stands. "I understand. Thank you for your time. I can't make any promises, but hopefully we can ensure Mr. Thwaite won't be able to bother you again."

"He doesn't have any parental rights, does he?" I wish I could remember her name, but I've met too many people since leaving Laketown that my brain is mush.

"No. You are the children's sole guardian."

That's a relief, though I should look into the official adoption process before I get too far into this thing. I don't want to risk the chance of losing them, no matter how small that chance may be.

It's definitely going to be a job for Tomorrow Hope, though. Or Next Week Hope. Or the Hope who isn't completely exhausted and wishes she had just asked Chad to come with her instead of being angry and frustrated. I never got my phone back from Todd, which means I can't even call Chad and explain it all to him because the man is a complete ghost on the internet so I can't find his phone number. I'm hoping the police in Laketown have my phone, or I'm going to be in trouble.

I'll drive back to Chad's in the morning and apologize for not acknowledging how scared he was of what Todd might do. Maybe, if he had given me a chance to explain exactly what happened at the diner, he would be here with me right now and giving me the support I wish I had while I dealt with all of the police and lawyer questions.

"I'll show you out," Aunt Phoebe says, appearing in the doorway and recognizing that the lawyer lady is done talking to me. She comes back to the lounge a few minutes later, picking up a blanket and draping it over me where I sit stiff and frozen on the couch. She's been so helpful, even if she was surprised when I showed up out of the blue. Having a rational adult with me was exactly what I needed. "How are you holding up?"

"I wish I had come straight to you a month ago," I admit, sniffling. I've been a veritable mess for the last couple of days, more emotional than I was even when I showed up to plan Bailey's funeral. Not that it was much of a funeral. It was me, the kids, and a few of her coworkers because my mom's family is all gone and I was still under the impression that my dad's side didn't care.

I've never been more wrong, according to the literal millions of dollars belonging to the kids.

"I might be too tired to have this conversation," I mutter, "but why didn't I know about the money? Why did it take so long for you to reach out? Why...?"

"Why did your mom think we were the worst of the worst?" Phoebe settles beside me. She's not much older than Chad, but there's a weathered look about her. She's soft and gentle, but despite the fact that she lives in a mansion and owns more cars than one person could ever drive, I don't think her life has been easy. "Because we were the worst," she says. "My big brother fell in love too young, and we all thought he was making a mistake by getting married, even with the baby. He and I were raised by parents who thought status was more important than action, and it took a long time for me to realize how backwards that was. When Parker died in that car accident, my parents finally figured out that all the money in the world meant nothing compared to having a loved one in your life. I'm sorry you had to lose your parents like that."

I accept her side hug with a teary smile. "It happened so long ago that it's really just been me and Bai for a while. I got used to being alone."

"Now you're never going to be alone," she says with a chuckle. "Those kids are incredible, but they're a handful."

I laugh. "You can say that again. They're such good kids, though. Even if I have no idea why Bailey thought I was the best person for them when they could have had someone like you."

"Bailey seemed to think your family was better off without us." She frowns. "We didn't even know about your parents being gone until after the funeral, and she told us you didn't want anything to do with us when we contacted her. I wish we had reached out to you too instead of listening to your sister, but at least you're here now. No point in trying to change what can't be changed."

Haven't I cried enough today? Swallowing, I shake my head and try to reconcile the sister I loved with the one who apparently kept running my life without me knowing. I'm sure she had her reasons for keeping our grandparents away and thought she was doing the right thing. Right? But I've been so alone, and if I'd known my family was closer than I'd realized...

Would I have asked them for help? Probably not. It took Chad forcing his help to convince me that I don't have to do everything on my own.

Phoebe pats my arm. "Whenever you need a break, I will happily take the kids for a few days."

"Could I take you up on that offer right now?" I'm absolutely falling asleep, but I won't be able to get any real rest unless I know I will have the chance to see Chad tomorrow and make things right. "I have some things I need to take care of, and it will be easier if I don't have to worry about the kids getting their hearts broken if things don't work out."

That thought is terrifying, but I know it's a possibility with the way I left.

Phoebe hugs me again. "Of course. You've been through some awful few weeks, and I can take them however long you need."

Some of the weeks have been awful, yes, but not all of them. The last week with Chad was one of the best of my life.

Tucking the blanket tighter around myself, I take a slow breath, hoping it cleanses some of the stress I've been feeling. Chad was pretty good at making me forget all my worries, or at least feel like I could handle them, and I am missing his strong, quiet presence more than ever.

"Do you have any ice cream?" I ask.

Phoebe blinks at me, apparently caught off guard by that question, but then she smiles. "I'm sure I do. I'll go lock up the house and meet you in the kitchen."

I've already served myself a bowl of Rocky Road when movement in the doorway catches my eye, but it isn't my aunt standing there. It's Zelda, and she looks like she has slept as little as I have. I put her to bed hours ago, but she clearly didn't fall asleep like I thought.

"Hey, sweetie." I gesture for her to come sit next to me. "Do you want some ice cream?"

Once settled, she stares at the bowl with her big eyes full of fear. Why fear? "Is something wrong?" she asks.

"What? No. Everything is fine. Why?"

She clearly doesn't believe me, but she still steals my spoon and takes a bite. "Because Mom only let us have ice cream when she had bad news."

She said something similar when we went to get ice cream before they started school, and it's just as baffling now as it was then. "That's the only time?"

Zelda nods and takes another bite. "When are we going to go back to Chad's house?"

My stomach twists. "Oh, I don't—"

"I like Chad. He's funny and nice and really strong."

Well, it's good to know I'm not just lovesick and looking at the man through rose-colored glasses. "I like him too," I tell her and wrap my arm around her shoulders. "Hopefully we can go back soon." Hopefully he didn't decide we were too much for him after my overreaction and radio silence. If the Laketown police don't have my phone...

Suddenly Zelda sniffs, and I turn to her in alarm. I'm not awake enough to deal with tears tonight. "Z, what's wrong?"

"You and Chad are so fun," she says, leaning into me. "Mom wasn't... She was always working. Sometimes I like you more than I liked her. Does that make me a bad person?"

Oh goodness. Tears sprouting in my own eyes, I pull her against me and let her cry into my shoulder as I scramble to find something to say. But what do I say to that? Apparently the Bailey I knew is not the Bailey the kids knew, and I don't know what to do with that. I don't think she was ever a bad mom, but I can totally see her getting absorbed in work and staying long hours at the office. I'm sure she told herself all the time that she would go home early the next day, only to get caught up in a new project. Just like the many times she said she would bring the kids to visit me while I was in school but never found the time.

"Just because I'm a really great aunt and super cool, it doesn't mean you love your mom any less," I say, trying to go for a bit of humor because that's the only way I know how to cope. "Your mom was my best friend, and I think she was awesome at a lot of things. She talked about you all the time, you know."

Zelda wipes her hand across her nose. "She did?"

"All. The. Time. She was so proud of you and Link, and she wanted to give you guys the best lives. Maybe that means she worked a little too much, but I know she loved you with all her heart."

"I miss her so much."

"Me too, Z. And it's okay to miss her. Missing her means you loved her so much and she's a part of you."

Wrapping her arms around my neck, Zelda pulls herself into the kind of hug I've always wanted from these kids. It's the sort of hug that speaks of her trust and love and vulnerability, and I hold her as tightly as I can.

There's so much we're going to have to work through as time goes on, and I know I can handle it. No matter how difficult it gets. But it would be nice to have someone to help me, to stand by my side and offer support when I need it. And the kids love Chad. I don't know if they could stand to lose him too.

Which means I'm going to have to do some groveling after being silent for so long. I'm not looking forward to it, but the hole in my heart where Chad should be is just going to get bigger if I put this off. It's time to go back and pray that the chance I got with Chad won't be the only one.

October 27

Well, that prayer didn't work.

Chad's house is not only empty but looks prepped for winter, things boarded up and protected against the elements. I guess I should have expected that was an option, especially when I finally turn on my phone after charging it in the car once I pick it up from the Laketown sheriff's office. Chad called me four times, spread out over Friday and Saturday, so I can't blame him for thinking things might be over. But it's only been two days since I left!

I guess no one can say Chad Briggs isn't efficient.

"What am I going to do with you?" I mutter, wandering back to my car to warm up. Sun City is only a couple hours away, but those hours feel long when I've got kids with a childless aunt who was nervous even as she waved me off this morning. She can only last so long without some help. I probably need to find a nanny or someone to step in for a couple of days. I wonder if their nanny from Florida would be up for a paid trip across the country...

It's not the best use of the money in the kids' accounts, but a round trip plane ticket and a few days of pay would hopefully be worth the chance to make things work with Chad. Zelda and Link need a man in their life, and I hope that man can be him.

Before I can drive back to Furley and make a plan with Phoebe, an old sedan pulls up behind me, and I recognize Hank behind the wheel.

"I saw you drive past," he says, climbing out of his car at the same time I step out of mine. "Wasn't sure if I'd see you back here, with the way Briggs was acting."

"Yeah, I'm getting that sense too," I mutter. "Did he go back to Sun City?"

"Yep. Moping the whole drive, probably." He stuffs his hands into his coat pocket and shrugs. "What in the world happened between you two?"

Oh, what a question. "A lot. But also...not. He tried to fix something that I had already fixed, and I got frustrated. So did he. It was a whole thing."

"Love is always a whole thing."

I wonder what Hank's story is and if he's ever experienced a whole thing with love. Something tells me he has.

"Any ideas for how to fix it?" I ask, folding my arms and hoping he has all the answers.

He nods toward my phone. "A conversation is a good start," he says, grinning.

He's not wrong, but Chad and I spent so much time talking that it didn't leave a lot of room for doing, which feels more appropriate for this moment. "You know that thing in books and movies where someone does a big gesture for the other person?" I say slowly.

Hank's smile grows. "Sure do. What are you thinking? I didn't take Briggs as a fan of surprises."

"Oh, I'm pretty sure he hates them. I should keep things small, just in case."

"Good idea. Just seeing you would be surprise enough when it comes to him."

"I think you're right." I imagine myself showing up on his doorstep and the look on his face, and my smile feels like it breaks through the last couple days of stress. "You don't happen to know where he lives, do you? He's not exactly easy to find."

If ever there was a reason to like Hank—not that I was ever questioning that—it's the mischievous smile he gives me right now. "There's a chance he gave me his New Mexico address in case of emergencies. He's a good guy, that Briggs. And you are good *together*. I spent less than twenty-four hours with you kids and have been feeling extra inspired ever since."

Though I haven't figured out if my almost-hermit neighbor is a hugger, I hug him anyway, wrapping him up in my arms and silently thanking him for getting Chad and me to dance together during the storm.

"You ever think about settling down?" I ask him. He may not be a Chad—according to the internet, that's a good thing—but I can see someone falling in love with Hank's easy charm and sweet smiles.

And maybe with the way he turns so completely red when he's embarrassed. It's adorable. "Oh, I don't... Who would even... It's not like..." He coughs and looks at his car. "I should get back to work, but I'll text you his address. Good luck, Hope. I'll be rooting for the two of you."

Good. I think we're going to need all the rooting we can get.

Chapter Twenty-One

Hope

October 31

It turns out I'm a coward.

I can make a whole plan—fly out the nanny, call the school and alert them to absences for the week, set Phoebe up with a bunch of streaming services to keep the kids entertained while I drive a couple of hours to a different state—but when it comes to the walking up to the doorstep and knocking on the door...

I don't think I can do it. At this point, I haven't seen or talked to Chad in six days. Considering our relationship lasted at best two weeks but really endured less than a week, I'm not liking the sound of my odds. I still haven't called him—*thank you, fear*—and there are enough cars parked outside his house that I'm really starting to think I *should* have called so I wouldn't end up interrupting a party or whatever Chad has going on.

It's probably his family, which is somehow way more terrifying than the idea of interrupting an actual party.

Let's not forget the fact that in the chaos of the last several days, I forgot that today is *Halloween* even though the heaven-sent nanny bought costumes for the kids and they wouldn't shut up about trick-or-treating through Phoebe's insanely nice neighborhood. I feel a little weird lurking in my car while there are children wandering around in princess dresses and army suits. I could get a hotel for the night and come back tomorrow, but if it's this hard to get out of the car now that I'm here, there's no way I'll be brave enough to come back in the first place.

I remind myself of what Link said to me when I was leaving Phoebe's house earlier today: "Tell Chad that I'm sorry and that I want him to come back." His poor little heart has been breaking since the moment Duke disappeared in the woods, and I can't let him feel guilty for the rest of his life. Duke is back—yay!—but forgiveness is in order.

If Chad is willing to give it.

"You're stalling," I tell myself, which isn't all that helpful. "The worst he could do is shut the door in your face."

Actually, there are a lot worse things he *could* do. But I don't think there's a lot that he *would*. Chad is too good of a guy to make the same mistake twice, and I know he'll hear me out if I ever get over this cowardice. That's really what's important here. We need to clear the air, speak our truths, and decide where to go from there. Otherwise we'll always wonder, and I refuse to live like that when I've seen how quickly a life can be over.

"Okay, Karen," I say (because it's a lot easier to be stern with Karen than with Hope). "You have ten seconds before you have to get out of the car or turn around and never look back. Ten. Nine."

I'm out of the car before I can count down to eight, marching up to the porch and ringing the doorbell before I can chicken out.

Oh no, is it too late to run? I glance behind me, wondering if that bush would be enough to hide me, and I have one foot in the air, ready to book it, when the door opens.

My heart pounds so loudly that I can't hear a thing, not that he's saying anything. Chad just stands there in the doorway, staring at me with wide blue eyes, and his whole body frozen in place. And what a body. Whether it's a costume or just his normal look, he's got the lumberjack thing on full display right now, with one hand on the door and the other reaching forward to grasp the door frame. Prime position for me to leap onto him and never let go.

"Oh," he finally says. Not exactly the warm greeting I was hoping for, but I'll take it.

"Hi," I say back, which is just as evasive as what he said.

"Where are the kids?"

I shouldn't love that he asks about them before asking anything about me, but I do. It means they've been on his mind. Hopefully I have too. "They're with my aunt. You left Laketown."

"I didn't see a reason to stay."

"So you just left? Without saying anything?"

"You left first."

"For two days! I came back." I huff. Arguing isn't going to help anything. Maybe we can go inside and…

For the first time, I notice a group of people gathered at the edge of the dining room, all of them watching this scene at the front door with clear interest. I recognize Houston immediately—though I have no idea why he's wearing a leotard and tutu of all things—and his twin, Brooklyn, is easy to pick out. And not just because she's in a matching tutu. Okay, why is the guy in between them *also* wearing a bright pink tutu? I would think it might be a thing if there weren't three others in completely different costumes. I'm guessing Micah is the cute one in the circus outfit, unlike the other blonde who looks nothing like the Briggs trio, and Micah's got a handsome man on her arm and a wide grin on her face.

It seems everyone in his house knows exactly who I am, and I feel my face growing steadily warmer under their stares.

Without a word or even a glance back, Chad takes a step forward and closes the door behind him.

"Does this mean we're going to talk on the porch or you're going to tell me to go back home?" I ask.

He doesn't have much of an expression on his face, outside of the shell-shocked look of someone who has just seen a relationship ghost and isn't sure if he can believe it's real. "I guess that depends," he says slowly.

"Depends on what?"

"On if you'll let me apologize for being an idiot."

I risk a smile, even though we're nowhere close to safety yet. "I think there's going to be some time for that eventually."

He frowns. Is it weird that I missed his frown? Granted, I missed everything about him, but seeing this slightly grumpy side feels more like the beginning of our crazy relationship, when I was still trying to figure him out. "But not yet?"

"Do you think we got too comfortable too fast?" That question leaps out of me, wild and desperate. "I'm not saying I regret anything that happened with us—not the good stuff, anyway—but none of it felt real, you know? We didn't have the awkward dating stage where I was afraid to come across as desperate and you were afraid to take my hand for the first time and neither of us was really sure of how the other person felt. It was just so…"

"Easy," he finishes for me.

"Yeah."

"Yeah."

Whether that means he agrees with me or not, I feel like my thoughts have been validated by that single word. It's not even a word. It's just a sound, a breath, a prayer.

"I don't think easy is a bad thing," Chad says. He takes a step closer that feels like crossing the ocean that's been between us all week. "And in case you were wondering, nothing about being with you is easy. You're the most infuriating woman I've ever known."

"Thank you."

He growls. "I'm sorry for not letting you talk. Todd had me scared out of my mind, but that's no excuse to treat you like…"

"Like a child," I throw out, if only because I know he won't like it. "I'm sorry I was too stubborn to tell you that the police told me I should get the kids somewhere safe, just in case Todd wasn't working alone. Plus…" I laugh a little, shaking my head. "I didn't want to slap you while I was feeling really slappy. Leaving felt safer."

A smile plays on his lips, and suddenly it's my one and only goal to make it truly appear instead of letting it remain just a hint of happiness. There's nothing I like more than Chad when he's happy. "For the record," he says, "you're allowed to slap me when I'm being a total idiot."

I take a step closer to him, the first one I've taken since he opened the door. I know he notices because his eyes slip down to my feet before resting on my mouth for a moment on their way back up. "Good to know," I say with a grin. "Are you prepared for that much slapping, though?" Also for the record, I don't intend to *ever* slap him, but he doesn't need to know that.

His smile is closer but not quite here yet, and I wonder what it will take to bring it out of him. It took a while after I first met him, but I'm hoping it's easier now that I know what makes him tick.

Leaning in, he gets so close that I can almost feel his warmth despite him not touching me. With the way he keeps his hands in his pockets, it's like he's afraid to make that first connection. "I can think of better things than slapping, though I may not learn my lesson if we follow my plan."

He nearly winks, everything about him so subtle that I might miss it if I weren't completely riveted on him. "I might just make the same mistake over and over to get the punishment."

What a flirt! "Is that so? That doesn't sound very helpful to me."

"Depends on where you're standing." Then he sobers, his expression turning sad. "Can you forgive me for being stupid and self-centered? I've missed you, Hope."

I can't keep myself from touching him anymore, and my fingers find his arm, pulling one hand from his pocket so I can slip my fingers between his. "You were trying to protect me. That's not self-centered at all. But, like I tried to tell you, I didn't need your protection. I needed your support. I just needed *you*, Chad. I've felt so lost without you with me."

I expect that to bring back his smile, but instead his eyebrows pull downward. "I can't have you need me," he mutters, which feels like an awful thing to say until he adds, "I've been needed my whole life, and I'm still figuring out who I am outside of that. But..." He leans down, forehead resting against mine. "You can *want* me."

I let out a little laugh. "Oh, wanting you is okay?"

"Preferable. I'm as far from perfect as it gets, but I hope you can—"

"I've never wanted perfect," I say, hating that this is making me cry again. They're good tears, though. "I just want you, Chad."

I rise up on my toes, and our mouths collide in a kiss that I've been craving for days. As always, Chad takes the lead, but things feel different now. He leaves room for me to step in if I want, though that means it feels like he's holding back. That's the last thing I want at this moment.

"Two things," I say, breaking away slightly. "One, why is Houston wearing a tutu?"

Chad chuckles. "I have no idea. And the second thing?"

"Are you going to kiss me, or what? I'm not getting any younger, you know."

"Thank goodness for that. Are..." He frowns again, tugging at the ends of my hair. "Are you sure you want to put up with me? I know I'm not easy to deal with."

I laugh, and my heart feels so much stronger than it has all week. "Thank goodness for that," I say, rubbing my hand along his scruffy jaw. Mm, I've missed that. "Chad, if you haven't figured out yet that I'm stubborn and do what I want, then you're not nearly as smart as I thought you were. Life would be boring if you made it too easy for me. Kiss me, old man."

There's that smile, the one that brings him to life. I love that smile, though he doesn't give me a chance to enjoy it for long because he pulls me in for a kiss. And oh, does he kiss me. All of his restraint vanishes as he dives into what will be written down in the history books as the best kiss of all time.

His hands lock around my waist and guide me back until I'm pressed against one of the large columns holding up the roof overhang, subsequently hiding us from the street, and then he captures my mouth with the desperation of a starving man. It's been almost a week since he last kissed me, and I feel each and every one of those days as he works hard to remind me how much I love this.

He puts everything into that kiss, and when it feels like he has nothing left, it's my turn, and suddenly it's a battle of wills, like we're both fighting to be the one in charge. It's hands grabbing arms and hair and faces, and mouths moving together in a desperate battle until we break apart in unison, like we both know neither one of us is going to win and that's totally okay. I've never in my life experienced a kiss like that, and with the way my heart pounds in my chest, like it's trying to escape, I know there's no going back.

This guy is it for me. And that's terrifying.

"Do you want to come inside?" Chad asks, the words coming out light and airy as he fights to breathe.

I let out a shaky laugh, tucking myself into his broad chest and letting his rapid heartbeat validate my complete lack of strength. At least I wasn't the only one affected by that madness. After a kiss like that, I'm not sure I want anything except more of that. I am *desperate* to experience that again. But I do want to meet his siblings, and we need to take things slow where we can. I have a feeling we can only go so slow before this changes into something we can't take back. Before this budding relationship is something permanent.

At this point, I can't imagine a world without Chad Briggs, but I don't know if that's what he wants. So we need to sit down and have a conversation about where this is going. I know where I want it to go, but what does he want?

"Okay," I say, still breathless. I'm still reeling from that kiss, but now I'm also imagining Zelda as the flower girl at our wedding and Link holding the rings, so I feel like this lightheadedness is justified.

Chad grips my hand as he opens the door, like he's afraid to let go of me now that he has me. Let's hope. "Don't let them overwhelm you," he says as he leads me inside. "My sisters proved with Houston's date tonight that they have no sense of boundaries."

"You forget that I also have no boundaries," I remind him. "I think I'll..."

All words I might have said vanish as soon as we catch sight of the dining room and kitchen, both of which are completely covered in food and pumpkin guts as Chad's siblings have a full-on food fight in the middle of his house. It's a horror scene of epic proportions, and Chad squeezes my hand so tightly that it almost hurts. He looks both disgusted and furious, with a bit of bewilderment mixed in for fun, and it is taking every ounce of strength I have not to burst into laughter.

Chad whistles sharply, and everyone immediately freezes. Everyone except Duke, who can't stop his tail from thumping even though he lies down in obedience. I don't think Chad has words for how he's feeling right now, and though I'm so tempted to grab a brownie and smash it into his face to break the tension, I give him a tug instead.

"I don't want to ask," Chad says before allowing me to pull him toward the door.

Neither of us says a word until we're back on the porch, and then I lose it, falling into a fit of laughter so hard that I have to sit down on the porch swing and pull Chad down with me.

"I'm going to kill them," he growls, shaking his head. But there's affection in his eyes, and it only takes three seconds before he starts laughing with me.

Leaning into him, I rest my head on his shoulder and decide that this might be my favorite place to be. Right by his side, laughing with him. "I think you scared them enough that they'll clean up."

"I don't remember the last time they all looked that happy."

Oh, is that the reason he's so shocked by what we just witnessed? I look up at him, trying to determine what his expression means. I'm sure there's some need for cleanliness in there too, considering he's the type of guy who does the dishes while he cooks, but maybe he doesn't mind the mess as much as I thought. Plus, for a guy who has always seemed pretty steady and non-emotional, he's been dealing with a lot the last few weeks.

"Are you analyzing me?" he asks suddenly, rubbing his thumb along mine. "You look so studious."

"Not words anyone has ever said about me. Actually, that's not true. I was a pretty good student."

"And you will be again when you finish your degree."

I can't stop my grin as I curl up closer to him. "You think I should finish school? Even with the kids?"

"I think there's a good chance you won't be doing everything on your own anymore. I don't have to work, so I could look after the kids while you do your thing. You deserve to have dreams, Hope."

I sigh, feeling so content. Part of that could be because the weather here in Sun City is alarmingly perfect, but mostly it's because Chad is so good at making me feel valuable on my own. I don't know how a career in astronomy is supposed to work when I have a family now, but I love that Chad wants me to try. "I like you."

"I know you do."

"So, how long do we give your siblings before we go back in?"

Chad's hand tightens around mine. "What if we don't?"

What is that supposed to mean? "You don't want me to meet them? Or are you afraid that I'll join in on the mess-making?"

"I wasn't worried about that until now." He kisses the top of my head. "I think... Can I just keep you to myself tonight? I'm still not a big fan of sharing."

I totally understand that feeling, just like I am totally okay with saving tonight for the two of us. "I'm all yours," I murmur.

After several peaceful minutes of silence, though, my thoughts decide they don't want to shut up, and I wince before I say, "So, all of your siblings are paired off tonight?"

Chad chuckles, like he was waiting for me to say something about them. "Your timing in Sun City was most appreciated. I'm not sure about Houston—I have some concerns about his date—but they've been busy falling in love while I was gone. Almost makes me wonder if I was the reason they've been on their own before now."

"Have you ever threatened one of your sisters' dates with a shotgun?"

"Not so far, though Fischer has me wary when it comes to Micah. It would be a Glock 43X anyway."

I love that that's the way he answers that question instead of simply saying no. For having such a meme-based name, Chad is as unique as they come. "Then it's not your fault that they haven't found their soulmates until now."

"Do you believe in soulmates?"

"Do you?"

"I didn't." He sits up and kisses my temple. "But then I had a feeling I should take some time off." He kisses my cheek. "Spend some time in Laketown." Kisses the side of my mouth. "Meet the most annoying woman I've ever met in my life." With one gentle finger, he turns my head and presses his mouth to mine in the softest of kisses. "I think I may have been wrong about soulmates."

Grinning, I pull him closer to give him a real kiss. "Oh, you think?"

For the next hour or so, we either kiss like we're not sitting on the porch in full view of any kids who may still be out trick-or-treating, or we sit beside each other and talk. There's nothing I like more than talking to Chad, and everything about our conversation feels easy. We talk about Todd; Chad fills in the details of Todd's embezzlement as much as he can while I tell him what I learned about him being Link and Zelda's dad. And we talk about the money that my grandparents have given to the kids. I mention my own account, which contains its own little fortune and was news to me when Phoebe told me about it two days ago, and Chad shocks me into silence when he tells me how much he has saved up over the years. It suddenly makes sense why he could afford two houses and doesn't need to work.

We talk about the future without putting things into any certain terms. I think we're both still a little on edge, and saying anything definitive out loud feels ominous.

Houston is the first to leave, his pretty (and apparently questionable) date in tow, and he looks at me with interest when they hit the porch. It's a little strange, seeing him in person after seeing him on TV more than once—especially because he's still wearing that tutu, which is now splattered with food—but he looks so much like Chad that it somehow makes him feel more real. He may be attractive, but he's got nothing on his older brother.

"Is my house still a disaster?" Chad asks.

Houston gets a cheeky little grin on his face as he glances at the closed door. "You taught us too well. I'm pretty sure it's cleaner than when we started."

"Good."

His eyes flick over to me again, taking me in with keen eyes. His strength may be in athletics—hello, giant muscles on display—but I have a feeling Houston is just as smart as his brother. "Are you going to introduce us?"

I want to smack Chad for smirking the way he does. He's going to have way too much fun with this, but I know he won't change his mind on keeping me to himself tonight. "Nope."

I'm tempted to introduce *myself*, but then Chad squeezes my hand. Grinning, I cuddle in closer and accept my fate to remain anonymous until he's ready to learn how to share.

Houston, on the other hand, doesn't like the idea of me remaining nameless, and I can tell he wants to argue as he looks between Chad and me. But the blonde girl with him nudges him a little. I recognize the look in her eyes, and even if Chad thinks there's something sketchy about her, she is clearly crazy about Houston. (Probably why her costume tonight is a baseball uniform.) She may not be what I would have pictured at his side, but her girl-next-door look fits really well with the larger-than-life athlete she clings to.

"Well, we're headed out," Houston says with a shrug. "Are you going back to Laketown?"

That's something that we *didn't* talk about, and yet Chad looks at me with a sparkle in his eyes. I have a feeling he has something brewing in that head of his, though I have no idea what it might be. Honestly, I don't care where I am as long as the kids are happy and Chad is with me. But where we live fits inside that "definitive" sphere that feels so precarious right now.

Still, I can almost hear his thoughts as he searches for my own. *What do you think?*

I bite my lip before I start laughing. *I'm not having this conversation in front of your brother*, I try to tell him, though I highly doubt that's the message I conveyed because Chad is twisting his mouth in such a way that I can't think about anything except kissing him.

"We'll see," he says, which is the best answer either of us can give right now. Then he turns to Houston's date. "It was nice to meet you, Darcy Paxton."

Oh, there's definitely something there, and though Houston doesn't seem to notice, Darcy does. It's small, but her expression shifts into something slightly fearful, and I know Chad notices because he tenses beneath me. It's all so subtle, but I have nothing to do right now but watch, and I'm suddenly deeply interested in Houston's dating life in a way I shouldn't be.

"See you around," Houston says, and then they're gone, climbing into a big charcoal truck and driving off into the darkness.

I sit up. "What was that?"

Chad is already pulling out his phone. "She's lying to him. I don't know what about, but it could be dangerous."

"You think she's trying to take advantage of Houston's status or something? His money? He's rich, right?"

Pausing whatever he's looking up on his phone, Chad looks at me out of the corner of his eye. "You're not his type," he says.

I roll my eyes. "Just do your thing, Bigfoot. I only have eyes for you."

"Is it weird that I like it better when you call me old man?" He shudders before resuming his search. "I can't believe I just said that."

Ten minutes later, during which I do my best to distract him but am ultimately unsuccessful—I give him points for staying focused even when I nibble on his earlobe—Chad growls a little and glares at his phone.

I look at his screen, but it's just a bunch of words that I am too lazy to read through. "What did you find?"

"She's not who she says she is."

"Her name isn't Darcy Paxton?"

"No, it is, but..." He seems more confused than anything now. "I can't decide if this is a bad thing or not, honestly."

"Are you being vague on purpose?"

"Yes."

"Oh."

He laughs, pressing a kiss to my temple and sliding his phone back into his pocket. "I'll talk to him tomorrow and let him choose whether he wants to hear it or if everything should just play out."

"Look at you, learning how to keep boundaries and let people solve their own problems!"

He groans. "You're never going to let me live the Todd thing down, are you?"

"Never." But I punctuate that word with a kiss, and even though his other siblings eventually make it outside on their way out, neither of us give them any notice. That's for Tomorrow Hope and Chad. Tonight, we're the only ones who matter.

Chapter Twenty-Two

Chad

November 1

I SHOULD HAVE THIS figured out already, but I'm still annoyed when I wake up in the morning exhausted because I could barely sleep knowing Hope was in a guest room right across the hall. I made sure to put her in a room that didn't share a wall with mine, but that didn't really help. Not when the rest of the house is empty. All I could think about was how easy it would be to take the few steps to her door and crawl into bed beside her so I could hold her and never let go.

It's not even about physical intimacy, though that crossed my mind as well. It's about being with her, next to her, breathing the same air and knowing that her heart is beating strong and calm.

Forcing myself to ignore her closed door, I make my way downstairs and start a pot of coffee so I'll be at least moderately personable when she wakes up.

Hope showing up on my doorstep was so much better than I could have expected. As much as I had hoped and dreamed for something like that to happen, I was convinced the most I would get was a phone call. When I didn't get that much, I resigned myself to being alone the rest of my life, knowing no one would ever compare to the woman who forced herself into my life in the best possible way. The way I feel about her isn't something that will go away with time or distance, so I'm glad I don't have to deal with either of those things right now.

When she appears on the stairs, her hair falling in a mess around her shoulders and her eyes sleepy and warm, my heart beats with a resounding rhythm of love. I hate that I haven't said those words to her yet, not even last night, but I'm not sure I can survive putting them out into the world if I am not absolutely sure that I am what she wants.

Seeing her in my house like this feels so much bigger than having her stay with me in Laketown. Laketown was a dream, a world set apart from reality, and it was easy to pretend that it had nothing to do with my actual life. But this? She comes up beside me and steals my coffee out of my hand without a word, and the sight of her here in New Mexico seems to solidify the idea that she can be a part of my life forever if I just say the words.

Can I do that? Can I trust her with my heart?

Of course I can. I don't think that was ever in question, no matter what I told myself. Hope never says something she doesn't mean, and she's already told me multiple times that she loves me. She basically told me last night that she has no intentions of going anywhere.

So what's stopping me?

"Morning," she says, grinning as she takes a sip of my coffee. "This is disgusting. Where's all the good stuff?"

"I was planning on making you your own cup," I tell her, rolling my eyes even though I don't care.

I'm too busy thinking about how my yard is ideal for kids, with a huge stretch of grass in the back and a pool that rarely gets used. The school bus stops just a couple of houses down. I can count nearly a dozen kids in the neighborhood similar in age to Zelda and Link. I know Hope just bought her house in Laketown and that moving to a new place is always a little traumatic for a kid, but have they really settled enough to cause problems if I were to ask them to come here?

"You seem to have a lot on your mind this morning," Hope says, brushing my cheek with her thumb.

There's a wildlife center not far from here. Link would love that. And Sun City just opened up a new observatory a few miles outside of town...

"Care to let me in?" she asks. But then she narrows her eyes and looks around. "Okay, is it weird that it feels too quiet? I kind of miss the kids."

I lean in and kiss her, taking the coffee from her hands and setting it on the counter so it isn't between us. "Are you sure about that?" I ask before lifting her up onto the counter and deepening the kiss.

"Mm, okay, you make a good point." Her fingers find their way into my hair, sending a shiver through me. "I think we need to take advantage of the privacy while we've got it."

I grunt. Too much talking. Except... "I have no idea if this house is well equipped for this kind of thing," I say in between kisses. "Care to test it out with me? The countertop seems sturdy."

Grinning, she glances at the walk-in pantry, which is partially open. "You mean like making sure there is plenty of space for a couple of people to move around in your pantry if necessary?"

I nod seriously. "Or seeing if the window seat down the hall can comfortably seat two people."

"Maybe figuring out which couch is the most comfortable," she suggests with a wink.

This is why I love her. One of the reasons, anyway. She understands the things I don't say. "I want to see how well you and I fit here," I say, perhaps a little cautiously. I'll ask her outright if she'd be willing to move to Sun City, but not yet. First, I want to enjoy this bubble.

"You are aware that I don't care where we're making out as long as you're kissing me, right?"

"I am fully aware," I growl and pull her against me so I can pick her up and move to try the window seat first, kissing her the whole way there.

Turns out there's no bad place to make out inside my house. Hope says this is a matter of serendipity, which has me feeling ridiculously hopeful, especially when she slips away to give the kids a call and see how they're doing, promising to tell them hi for me.

I use this momentary free time to see if Houston's girlfriend, Darcy, ever texted me back. I shouldn't have texted her last night, but it was a good way to keep myself distracted after sending Hope to her guest room. Darcy didn't reply last night, nor has she sent anything this morning, but that doesn't surprise me. I warned her that Houston was going to learn the truth about her identity eventually and told her that if she didn't tell him, I would. I wonder which option she'll pick.

Houston likes her. A lot. After talking to him last night before Hope showed up, I'm pretty sure he's fallen for Darcy hard and may even be in love with her, but that means nothing if she's lying to him. Especially because there's the whole thing with Tamlin Park, the reporter who, according to Micah, has some serious chemistry with my brother but may or may not be out to ruin his career.

This wouldn't be quite so complicated if Darcy was who she says she is.

"You always look so serious when you think hard," Hope says, settling herself on my lap and wrapping her arms around my neck. I must have gotten lost in thought for a while if she's back already.

I brush my thumb against the red skin on her chin. "Sorry."

She shakes her head. "I knew I was signing up for beard burn the moment I first thought about kissing you."

"Which was when, exactly?"

"Spaghetti night, probably."

For some reason, I feel a strange rush of pride when I say, "I was first, then."

Her eyes go wide. "What? When did you think about it?"

"When you picked me up after my run."

"That was, like, a week before me! And here I thought I had to wear you down."

Chuckling, I kiss the tip of her nose. "Oh, you absolutely wore me down, but not because I didn't want it. I was trying to stay far away from you but only had so much resolve. Why do you think I decided to chop wood within sight of your kitchen?"

Her eyes glitter as she pulls herself in close. "I still haven't gotten to see that, by the way, and I *will* be demanding that sight at some point. What were you thinking about earlier?"

The way this woman moves from thought to thought is exhausting, but I wouldn't have it any other way. "Houston and Darcy."

"Did you find out something new?"

"No, but I think I should talk to him sooner than later. I don't want him to fall too hard and get hurt."

"You're a good brother."

I noticed early on that she is so good at saying little things like this that sound inconsequential but mean everything. But this one hits harder than anything else she's said to me, and my heart feels like it's expanding in my chest.

"You think so?" I ask, genuinely wondering if she meant it. Then again, Hope never says anything she doesn't mean.

Sensing my need for validation, she grins and places her hands on my cheeks so I can't look away. Not that I want to. "Chad Bigfoot Briggs," she says, ignoring my eye roll. I guess I should tell her my middle name at some point. "You are the best man I've ever known. That makes you a good neighbor, a good friend, a good brother, and someday a good father. Hopefully sooner than later on that last one."

Well, I'm a goner. This moment will forever be named as the moment Hope Duncan completely and entirely stole my heart. I will never get it back.

"I'm going to text Houston and see if he's available for lunch," I say slowly, most of my energy going into sending said text because it won't happen otherwise.

She smiles wide, fingers already curling into my hair at the back of my neck. "And until lunchtime?"

I don't bother speaking my answer, diving into a kiss instead.

Chapter Twenty-Three
Chad

"I'm starting to think this was a bad idea." I take a step away from my truck, accidentally stepping right into Hope. I grab her before she crashes to the ground, wincing. "Sorry."

Rolling her eyes, she gets steady on her feet again and then pokes me in the chest. "You're the one who thought he should get involved, and now that you've texted Houston about going out to lunch, you can't back down now or he'll think it's something terrible!"

I grab hold of her hand and hold it over my heart. "What if you come with me?" Mostly, I don't want to leave her side now that I have her back. Anytime I've been away from her, disastrous things have happened.

Her eyes go wide. "You want me to come to your heart-to-heart lunch with your famous brother? You wouldn't even introduce me to him last night."

Mm, that was one of my better decisions. I lean in to tease a kiss against her lips, which she allows with a sigh. "Maybe I'm trying to give you a reason to stay in my life."

"I don't need a reason, Bigfoot. I'm here."

I hope she means that; I'm not sure I'll be strong enough to let her go if she doesn't.

"Are you ever going to tell me why you're so suspicious of Houston's girlfriend? Because they were adorable last night, and he's clearly into her."

My phone buzzes before I can answer, a number I don't recognize, and I reluctantly answer the call in case it's something to do with work. "Briggs."

"Chad? It's...it's me. Your dad."

I hang up and curse under my breath. He's out?

Hope frowns. "What was that?"

"My dad's out of prison," I say right as he tries calling again. The words come out strangled, mostly because I have no idea how to react right now. Did I know his sentence was almost up? I didn't care, so I didn't pay attention.

How did he get my number? He must have looked up my business and gone through the questionnaire I set up. He would have had to answer a specific way for the website to decide he needed immediate access to me. It's the only way it would have given him my info.

How many tries did it take him?

"Chad?" Taking my hand, Hope guides me to the porch and forces me to sit as the call goes to voicemail. "You okay?"

Well, my hands are shaking, so probably not. "I didn't think I would ever talk to him again."

"Technically you didn't."

I manage a small smile to match the grin she's giving me. I'm so glad she's here right now so I'm not stuck dealing with this new development by myself.

My phone buzzes again, this time with a text.

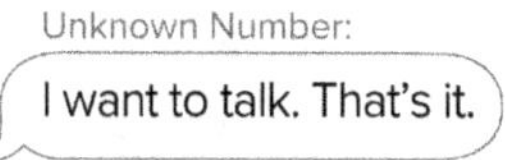

I feel both nauseous and amped up as I stare at his words, which is a terrible combination. "What do I do?"

Hope laughs. "You're asking me? You're the one who always has all the answers."

"Not this time."

This man left me—a fifteen-year-old—in charge of two seven-year-old siblings. I had no idea what I was doing, and that responsibility changed the course of my whole life. Who knows what my life could have looked like if he'd been the father he was supposed to be?

Another text comes through, but I refuse to look at it. Hope takes my phone, reading silently. "He says he's sorry," she tells me gently. "And that he can never make up for what he did but he wants to move forward."

I clench my hands into fists on my thighs. Do I want that? Do I want to move forward? It's been more than twenty years since the man forced me to become a parent, and I haven't spoken a word to him since the day he was arrested. Not a great place to end things.

"What would you do?" I fix my gaze on Hope, silently begging her to help me process this.

She winces. "I would give anything to talk to my dad again."

"But he was a good dad."

"The best."

"That doesn't really help me."

"I know." She takes my hand, even though it's still balled up in a fist. "How about this? Say it was your kid. Say you made some terrible mistakes but you have a chance to apologize. Would you take it?"

I furrow my brow. The obvious answer is yes, and the ball of guilt in my stomach that hasn't left since I shouted at Link seems to grow bigger as I think about her question. I really need to tell him I'm sorry and make sure he knows that what happened with the mountain lion and the bear trap wasn't his fault. "You think I should talk to him," I guess.

Hope smiles. "I think it depends on if you want to give him some closure. I don't think you need it on your end."

She's right. I rarely think about my dad because everything he did is in the past, and I don't regret the chance I got to help raise my siblings into the people they are today. I'm proud of them and everything they've accomplished, and no conversation with my dad will change that.

I lean in until my forehead rests against Hope's. I'm going to be late to pick up Houston for lunch if I'm not careful, but I almost don't care. "Does it make me a bad person if I'd rather let him live his life full of regrets?"

Hope snickers. "I don't know if it's bad or good, but it's certainly human. What would you say to him if you did talk?"

I give her a soft kiss in between each thing I say. "I would tell him that we're better off without him. That the twins don't need him messing up their lives because things are good. That I'm glad he did what he did because it led me to you."

Hope deepens the kiss, making me think canceling on Houston is a great idea, but then she pulls away. "You're going to be late."

My phone buzzes with another call, but I block my dad's number. Maybe someday I'll talk to him, but not today. Not anytime soon. Things are too good to risk him messing things up.

"You'll be here when I get back?" I ask her, a bit of fear coloring my question.

But Hope smiles and kisses me again. "I'll be here. I promise."

That promise is the only reason I'm okay with climbing into my truck and driving off to the stadium where Houston is practicing with his team. Though I saw him last night, moments with my brother are rare, so I can't regret the fact that Hope didn't let me skip out on this.

Especially when I see the smile on Houston's face when he comes out and tosses his gear into my bed. "Missed me that much?" he says, clearly jazzed that I reached out like this. "What about your lady friend?"

Okay, I may still have some regrets. But this lunch is about him, not me. I want to make sure he doesn't get hurt by whatever Darcy is doing. "Don't call her that," I grumble and climb into the cab. Once we're moving, I decide I should share a little more about the woman I love. He'll just make assumptions if I don't. "Her name is Hope."

Houston sniggers. "And who, pray tell, is Hope?"

"She's..." How do I even put it into words when I have yet to tell her how I feel?

"Your lady friend." He winces when I punch him, even though I don't hit him hard. That's his bad shoulder, and I remind myself to take it easy with him. He admitted last night that he may not be able to play anymore without surgery, and I won't make it worse for him. "It seems like she makes you happy," he says, raising his eyebrows. "I'm happy for you, man."

I'm happy too, but I am terrified. Now that she isn't next to me, all of my fears are creeping back in. "She has two kids," I mutter. One of whom still thinks I'm angry with him, and who knows how Zelda really feels about me?

Houston shrugs. "And?"

And this is going to be so much easier if I just let it all out. I didn't come here to spill my guts, but it might make it easier for Houston to listen to me if he knows I'm just as lost as he is when he comes to love. "What if I can't be enough for her? I've already messed things up once, and we're going to give things another try. But I'm not sure if..."

"I'm going to be serious for a second, okay?"

I look over at him, lifting one eyebrow. "Is that possible?"

He snickers. "Only on rare occasions."

"Blow me away, Texas."

"I know for a fact I haven't ever thanked you, but you were the best big brother anyone could have asked for."

We reach the restaurant right as he says this, which is great because emotion rises in my throat and touches my eyes, making it difficult to see. No, he hasn't thanked me for taking care of him, not in a general sense, but I've never asked for thanks. I've never needed it. But that doesn't change how deeply his words hit me. It almost makes me feel okay with my decision to ignore our dad because we were fine without him. The three of us made it through because we had each other.

I think about Hope and the kids. If I'd never met them, they would have been fine. Hope loves them and will make the most incredible mother, and Link and Zelda will become wonderful people as they grow up. But what if they had someone else looking out for them too? A father who didn't abandon them like mine did?

"You got the short end of the straw," Houston continues quietly, "being so much older than us, and when Mom died, you never got a chance to really mourn. The State made us go back with Dad, which meant you suddenly became a parent at fifteen, but I never once heard you complain. You may think we didn't realize how crazy it was that a teenager would have to get a job to make sure there was food on the table, but we did."

I think I've spent too much time trying not to feel anything because all of these emotions the last few days are kind of killing me. What if Houston's right? He didn't directly say he thinks I'd be a good husband and father, but I'm pretty sure that's what he's getting at.

I don't want to mess things up with Hope, but maybe that burning desire to do right by her is enough to ensure that I do. I'll obviously make mistakes, but who doesn't?

Houston clears his throat. "It might make me sound ungrateful, but I was mad when Lloyd worked the courts so he could take us in. I felt like he was shoving it in your face that he was so much better than you, even if that's stupid."

I let out a single laugh. "It's not stupid. I hated him for the first few years because he did what I couldn't. I didn't have the stability to get guardianship after I turned eighteen."

"But you tried?"

Of course I tried. I want to tell him that, but my words stick in my throat. I'm going to hazard a guess that Houston hasn't paid any more attention to our dad's sentence than I have, and I wonder if Dad has reached out to him or Brooklyn yet. Brook will be fine; she forgave him years ago. Houston... I have no idea how he'll react, and I'm not going to bring Dad up. That's a surefire way to ruin the day for both of us.

"My point is," Houston says, "you've always looked out for us, and you are always going to do what's best for the people you love."

We keep talking as we head into the restaurant, though I'm only partially paying attention to what we're saying. I didn't expect to have such a heartfelt conversation with my brother, and now I'm questioning my motives for bringing him to lunch. Is this really what's best for him? He already hates when I meddle in his life, and this is so much worse than anything I've done in the past.

I glance at my phone as we sit, which holds all of the info I found on Darcy. Houston is in love with her, whether he is willing to admit that or not. Maybe telling him the truth about her isn't a good idea. Maybe he needs to figure it out for himself. We're here, though, so I'll have to tell him *something*. Hopefully I can do this right and lead him to a happy ending.

He deserves that much.

"You trust me, yeah?"

Houston narrows his eyes. "What did you do?"

"How much do you really know about Darcy Paxton?"

"I told you not to look into her! We're not talking about this, Chad." And yet the curiosity is clear as day in his eyes. Something tells me he has already had doubts about her. He's not stupid, and Darcy's secret isn't something she can easily hide.

After a moment of trying to read my face, he drops his head onto the table. "Do I have reason to be worried?"

"I'm not sure."

"Then why bring this up?"

"Because I don't like not being sure. I'm just looking out for you, Hou."

Groaning, he seems to debate with himself some more before he asks into the table, "Is she dangerous or something?"

What a loaded question. I barely have much info as it is, and even if I'm mostly convinced that what I found is true, there's always the chance that I'm wrong. I hate being wrong. "Again, I'm not sure. It depends on how you define dangerous."

"Just tell me."

I cringe. "I don't think you really want to know. If I tell you, it's not something you can unknow."

"Then don't tell me. If it's important, I'll figure it out on my own."

He will, and I hope it doesn't take long. I look at my phone, wishing Darcy had texted me back. If nothing else, she could have confirmed or denied my accusation, but she's been silent. In a perfect world, Darcy would tell Houston the truth herself.

My phone dings, pulling up a website that must have a hit on something I'm following. In this case, it looks like it's the reporter Tamlin Park, and I'm curious how Houston will react if I start playing it. We're waiting for our food anyway, so I might as well see what she's up to.

Houston perks up as soon as he hears her voice, his whole bearing growing lighter as he focuses on her face. That's not the look of someone who is fully invested in the girl he's dating, and I'm starting to think Micah is right about the chemistry between these two. I can feel it now, when they're not even interacting. Sure, he is deeply interested in Darcy, but there's a lot more to his story than what I've seen so far.

Things are going to fall into chaos for him soon whether he likes it or not, and I'll be here for him when it does. I'll always be there for him.

Just like I'm always going to be there for Hope and her kids. I've got to stop running scared and start going for what I want because there's no telling when I might lose it. If I've learned anything from watching Houston these last couple of days, it's that I need to tell Hope how I feel or we'll never be able to move forward. And I know just the way to do it.

Chapter Twenty-Four

Hope

November 2

SATURDAY MORNING LOOKS ABOUT the same as Friday morning looked. Sun City lives up to its name, though it's hard to believe that we're only a couple of hours away from the mountainy Laketown where we got snowed in a couple of weeks ago. It's not just the weather that is perfect here, though. Chad's house is phenomenal, with its well-maintained yard and pool and multiple bedrooms that could be turned into playrooms and offices and nurseries.

I know I'm getting ahead of myself, and Chad hasn't even said he loves me. He's shown me in so many ways, but it's the words that seem the most difficult for him. It almost makes sense, with the life he's lived and the relationships he's had with his family and his ex. But even if he hasn't said those words, I know I can't be the only one imagining what our life could look like if we lived it together.

We spent the afternoon yesterday touring Sun City, Chad showing me his favorite places and taking me to his little PI office. He was quiet most of the time, clearly deep in thought, but I'm not going to push things. I'll just make sure he knows I don't plan on running away again. And when we spent the evening snuggled up on the couch together until Chad forced me to go to bed, things felt like they're supposed to. We just need the kids to make it all perfect again.

I beat Chad to the kitchen this morning, so I've already made myself some coffee when he joins me. He glances inside my mug as he slides his hands over my hips, chuckling when he sees that I've left it black in case he wants to steal it instead of adding heaps of cream and sugar for myself. "Trying to prove you're a better person than me?" he guesses.

I scoff. "Of course not. Maybe a little. Mostly because I'm dying to hear about what happened with Houston yesterday."

He smiles, a sleepy look in his eyes. "I'm surprised you lasted this long. He decided he doesn't want to know. But he'll figure out the truth before long, and I'll be here to help him through it when he does."

I both love and hate that he won't tell me what he figured out about Darcy. It means he's good with boundaries, but I also want to know everything about what goes on inside his brain.

Wait. He said he'll be here for Houston. Does that mean he won't be in Laketown? I swallow, gripping the coffee mug a little tighter. "I should go back for the kids soon."

He doesn't move outside of touching his forehead to mine. "I know."

"Will you come with me?"

He swallows, and my heart sinks a few inches in my chest. "Actually... I've been doing a lot of thinking."

Oh no. Thinking is bad. Thinking leads to ideas and decisions and someone being left behind because logic never listens to the heart.

Chad snorts a little laugh. "You just got so tense. Are you really that pessimistic?"

"You can't just drop a line like that with no follow up!" I complain.

"I was thinking you could move the kids to Sun City. Your house is terrible anyway. So, you could move here."

Oh. That's not so bad. And he's right. But... "The housing market is so much higher here," I say, my mind spinning too fast to stop me from using such a lame excuse when I just got informed I have a pretty decent fortune in a bank somewhere.

It's Chad's turn to tense, his hands pressing tighter to my sides. "No, I mean *here*. In this house. My house. With me."

The coffee mug slips from my fingers, shattering between our toes. Chad leaps back, pulling me with him, but I yelp when I step on a shard of ceramic and leap into him, knocking him off balance. We go down hard, and though Chad braces most of my fall, this collision actually hurts.

"Sorry," I groan, curling in on myself on top of him. "You sure you want this chaos around you all the time?"

Chad bursts into laughter, his whole body shaking beneath me as if the sound of his laugh isn't enough to get his amusement out of him.

"You are such a disaster," he says through his laughter. After he can breathe again, he adds, "I have never been more sure of anything in my life. I'm in love with you, Hope."

My head snaps up so I can see his face, which has the most beautiful smile on it as his blue eyes take me in. But he isn't done. "I'm so madly in love with you, and Zelda, and Link, and I can't imagine a life without the three of you in it. I know we just met, but it feels like fate brought us together, and there's nothing I want more than to wake up next to you every day for the rest of my life." He swallows, his expression growing serious. "Hope, will you—"

I clap a hand over his mouth, which he clearly takes as a rejection because his expression drops, and now I'm the one laughing because I couldn't have chosen a worse thing to do if he was about to say what I think he was about to say. "I'm sorry," I say and kiss his nose, though I'm laughing even harder now, and now he just looks confused. "That was rude of me. I'm going to let you finish that question, but not here. Not now. My socks are soaked with coffee and it's driving me crazy, and I will not have that be my memory of this moment. Okay?"

He grins at me beneath my palm, a full wide smile unlike anything I've ever seen before because it seems to reach his eyes differently. I move my hand so he can speak. "Are you telling me that I'm bad at proposing?" he asks.

That last word alone sends a shiver through me. Looking around at the mess I made and the way we're lying on the kitchen tile, I shrug. "I mean, yeah, this isn't exactly romantic."

"You want *me* to be romantic?"

"I'm sure you have it in you somewhere. Just be glad I'm letting you ask instead of doing it myself. That's the way all the cool kids are doing it nowadays."

"You are the most frustrating woman I've ever met."

I grin. "I know. And I promise I'll say yes to your question, but only if you ask it properly."

"Can I kiss you, or do I need to ask properly for that too?" He's definitely getting grumpy.

I brush my hand along his scruff before leaning in. "You're ridiculous, old man. And you never have to ask for that."

We make out on the floor until I find a string of pumpkin guts beneath the cabinet, and Chad lets out a deep and weary sigh.

"I should probably introduce you to my family," he says, like not doing so was ever going to be an option. "My sisters will be mad at me if I propose without letting them help."

Then he fixes me with a stern stare that sends a shiver through me. "But I *will* be asking you to marry me, Karen Hope Duncan, and I will not be patient about making that wedding happen sooner than later. Are you okay with that?"

I snicker. "Are you going to give me a choice?"

"Always. But I know what I want, and I will never stop trying to keep you in my life until the day I stop breathing."

"Now I understand the sooner than later part. You're getting up there in years."

I cut off his answering growl with a kiss that is the first of many, many more to come.

Chapter Twenty-Five
Chad

"Are you sure you didn't get mountain fever or something? Altitude sickness? Eat a poisonous mushroom?" Micah blinks at me, maybe for the first time since I announced my intentions with Hope a couple of minutes ago. "You do know you're talking crazy right now, right?"

Micah Taylor calling me crazy. That's a new one. Sighing, I scoot to the edge of my seat and reach out for her hands. She places her fingers in mine, the same gesture of trust that she's always given me since she was a baby. She's grown up so much, but sometimes I still think she's that little four-year-old who fell asleep in my arms the night after our mom died. I may have only been fifteen, but I didn't move off the couch for hours because I was too afraid to wake her. And maybe I'd needed the same comfort because losing Mom felt like losing the one thing in my life that I was supposed to have forever.

Her opinion won't change my mind, but I want her to be on board with this decision because she and the twins mean so much to me.

"You know I'm going to ask you to help plan the wedding, right?"

Micah rolls her eyes. "As if I would give you a choice. It's only all I've ever wanted to do for you since I was five. And yes, Fischer knows I am obsessed with weddings."

I glance at Fischer, who is deep in conversation with Jordan on the other side of the room. I still haven't had much of a chance to talk to Micah's new boyfriend yet, something I hope to fix soon. He has enough red flags that popped up when I looked into him a couple of weeks ago that I need to make sure Micah fully knows what she's getting into now that things are looking more serious.

"Hey!" She squeezes my hands, pulling my attention back to her. "Yeah, I know about his whole embezzlement thing. Stop glaring at him and start telling me about your plans to *propose* to the woman you met three weeks ago. Brook!"

I wince as Brooklyn comes into the living room after finishing up a phone call she'd gotten soon after she arrived. I know what Brooklyn is going to say, so before she can ask why Micah looks ready to explode, I grab her hand and pull her onto the couch next to me. "I'm going to marry Hope. Soon. And I know it's fast, but I wouldn't be doing something like this if I wasn't completely sure that she's it for me. Okay?"

Brooklyn, who is usually an open book, stares at me with a blank expression, like my words broke something in her brain. "I'm sorry," she says after a moment. "Did you just say..."

"Marry," I confirm. "I tried to propose to her this morning, but she wouldn't let me."

"Because it's *crazy*," Micah repeats.

"It's not that crazy," Houston mumbles.

Honestly, I forgot he was even sitting there despite his chair resting only a few feet from the couch. He's been there since he got here, but Micah was quick to take all my attention as I told her about my feelings for Hope. I frown at him. "You don't think it's crazy?"

He shrugs without looking up. The floor must be incredibly interesting, considering he's been staring at it for the last five minutes. I invited my siblings over for brunch so I could break the news to them before things got too far, but it quickly turned into a solo conversation with Micah. I didn't think it was possible to forget Houston Briggs was in a room, but I did.

And there's something bothering him. He wasn't like this yesterday.

"Did you talk to Darcy?" I ask, wondering if Brook and Micah know anything about my brother's situation. I still haven't heard a word from Darcy, though I've been tempted to text her again.

Houston looks up at me, but only for a second. I've never seen him this unsure, and now I'm wondering if I should have told him more yesterday. Letting him come to his own conclusions felt like the right thing, but that might have been a bad move, no matter what he decides. "No," he says after a long, pregnant pause. "She's in Albuquerque."

I'm pretty sure she's not.

"What did I miss?" Micah asks, looking between us. "And what does this have to do with Hope?"

"Where is Hope, by the way?" Brooklyn asks.

"Upstairs," I tell Brooklyn. I ignore Micah's question for now, turning back to Houston. "If you really want me to tell you, I can—"

"No." He swallows. "No, I need to focus on my interview with Tamlin today."

Micah squeals. "You're seeing Tamlin today? She's awesome!"

Houston growls, running his hands through his hair. "I *know* she's awesome."

"Last week you hated her," Brooklyn points out. "Besides, aren't you dating Darcy?"

I really wish I hadn't missed trivia night. From what I've gathered, all three of my siblings had a lot happen the last couple of weeks—they were all single before I went to Laketown and now they're not—but I would have liked to meet Tamlin and seen their chemistry for myself. If Houston's reaction to the video yesterday meant anything, he's more interested in her than he should be, given her profession.

That's dangerous.

"Hou," I say.

He shakes his head. "I don't want to know. I want to figure this out on my own. I *need* to."

"We are getting *off topic*," Micah says, waving Houston's angst away like it's nothing. "Our big brother just told us he's planning to get married after knowing this girl for less than a month, and we need to talk him out of it!"

"Why?" Brooklyn and Houston ask at the same time.

Micah blinks, glancing between the twins. "Seriously? How am I the one questioning this?"

She makes a good point. Micah is the queen of love stories. She sees love everywhere, even between strangers, and she's always wanted a perfect love story. I'm not so sure she got that with Fischer, but she does seem happy. Whoever he is—I will definitely be doing more digging—he did something right when it comes to my baby sister.

Brooklyn shrugs, and her eyes stray over to Jordan, who seems to sense that she's looking at him because he looks right back and gives her a broad smile. That's a pairing I never would have predicted, but they have history. That history might have been rough at times—Jordan has grown up a lot since his high school days—but it seems to have been good for their new relationship. Not sure how Houston feels about his best friend making eyes at his twin sister, but Brook is happy.

Just like Micah.

It's not like I would ever want to give up my whirlwind love story with Hope, but I hate how much I missed while I was gone. These three have stories that I need to hear before I'll ever be comfortable with them falling in love.

"Micah, you've only known Fischer for a few weeks," Brooklyn says once she tears her eyes away from Jordan. "Houston fell in love with Darcy pretty much the minute he met her."

"I did not," Houston grumbles, turning bright red. I didn't even know Houston knew how to love, with the way he's gone from girlfriend to girlfriend. But based on how he looked at Darcy when they were here on Halloween, it's obvious he fell hard and fast. That's what makes the Tamlin thing so interesting.

"I think I was doomed the minute Jordan gave me a concussion," Brooklyn continues.

I choke. "WHAT?" I'm halfway to my feet before Brooklyn and Micah both grab my arms, tugging me back down.

At least Jordan looks properly terrified. "It was an accident," he tells me, holding his hands up. "I promise I took good care of her."

"Too good of care," Houston mumbles, probably not as quietly as he intended because he turns red as soon as he sees Jordan's glare. "Sorry."

Jordan folds his arms. "We cool?"

"We're cool."

I'm not so sure they're *cool*, depending on how Brooklyn and Jordan ended up together. Again, I'm sort of cursing the fact that I missed everything in the few weeks that I was gone, but now her phone call makes more sense. She called me the night I made spaghetti with the kids, and she mentioned Jordan, though I never quite figured out why she would bring him up. Understandably, my attention was quickly pulled...elsewhere.

"Chad, I'm fine." Brooklyn pats my arm. "Outside of the concussion and the sprained ankle, Jordan has been so good for me."

I raise an eyebrow, pleased to see Jordan flinch when he meets my gaze. "Sprained ankle?" I growl.

He swallows, looking at Fischer as if hoping to get some backup. But Fischer has already proven he's smart enough to stay on my good side, and he keeps his mouth shut.

I should finish this conversation before things go too far off the rails. Preferably before Hope loses patience and comes barreling down the stairs to introduce herself before I can make my arguments to my siblings. I don't want them to think I'm making a mistake by jumping into things so quickly, even if that's exactly what all of my siblings are doing.

"Look," I say to my siblings, rubbing my jaw. "The only reason I'm telling you three about my intentions is because I don't want you to worry about me."

"What about her?" Houston asks. "Is anyone worrying about her?"

My eyebrows lift. That was surprisingly thoughtful. "The only family she has is her aunt," I say. "And the kids. But if you knew Hope, you'd know she will never do anything she doesn't want to do. She's a force to be reckoned with."

"We would know her if you would stop hiding her upstairs," Micah says, and she's almost surly as she stares at me. Maybe she doesn't like being the only voice of reason in this conversation. "I'm withholding judgment until I can actually talk to this woman. And you're not allowed to make out with her to avoid conversation like you did on Halloween!"

"I need to leave soon," Houston mutters. "I've got that...thing."

"You mean the thing with Tamlin Park with whom you have heaps of chemistry, right?" Micah says, bouncing her eyebrows. "Also, did you know that if you try to use the swipe feature on your phone to spell her name, it comes out as Tampon instead?"

"Yep," Brooklyn agrees. "I may have sent Jordan an extremely misleading text the other day."

"Why are you guys typing Tamlin's name?" Houston asks with a groan. "I'm dating Darcy. End of story."

I don't think it *is* the end of his story, and I'm curious how this is going to play out. The need to step in is almost killing me, but Houston is right. He needs to get through this on his own. He's right on the cusp of knowing the truth about this woman he seems to love, and I don't know how he's going to react. Hopefully it goes well for him rather than blowing up in his face.

Regardless, Micah is *also* right, and it's time for Hope to finally make an appearance. She's been freaking out about this all morning, as if my siblings are capable of disliking anyone. Pulling out my phone, I send her a quick text to tell her she can come downstairs.

She responds immediately.

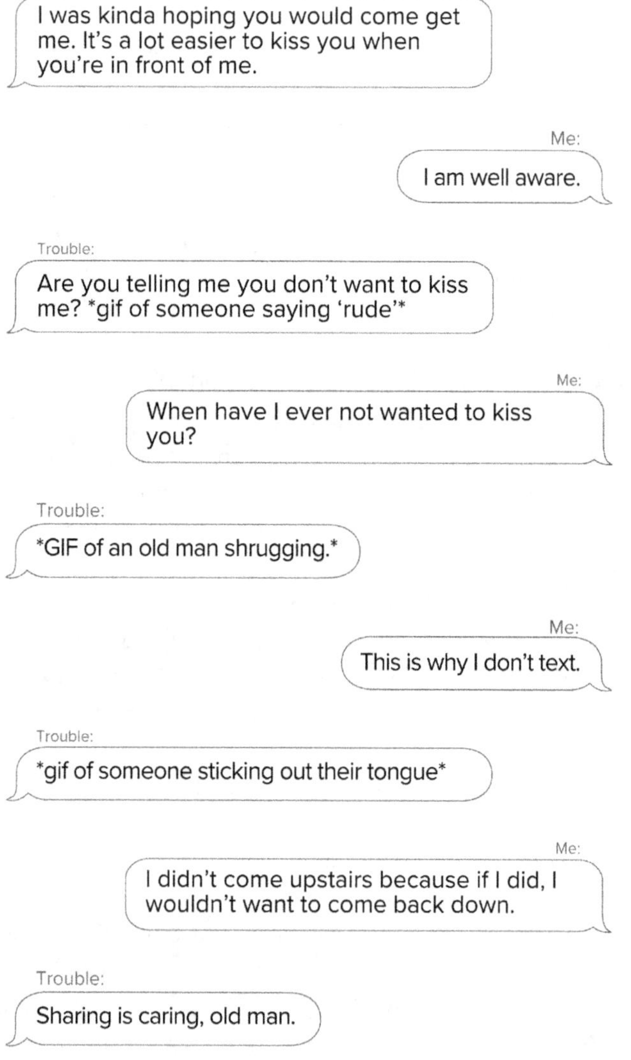

Instead of responding in the negative, like a part of me hopes, she appears on the stairs, and the whole room seems to grow brighter as soon as she's in it. Her smile is warm but tentative, and she can't seem to decide where to look as she takes in the Briggs clan. I'm perfectly happy if she only looks at me.

"Okay," Micah says quietly as Hope approaches our little gathering.

Jordan and Fischer come over too, apparently deciding that if Hope can join me and my siblings, they officially can too.

Though I take Hope's hand and guide her onto my lap, I turn my focus to Micah. "Okay?" I repeat.

My sister smiles for the first time since I told her my plan. "I've never seen him look at anything the way he looks at you," she tells Hope, tears filling her eyes. "Like he's happy for the first time in his life."

She may be talking about me like I'm not here, but I don't care. Now that I have Hope in my arms, everything is better.

Tucking her arm around my shoulders, Hope leans into me. "Yeah, for a minute there, I wondered if he ever smiled. But you Briggses have some good smiles."

"They really do," Jordan says as he wedges himself onto the couch with Brooklyn between us and puts his arm around her. Impressive, given the wary glance he throws my way. He may have been friends with Houston for the last decade and a half, but he and I haven't interacted much. I'm perfectly okay if he's intimidated by me since that means he'll be careful with Brook from here on out. I won't be easy with their relationship until I know more about how it came about, which means he's due for an interrogation.

I'm looking forward to that too much.

Fischer isn't as outwardly affectionate as Jordan, but he still reaches out for Micah's hand, like he fully understands how necessary it is to have that physical contact whenever possible. "Their smiles are a defining feature," he agrees when she beams at him.

Houston grunts, pushing himself to his feet. "Hope, nice to meet you. Hopefully Chad doesn't drive you crazy. I have somewhere I need to be."

"Texas," I call.

He pauses by the front door, looking back at me.

"It'll be okay."

He doesn't seem all that sure, but he nods once before slipping out of the house, leaving me with my sisters and their boyfriends. Thank goodness I have Hope here to keep me from getting overprotective, or I would start grilling Fischer and Jordan right now in search of anything that might make them unworthy of my sisters' affection.

As if she reads my thoughts, Hope plants a long kiss on my cheek. "You've got your own love story to deal with," she whispers to me. "Did you tell them?"

"Did he tell us that he's planning to marry you in the next month because he's crazy?" Micah says with a roll of her eyes. "Don't let him steamroll you, Hope."

Hope's eyebrows shoot up as she leans back to look at me. "Next month, huh?"

I fight my grin. "Were you hoping for sooner?"

"I'll drive down to the courthouse with you right now if it means I can keep you," Hope replies.

Brooklyn snickers, patting my arm again. "I think Chad knows exactly what he's doing," she tells Micah, and she, at least, sounds perfectly at ease. "Sorry, Hope, but our mom was a big fan of cele-brations, so we won't let you get married at the courthouse. Mic and I will help you plan the wedding."

"I don't care about a wedding," Hope says to me. "I just care about you."

I roll my eyes. "Says the woman who wouldn't let me propose this morning because it wasn't romantic enough."

"We were lying on top of a puddle of coffee and pieces of broken mug!"

"Chad!" Micah scolds. "You didn't even make a plan?"

I shake my head. "I never could have planned for you," I tell Hope. "Seems silly to plan anything now."

"You are just as hopeless as Fischer," Micah says.

Fischer frowns. "Hey!"

"You know it's true. The only reason you're romantic is because I taught you what to do."

"You didn't teach me this." Despite his audience, Fischer leans down and kisses Micah in a way that gets Brooklyn blushing and Hope giggling.

Jordan chuckles as he pulls Brooklyn closer to his side. "I like the way he thinks," he says, eyes dancing with amusement.

I glance at Hope, warning her to keep her mouth to herself. If I start kissing her now, I'm not going to want to stop. The hungry look she throws back almost wins out; I have to bite my tongue to hold myself back.

"So, you're happy?" Micah says once she's free, though she barely gets the words out.

I smile, grateful for her concern, but it isn't necessary. "I've never been more hopeful in my life."

Hope snorts. "Please tell me that pun wasn't intentional."

"If only Houston could settle down like the rest of us." Brooklyn sighs. "Maybe things will go well with Tamlin today?"

"Or with Darcy," Micah says. "I liked her, and Houston seems to as well."

Neither woman is who she says she is, and I can only hope Houston figures that out sooner than later. I'm still tempted to tell him, but I'll trust him. For now. I might have to keep an eye on him, maybe even track his phone and figure out where he's meeting Tamlin today so I can see her for myself and get my own in-person take on this supposed chemistry she has with my brother.

I'll probably find them on one of the Little League fields. He hasn't told any of us that he coaches and has been doing so for years, but I show up to his games now and then. Just to make sure he's doing okay. My guess is Tamlin figured out his secret hobby and is about to expose him, which could be good or bad. I should go, just in case she—

"Wow," Hope says, stroking my jaw and pulling my attention back to her. "You are so distracted today. Busy planning your fancy proposal?"

I smirk. "No, that's Micah's job."

"Really?" Micah squeals and claps her hands. "I'm totally going to be planning the wedding, but you'll let me help with the proposal too?"

I roll my eyes. "What do you think?"

While Micah squeals, Hope runs her fingers through my hair and purses her lips. "Houston will be fine," she says quietly. "No matter what happens, he's got you."

Man, I love her.

And while being able to admit that is all well and good, I think I've reached my limit of sappy sibling stuff for the day. "Food's in the kitchen," I say, adding a little growl into my voice. "And then I'm kicking you all out. I have things to do." I meet Hope's gaze again, diving deep into her warm brown eyes as we sit there together. We need to go get the kids and figure out how this housing situation is going to work until we make things official—she presents so much temptation, and I only have so much restraint. I want to do this right. But for now, I just want to be with her and enjoy these last few moments we'll get on our own.

As soon as we leave this bubble we've been in, I have a feeling we won't get many more moments alone. Not with Link and Zelda and hopefully more kids on the way.

I'm totally okay with that.

Epilogue

Hope

December 11

YOU KNOW THOSE MOMENTS when you are convinced you've died and gone to heaven because everything is so perfect and there's no way it can be real?

This is one of those moments.

"That one is the Big Dipper. See the handle?" Chad lifts his arm to point at the sky, his words overlapped by the sound of frogs calling to each other in the darkness.

"Hope says it's called Ursa Major. Ursa means bear." Link, who was already about as close to Chad's side as he could get, somehow snuggles in even closer on the blanket they're sharing. "I don't think it looks like a bear, though."

Chad laughs. "Me neither, but Hope is probably right."

"I'm always right," I say, pulling their attention up to me where I stand on the porch. I got distracted by the sight of them on my way back from using the bathroom; otherwise I would have joined them. "Besides, Chad sounds like a bear, so that's close enough."

He glares at me while Link giggles. The two of them have basically been inseparable since the day I moved the kids to Chad's house in Sun City, which was absolutely a good move. The school is way better, his house has more space, and Chad bought memberships to the wildlife center before we'd even started packing our stuff, something that pulled Link out of his shell more than I could have hoped for. Now, if we get him talking about animals, the kid won't stop talking. Everything about Chad has been good for us.

"Which constellation is your favorite?" he asks Link, though he's still looking at me.

"I like the one you like."

"I like the stars in Hope's eyes."

I snort. "Cheesy, much?"

"Guys," Zelda hisses from her own blanket, "stop talking. Duke is sleeping."

Based on the thump of his tail as he cuddles with her, he's wide awake, but I don't correct her. I just take in the moment, marveling at how perfect everything is right now. Three months ago, I never could have predicted this for my life, and it all feels like a dream.

Chad looks at me again after grinning at Zelda, and in the moonlight I can see the fire ignite in his eyes. "Okay, kids, it's time for bed."

They whine and grumble, but Chad and I both stay silent. It's a weirdly effective way to get them to stop arguing, and I can only hope it lasts as they get older. I am not prepared for actual fighting or disobedience, so I'm more than okay with avoiding it while I can. When their protests yield no results, they both trudge into the rental house with Duke right behind them.

Chad doesn't move from his blanket, though he's giving me some serious eyes.

"Let me put them to bed," I say with reluctance. It's better to make sure they're good and tucked in rather than risk one of them deciding they need a glass of water or a quick check of the closet, like last night when Zelda chose to be afraid of the dark for the first time in her life. I'll blame the few hours' time difference and the fact that this is the first vacation the kids have ever had. They didn't sleep much the night before either, too excited about everything happening to settle down.

Chad groans, pushing himself to his feet. "I'll take care of Link." He runs his hand across my waist as he passes, sending a shiver through me.

When I'm thoroughly convinced Zelda is in bed and will stay there, I head back outside in the hopes of finding Chad waiting for me. The beach is currently empty, but I don't mind having the night to myself for a little bit. For a chance to breathe and be still. We've been in Hawaii for a day and a half now, and everything has been non-stop since the minute our plane landed.

Since before then, honestly. Time hasn't slowed since the morning Chad first tried asking me to marry him a month and a half ago.

The sounds of the frogs and the waves on the shore and the gentle breeze rustling the palm trees that surround our rental house all blend together as I close my eyes and breathe in the night. This is perfect.

And when a pair of arms embrace me from behind, I can't stop my smile. "Yeah, this is heaven."

Chad nuzzles his nose into my neck. "You think so? Is this everything you dreamed it would be?"

"Well, I never imagined I would have two kids and a dog with me on my honeymoon. Or that I would have a big old bear for a husband." His hands tighten around my belly as he growls, making me laugh. "You know I love you, old man."

"I would hope so, because now you're stuck with me, Mrs. Briggs." Before I can react, he spins me around so I'm facing him.

I wrinkle my nose. "I don't feel old enough to be Mrs. anything."

He trails kisses down my nose, smoothing out the wrinkles with his touch. "Mrs. Karen Briggs. Just embrace it. Maybe get a haircut—short in back, long in front. Start wearing yoga pants and—"

I cut him off with a kiss before he makes me puke from too much middle-agedness, and he accepts my deflection with enthusiasm, hands gripping my sides and pulling me close. Then he picks me up, taking me over to the blanket and laying me down so he's got a backdrop of stars above him as he settles over me. It might be the best sight I've ever seen in my life.

"You sure the kids are asleep?" he asks, his voice rough.

I nod. *They'd better be.* We haven't had any time to ourselves since our wedding two days ago, and I am regretting not taking Micah's offer to take the kids. I couldn't imagine going on this trip without them, though, even if it means we only get stolen moments after they're asleep. That's how it's going to be for the rest of our lives. We'll take a trip alone once the kids are more settled.

It would have been smart to at least postpone our flight until the day *after* the wedding, though. Not sure why Chad allowed that oversight when I was making the plans for our honeymoon. Regardless, we finally have a chance to make up for it here in our own little slice of paradise.

Chad brushes his finger across my cheek, his gaze so warm and soft. Who would have thought my gruff and grizzly neighbor would have so much capacity for love? But I am so glad he does. He kisses me softly, speaking against my lips. "I love you, Hope. My wife." He says that word like it's the only thing he's ever needed in life.

I grin, scraping my fingers against his scruff. He shaved for the wedding, but I'm glad to see the beard coming back even though it's only been a couple of days. This rough side of him is the side I love the most. It's the side that speaks of his imperfections and humanity. The patch of gray on his chin is a testament to the hard life he's lived and his capacity to persevere even when things get tough, which is exactly the kind of man I want by my side as I figure out this thing called life. It's not going to be easy, but with him by my side, I can do anything.

I run my thumb across his bottom lip as I marvel at the fact that I get to call him mine. "I love you, my husband. So, so much. Now, kiss me like you mean it."

He grins. "Yes, ma'am." And he does, kissing me like he can't wait to see where this crazy life of ours takes us next.

The End

Also by Dana LeCheminant

Love in Sun City
Kiss Me if You Can (a novella)
She Likes It, Hey Micah
The Chad Next Door
Crossing the Brooklyn Briggs
Houston, We Have a Problem

The Wonder Boys
Love on Camera
Love in Writing
Love on Display
Love in Disguise

Simple Love Stories (Sweet Love Stories)
Simplicity
Growing Young
Bittersweet Brews
In Front of Me
As Long as You Love Me
Dear Dalia
Let Go

Terms of Inheritance (Sweet Romance)
Forever You and Me
Holding On to Everything
A World without You
Love, Strictly Speaking

Historical Romances
The Thief and the Noble
A Twist of Christmas (part of The Holly and the Ivy anthology)
What Dreams May Come
This Above All

About the Author

Dana LeCheminant has been telling stories since she was old enough to know what stories were. After spending most of her childhood reading everything she could get her hands on, she eventually realized she could write her own books too, and since then she always has plots brewing and characters clamoring to be next to have their stories told. A lover of all things outdoors, she finds inspiration while hiking the remote Utah backcountry and cruising down rivers. Until her endless imagination runs dry, she will always have another story to tell.

www.ingramcontent.com/pod-product-compliance
Lightning Source LLC
Chambersburg PA
CBHW070459200726
48293CB00007B/2291